Shelby's Story

Book 2:
The Love After Loss Series

Danette Fogarty

Losing your spouse,

your "other half,"

is like being left adrift on a life raft.

You know it would be much easier

if they were with you as you

navigate the waters of life.

This book is dedicated to

my mom, Pam,

my cousin, Peter,

my mother-in-law, Barb

We can't understand what you went through,

But we love you and wish you happiness.

Three women, all suffering from losing a loved one
get an invitation to a retreat in Galveston, Texas.
Shelby lost her husband in a horrific
motorcycle accident.
After almost a year, she's still in a fog of grief.
At the prompting of her parents, she
accepts the invitation to go to the retreat.
During her time away, Shelby gets a call
from her friend, asking her to take
over running a gymnastics gym.
Stepping in, even if it's for a friend,
churns up old feelings inside of Shelby.
When she meets the direct, and very nosy,
uncle of one of her students,
Shelby becomes even more confused.
Gannon Riley did his sister a favor
and picked up his niece, Kendall.
He didn't know that the gym teacher
would be so beautiful, and so aloof.
But, being Irish, Gannon had a stubborn
streak a mile long and he would use
every bit of it to draw out the standoffish Shelby.
Can two people, who meet by happenstance, find the
Love After Loss they seek?

Chapter 1

Shelby scrubbed the bathtub, and fumed with anger. Kent was late, yet again, and she was getting really tired of it. She understood that his job was his passion. She'd tried to be supportive hadn't she? She'd quit her job to help him run the gym, she'd been there for uniform fittings, doing the girls' hair, and helping calm more than one emotional gymnast after he'd given her a verbal blasting. She thought the least that he could do was be home, on time, for date night.

Now, she was cleaning their, already clean, bathroom, and he was going to pull into the driveway, get out, and give her the smile that always melted away the anger she was currently holding inside.

Smiling at the prospect of what she had planned for the evening, Shelby decided to forgive him in advance. She knew that the gym, thankfully, was really taking off. He had a few new athletes that held a lot of potential. They didn't dare say Olympics, but Shelby knew all the coaches were thinking it.

Gymnastics was an all-encompassing business. You loved it or hated it and Kent, well, he loved it with every fiber of his being. He loved the hours of hard work, loved trying to mold his gymnasts into the kind of competitors others would respect, and even fear a little.

The tub was now sparkling clean.

Shelby smiled because it was going to be filled with a bubble bath for two later on this evening.

Looking at her phone, Shelby sighed. She tried to call him but it went straight to voicemail. It was probably better to just get showered and changed. If he wasn't answering his phone, that meant he was on his way and she had approximately a half hour.

Using the shower, Shelby quickly got cleaned up. She pulled on a light sundress, put on some lip gloss and mascara only since Kent didn't like her to be too "done up." Her hair was already pulled back into a clip that would be easy to let loose later. She just finished putting on her perfume when the doorbell rang.

Strange, she thought. They weren't expecting anyone tonight.

Walking down the hallway toward the front door, Shelby thought she saw more than one person through the curtained window on the door. She wondered if Kent invited parents over to dinner. He did that on occasion when they were trying to get new gymnasts to come to the gym, but he always told her first.

As she opened the door, Shelby frowned. There were two police officers standing there on her front porch. "Hello?" She asked, sure they were at the wrong address.

The first officer, a woman, asked her, "Are you Shelby Forrester?"

Shelby nodded, and wondered why her skin was becoming prickly, the hairs on it standing straight up.

"Is your husband Kent Forrester?" The other officer asked, his voice a little squeaky.

Swallowing hard, Shelby answered him, "Yes, he is, what's going on?"

The woman officer stepped forward, "Mrs. Forrester, I'm Officer Simon, and this is Officer Franklin, can we come in for a moment?"

Still not knowing what this was about, Shelby silently nodded, and led them inside.

Officer Simon asked, "Why don't we sit down?"

Shelby was becoming more upset by the second. "Okay, you're scaring me," Her voice was becoming louder, "just tell me what's going on."

Looking at one another, the officers waited a couple of seconds, then Officer Franklin told her, "There was an accident on the freeway. A semi-truck was heading down the freeway and didn't see a dog that ran out. He tried to swerve to avoid the dog, and his vehicle went into the next lane, which he thought was empty. Your husband was on his motorcycle, so the driver of the semi-truck didn't see him. The truck struck his motorcycle and he was forced into another lane, and hit another vehicle."

As she was listening, Shelby's heart was beating in triple-time. Swallowing hard, she asked them, "What hospital is he at?"

The officers exchanged another look between them before Officer Simon stepped forward. She took Shelby's hand, and told her, "I'm sorry to tell you this, Mrs. Forrester, but the impact of your husband's motorcycle into the other vehicle was severe. I'm sorry to say that he expired at the scene."

'Okay, I'm having a nightmare,' Shelby told herself. 'Wake up, Shelby' she demanded of herself. 'Wake up!'

Officer Simon watched Mrs. Forrester, and knew the news wasn't taking root yet. She was in shock. "Let's sit down," She told the shaking woman, and joined her on the sofa. Looking at her partner, she instructed him, "Please get Mrs. Forrester some water," and watched as he left the room quickly.

No one wanted this kind of assignment.

Looking at the police woman next to her, Shelby asked, "Are you telling me that Kent is dead?"

Taking a deep breath, Officer Simon answered, "Yes, Mrs. Forrester, I am."

The next few hours were a blur for Shelby. She managed to give the officers the phone numbers of her parents and Kent's, so they could call them. Getting the news over the phone was certainly not the best way, but there was no possible way Shelby could get the words out.

When she surfaced into reality, the house was full of people. Her family, close and extended, and Kent's were milling around. Everyone was speaking in hushed tones. Looking over to her right, Shelby saw her cousin, Denise. She was saying to someone, "I just can't believe it."

A wave of pain flooded through Shelby's body. 'Kent,' she thought to herself, 'where are you?' She couldn't speak out loud, 'You should be here, taking care of all of this, that's what you're good at.' And then she giggled at the absurdity of her thoughts.

Covering her mouth, Shelby looked around the room to find everyone had stopped talking and were staring at her. "I was just thinking that Kent would be able to handle this much better than I can," She spoke the words out loud, and then started to cry.

Her mother pulled her close, and whispered, "It's alright, sweetie."

Danette Fogarty

A crazed look on her face, Shelby lifted her head, and yelled, "It's not alright! My husband is dead!"

And there they were......the words that everyone was trying to wrap around their minds. Kent was dead, and he was never coming back.

On the verge of hysteria, Shelby shoved her mother away, and got up quickly. "I don't believe it!" She shouted to the people in the room. "He wouldn't leave me!"

She was backing up, and out of the room now. People were coming closer to her, and she felt claustrophobic. Her parents, Kent's parents, their families were all surrounding her. They thought it was comforting but it was really not. "Get away!" She screamed, and backed up into the kitchen.

Her uncle Rick, who was a doctor, gently put his hands on Shelby's shoulders, and said, "I'm going to give you some medication to help you."

Shelby shouted, "No!" and tried to back away.

Her parents were on either side, her mother pleading to Shelby with her eyes.

Knowing there was no use, Shelby finally nodded, and took the pills, with some water. "This doesn't change anything," She shot the words at them. "Kent is still dead!"

The last thing Shelby remembered was seeing Kent's mother, sobbing in his father's arms, then the room went black.

Hours later, Shelby woke up. Her mother was on the bed beside her, sleeping, and her father was in a chair next to the bed, also sleeping. She didn't want to wake them, so she quietly got out of bed and went into the bathroom.

Leaning against the sink, Shelby looked at herself in the mirror. Her eyes were swollen, and had dark bruises underneath them. She honestly didn't know how long she'd slept, only that her dreams were filled with Kent. He was soothing her, as he always did when she was upset. She could still feel his fingers as they stroked her hair. Putting her own fingers up, the strands felt course and mangled. Turning on the water of the sink, Shelby watched it fall into the round bowl, mixing with her tears.

She stayed there, looking at the woman in the mirror, and saw someone she didn't recognize right now.

When she finally came out, she saw her parents were awake, and waiting for her. "I'd like to see Kent," She told them, the determination in her voice clear.

Her mother, who was still lying on the bed where she was next to Shelby, sat up. "Um, I'm not sure we can do that sweetheart," She told her daughter, her gaze shooting over to where her husband sat, as dazed as she was by their daughter's question.

Pushing up from the chair, John Brentman walked over to his daughter, cupped her face in his hands, and told her, "I'll make some calls."

Shelby watched her father leave the room, and then walked back to the bed. She sat on the edge of it and stared at her mom, saying, "I just need to see him, to make sure."

The look of pain on Rose Brentman's face was something she couldn't remove. It reflected the agony her daughter was facing in trying to realize that Kent was gone. She herself couldn't comprehend such a thing, so how could she expect Shelby to accept the fact? It was clear that Shelby couldn't, and she didn't. Leaning over, she held her daughter's hand and said a silent prayer for all of them to get through this.

An hour later, Shelby was in her father's car, with him and Kent's dad, Tony. They were on their way to the hospital to identify Kent's body.

Shelby was a little upset that the fathers knew someone would have to do this, but no one bothered to tell her. They just took it upon themselves to shield her from this. It wasn't their job to shield her anymore, she and Kent were adults and could handle their own stuff. Just saying the words in her mind, broke Shelby down. There was no more she and Kent, there was no more we, there was only her now. The tears slid down her cheeks and she was glad that the fathers let her sit in the back seat.

Once they arrived at the hospital, the three of them were met by the medical examiner. She led them downstairs to the morgue area. Shelby hated that word, it just sounded so cold.

"In here please," The woman instructed them, and pointed to a small room.

They stood there, looking at a window of glass. On the opposite side, there was a pulled curtain. After a few moments, the medical examiner pulled back the curtain so they could see Kent.

Shelby's face contorted into sobs. It was him! Her father pulled her against his side, in an effort to help her, but it was no use. Her husband, only a few feet away, was no longer alive.

Looking to her right, Shelby saw Kent's dad turn away, his pain was deep and jagged and he couldn't seem to handle seeing his son.

The curtain closed again, leaving the three of them quiet, and adrift on the waves of their own thoughts.

"I want to go in to see him," Shelby told the medical examiner when she came back into the room to collect them.

Her father spoke first, "Shelby, I don't think you should."

Tony Forrester nodded, "I agree with your dad, Shelby, we were told Kent was badly injured."

With a look, she silenced any further discussions. "I'm going in to see my husband," She said slowly and quietly.

The medical examiner nodded, and led her out of the small room they'd been standing in and through a door. There was a large room with exam tables. It wasn't exactly like what you saw on tv, but it was similar. Shelby tried not to focus on anything else except seeing Kent.

They walked up to where he lay on an exam table. There was a sheet pulled up to his shoulders.

Shelby stood there, just looking at him, for several minutes. He didn't look real; certainly nothing like the vibrant man she was married to. It was if they'd taken a mannequin that looked like Kent, and put it on the table. She almost giggled at the thought, then covered her mouth at the strange thought.

It was starting to sink in now, the knowledge that Kent would never again pull into their driveway, or walk into the house yelling her name, he would never sweep her up into a hug so wonderful that she giggled in delight, and he would never smile at her and tell her how much he loved her. That was the worst of it, never hearing those words again.

Shelby stepped forward and placed her hand on his shoulder. He was so cold! She had to resist the urge to ask for a blanket for him. Looking up, her eyes met the medical examiner's gaze as she asked, "Did he suffer?"

The woman hated that question because it was unknown sometimes, depending on the injuries a person experienced. "In my opinion," She told the young woman in front of her, "I don't think he really knew what was going on. It happened very fast, from what the EMT's were saying."

Nodding, Shelby started to shake. She bent over and kissed Kent's forehead. "I love you," She whispered to him before allowing the medical examiner to lead her back out of the room.

When they arrived back at Shelby and Kent's house, there were even more people there.

From the car, Shelby thought it looked like they were having some big party, rather than mourning a loss. "Dad," She leaned forward, "I can't deal with all of those people right now."

John nodded to her plea, "Okay, sweetie, we'll take you over to our house and let the moms know."

Tony was already dialing his wife's phone. He explained what they were doing and hung up shortly afterward.

Shelby sat back in the seat, and sighed. Suddenly breathing seemed so difficult. She thought it was crazy that she'd just seen her husband, dead, on a table, and yet, now, seeing all the people at their house was what was making her freak out.

Twenty minutes later, John pulled into the driveway of his house. He put the car in park but didn't make a move to get out right away. Tony sat there as well, just staring straight ahead. His daughter seemed to have fallen asleep in the back, if his check of the rearview was right. He was feeling a tremendous amount of guilt right now because, although he loved his son-in-law dearly, he was glad that his daughter was still here. Tony and Angelica, Kent's parents, could not say the same thing. Reaching over, John clasped his friend's shoulder, and said, "I'm so sorry, Tony."

Tony buried his face in his hands and allowed himself the tears that had been threatening his heart since he heard about his son's accident. "You know," He looked over at John, "you hear all the time about how only the good die young, and all that other bullshit that we tell ourselves to try and understand." His voice hitched, "But I don't understand," he started crying and raised his hand to hold his friend's, "I don't understand why my boy had to die."

His own tears falling, John replied, "Tony, I sure as hell don't know, but I wish I could tell you something to make this all okay."

Sitting in the backseat, Shelby kept her eyes closed. She knew that Kent's dad and her dad were friends and they needed this time to show their own grief. She tried to drift off into memories, in an effort to escape the present......

"You aren't doing it right," a voice called out.

Shelby had just completed a back handspring and back tuck on the beam, and thought she'd nailed it. Who the hell thought otherwise? Looking up, her eyes fell on this muscled guy walking toward her. His look was all business. Shelby recognized him from some of the college functions. She couldn't remember his name, but that face and body, well, they were pretty spectacular. Shoving her raging hormonal infused thoughts aside, she sat down on the beam, straddled it, and returned, "What was wrong with it exactly?"

His hands on his hips, he shouted, "Well, your arms weren't stiff enough, your legs weren't straight, and you just barely missed falling off that beam and landing on your ass."

"Okay, smarty pants," She challenged, "I'll do it again and if I nail it, you can kiss my ass."

Stepping forward, he whispered just loud enough so only she could hear, "IF, and that's a pretty big if, you nail it, I'll by you dinner, and then I'll kiss your ass."

With a smile on her face, Shelby redid the skill, and nailed it. She smugly jumped down off the beam, wiping her chalk dusted hands on a towel and asked the handsome critic, "So?"

Wearing a smile, he told her, "It's a good thing I like your ass."

"Shelby, honey," John whispered, and place his hand on his daughter's shoulder to wake her.

Rousing from her memory/dream, or whatever it was, Shelby focused. She nodded to her dad, and got out of the car.

With her father on one side, and Kent's dad on the other, they went into the house.

Everything was so quiet. She'd told herself that's what she needed right now, but suddenly it felt as if the silence itself was oppressive. Going down the hall, she went into her childhood home and threw herself on the bed.

Closing her eyes, Shelby allowed the memories to come and take her away.......

They were on a bus, headed back to campus from a meet at a competing college. Shelby was sitting with her friend, Bridgette, and wasn't paying attention as the bus pulled into the parking lot.

Bridgette was explaining her "complicated" relationship with a new boyfriend and Shelby didn't notice the crowd, until they were getting off the bus. As she started down the bus steps, there was music from a group of the marching band members.

Completely confused as to why they were playing here, Shelby was about to walk past them when the drum major stepped in front of her. Frowning, she turned around to skirt him, and the musicians, when she saw Kent. He was surrounded by his teammates and smiling his cocky smile. Walking toward him, Shelby knew he was up to something.

"Do you recognize the song?" He asked her when she was a foot in front of him.

Shaking her head, Shelby answered, "No, I don't."

Still smiling, Kent told her, "It's the song that was playing on the radio the first time I kissed you."

A sneer on her face, Shelby commented, "I believe it was me who kissed you first."

Kent waved his hand as if the details didn't matter. "What's important now, is will you?"

Thoroughly confused, Shelby inquired, "Will I what?"

During their discussion, Kent's teammates lifted up a banner that read WILL YOU MARRY ME SHELBY?

As soon as Shelby read the banner, she started to cry. Oh, he was always making the grand gestures. Didn't he realize that he was all she ever wanted, not these big productions? "Of course," Shelby answered, and allowed Kent to take her into his arms.

There was a knocking on the door, so Shelby turned over in the bed and faced the door. "Come in," She said softly.

Her mother came in, and sat on the edge of the bed. "Dad said you came right in here."

Shelby nodded. "I wanted my old bed, I guess," She answered her mom, then asked, "How are Kent's parents doing?"

Rose Brentman had always been proud of her daughter, but right now, when Shelby was probably going through the worst pain in her life, she was still thinking of others. Her daughter was a true gift, "They're holding up," she answered.

Sitting up, Shelby scooted back so she was leaning against the headboard, "I had him for eight years, but they had him for twenty-nine years, I want to help them."

Tears slid down Rose's cheeks, "Sweetheart, they want to help you right now."

"Mom, I'm not ready yet. I'm not ready to admit it, I'm not ready to accept it, and I'm not ready to break down," The admission hurt, but she couldn't lie, not now. "Let me help them, and you and dad, and then, when I'm ready, I'll let you know."

Not understanding exactly what her daughter was saying, Rose frowned. "I'm here for you," She told her daughter.

Shelby replied, "I know you are."

Chapter 2

Shelby stayed over at her parents' house that night. The next morning, Kent's parents were kind enough to come over so they could decide on some funeral arrangements.

Hugging them, Shelby noticed how much Kent favored his father. So much so, that it was difficult for her to look at Tony. Finally, she noticed that her parents were staring at her, and asked them, "What? I'm sorry?"

Rose asked her daughter, "Is there a funeral home you'd prefer to use?"

Shrugging, Shelby shook her head no.

The four parents started discussing options, and Shelby tuned them out, preferring to let memories invade her thoughts…

They were married! As Kent carried her across the threshold of the hotel room, Shelby laughed. There were rose petals on the bed, a bottle of champagne in an ice bucket, chilling, and chocolate covered strawberries on a tray. It was a big show for him, and Shelby just looked forward to them taking a few days, just the two of them.

She went into the bathroom to change out of her dress, and into a ridiculously sheer teddy that her bridesmaids gave her. When she came out, Kent was sitting on the bed, his tie undone, and looking nervous.

"I look ridiculous!" She sighed.

Standing up, Kent cupped her face in his palms, and said, "I don't see anything except my wife. My beautiful, frustrating, stubborn, magical, wonderful wife."

How could she find any fault with a man who told her that? "I guess I do look kind of hot," She added. They laughed as they fell onto the bed and made love for the first time as man and wife.

"Shelby," John said to get his daughter's attention. When her eyes focused on him, he smiled, and said, "We're going to the funeral home now."

Feeling a little silly for being caught daydreaming, Shelby stood up and followed the parents out to the car.

Her father drove, with Tony riding in the front, and the two mothers flanking her in the backseat. There was little conversation during the drive, except her mother giving her father directions to their destination.

When they got out of the car, Shelby thought the place was huge!

A woman came out to meet them, and walked them all inside. She introduced herself as Helen, and led them into a small alcove with a seating area.

Helen asked them questions, Shelby heard all of them, but deferred to Kent's parents for the answers. It wasn't that she didn't know what her husband's preferences were, she just didn't want to make the decisions right now and let in the pain.

Rose watched her daughter closely, concern filling her up more by the minute. She wasn't doing anything for the funeral preparations and she needed to. This was where you started to understand that you've lost someone. It wasn't easy, it hurt like hell, but it was necessary. If Shelby refused to do this, then her grieving process would be stalled.

Hours later they left the funeral home, having picked a date, the memorial cards, the guest book, the casket, and a myriad of other details that Shelby couldn't, or wouldn't make a decision about.

They drove back to her parents' house. As soon as Kent's parents left, she retreated back to her room.

Later that night, Shelby came out when she heard her parents' voices raised. She could only remember her parents yelling at one another a few times during her childhood. As she rounded the corner of the kitchen, she heard her mother say, "You are all just letting her hide! We can't do that, John."

Her parents saw her standing there, and immediately stopped yelling. "Mom," Shelby looked directly at her mother, "they're letting me find my own way."

Rose's chest heaved with emotion, "Baby, they mean well, I know that, but YOU have to be the one who does this or you won't get closure."

"What kind of closure do you expect me to get, Mom?" Shelby couldn't keep the sarcasm out of her words. "Do you want me to pick out which color we put in the damn coffin? He won't care! He won't feel it! He doesn't give a shit, Mom!" She started to walk away, then stopped and turned back to her mom, screaming at her, "He's fucking dead, is that closure enough for you, Mom?"

Rose watched their daughter leave the room, and crumbled to the floor, her husband rushing to her side. She was crying into his shoulder, saying, "I'm sorry, John. I know what she's feeling and I just want to help her."

John nodded, wanting to protect the two most important people in the world to him, and knowing he couldn't, not now. "Baby, she'll start healing, but you've told me a million times that people all grieve differently."

Nodding, Rose told him, "I know, but this," she pointed in the direction of their daughter's departure, "this isn't right."

Knowing his wife was right, but not knowing how he could change any of this, John did the only thing he could, he held his wife close.

The next morning, Shelby returned to her house. She called ahead and made sure that everyone was cleared out. They needed to find their closure, Shelby could understand that, but she couldn't handle their issues right now.

Opening the door, Shelby felt the void of the empty house. Her parents offered to come inside and stay, but she told them to just go on home. She assured them she could do this.

Walking into the living room, Shelby sat down on the chair that faced the big bay window, and let her mind go back......

They were driving down a street that Shelby didn't recognize. "Where are you taking me?" She asked Kent.

He smiled at her, but didn't answer right away. A few blocks later, he asked her to close her eyes. Shelby did as she was asked, and kept her eyes shut.

After the car stopped, she heard Kent get out, and wondered what he was up to. He opened her door, and helped her out, saying, "Keep them shut!"

Shelby shook her head, he was so into these surprises. Just two years ago he "surprised" her with buying a gym. That didn't go over too well, but Shelby had been supportive. Now the gym was a bonafide success, and training several high level gymnasts.

"Okay, now!" She head Kent say, and opened her eyes.

There, before her, was a newly built house. She looked at her husband, her eyes full of questions.

Kent kissed her on the lips, and announced, "It's ours!"

Shock covered her features, and Shelby asked him, "What do you mean, it's ours?"

Shaking his head at his wife's silly question, Kent replied, "We bought it."

She was about to voice her concerns when he stepped in front of her, took her hand, and led her to the door. "You'll love it," He explained as he led her inside. "I made sure it had all the things you said you wanted in a house."

They toured the house, and Shelby had to admit that she would've picked out the features he showed her. But, she wasn't even aware that they could afford a house. The last thing she was told was that they were investing all of their money back into the gym.

"Do you love it?" Kent asked her, his face bright with hope.

There was no way that Shelby could be mad at him for trying to take care of her, she smiled, and replied, "Yes."

Lifting up his wife, Kent swung her around. "Now," He smiled at her slyly, "let's go get our bed so we can start filling it with kids."

Danette Fogarty

The knocking on the front door brought Shelby out of her memories. She got up and looked through the glass. It looked like Kent's business partners, and friends, Jeff and Lisa.

Opening the door, Shelby knew she should at least attempt to smile, but couldn't do it.

Lisa stepped forward first, and hugged Shelby. "How are you doing, sweetie?" She asked.

Shelby nodded, not bothering to actually answer the question. She stepped back and motioned for them to come in.

After a quick look at her husband, Lisa took a deep breath, and followed Shelby inside.

The three of them sat down in the living room.

As if she was forgetting something, Shelby was looking around the room. "Oh," She finally remembered, "Can I get you some water?"

Jeff smiled, and answered, "No thank you, we're fine. We came to see if you needed help with anything."

"I'm okay," Shelby responded, but the words were flat.

Lisa spoke first, "Okay, well, we also came over to let you know that the gym has provisions in place for this kind of situation, so you don't have to worry about anything."

Shelby stared at her friend as if she were speaking another language, "Provisions?" She asked Lisa.

"Life insurance," Jeff answered. He knew Lisa didn't like him saying it like that, but this was what they needed to do, just tell Shelby what was what. "Kent and I made sure there was enough life insurance on each of us so our spouses would be okay and the gym would be okay."

Standing up, Shelby spat out, "Heaven forbid that precious gym not be okay!"

Not expecting her reaction, both Jeff and Lisa sat where they were, and didn't say anything.

Shelby realized she sounded crazy, but all anyone seemed to care about was the damn gym. And, frankly, she was sick of it. "I have been a second to that place for almost my entire married life, Jeff, so I really don't care what you do with it. I don't ever want to set foot in there again." She calmed down, "I know that neither of you did this, hell, I know Kent didn't plan this, but he was never here, and when he was, his mind was there, at the gym." Feeling drained, Shelby turned to leave the room. "I'm going to lie down, if you both could just see yourselves out that would be fine. I do appreciate you stopping by."

After they heard the bedroom door close, Jeff and Lisa sat there, staring at one another, and wondered what to do.

The next day, Shelby emerged from her room. She'd slept in bits and pieces. Her conscious mingled with memories as if it were dancing around it.

When she made her way into the kitchen, she smelled coffee. 'Funny,' She thought to herself, and jumped when a familiar voice said from behind her, "Oh, good, you're up."

Kent? Her mind wondered. She was smiling when she turned around to answer her husband, only to find his father standing there. Reality hit her full force! Kent wasn't here. He wasn't ever going to be here again. Dammit! Dammit! Dammit!

Kent's mom walked into the kitchen, and saw the look on Shelby's face. She knew what had happened. Kent sounded just like his dad and, for a second, their daughter-in-law thought this was all a bad dream. She'd done the same thing a million times in the last couple of days. "Shelby," She said softly, "why don't we take you in and get you in the shower."

Angelica gently steered her daughter-in-law into the master bathroom. She started the shower, got out some fresh towels, and tested the water temperature while Shelby just stood there, still as a stature. "It's crazy isn't it?" Angelica asked out loud. "I think he's going to just walk into the house and yell, hey mom."

Hearing her mother-in-law's words, Shelby snapped out of her trance. "Yes," She said in return.

"Why don't you get in the shower?" Angelica quietly urged Shelby, "And I'll get some cheese and crackers together for you to munch on."

With a small nod, Shelby stepped forward, and started to undo her shirt. Normally she wouldn't just undress with someone other than Kent, or one of her close girlfriends in the room, but she truly just didn't care at the moment. "Thank you," She said to her mother-in-law.

Angelica nodded, her heart breaking even more for her daughter-in-law.

The shower felt good to Shelby. She didn't realize what three days of little sleep, and practically no food, did to a person. It made them take a little raincheck from reality.

It was easier, in Shelby's mind, to just delve into the happy memories, not this mess that she found herself in now. It was a minefield of pain and agony, no matter which way she turned, there was a reminder that her husband was gone.

She came out of the room a while later, her hair in a clip, still wet because she didn't care to do anything with it. Not only were Kent's parents in the kitchen, but hers were too.

Rose stood and walked over to hug her daughter. She heard about Shelby's reaction to Lisa and Jeff's visit, and called Angelica to come up with some kind of plan. She knew her daughter would not take kindly to being "handled" but they would have to do just that for a while. "Hi, baby," She whispered in her daughter's ear.

"Hi, mom," Shelby returned, her tone flat.

They sat down at the kitchen table. The parents were talking about flower arrangements for the funeral, and all Shelby could focus on was the empty seat her husband used to sit in when they had family dinners.

"A toast!" Kent raised his glass, "To my wife, the one who puts up with me, and still thinks I have a cute butt."

They all laughed. Shelby just rolled her eyes, and shot back, "I thought I was the one with the cute butt."

Kent wiggled his eyes, a silent promise for a later adventure, after their parents were gone.

Angelica watched Shelby closely, and knew she was remembering something funny. There was a hint of a smile on her face. It was good to remember, it kept you from going crazy. But memories had their place, and although soothing, they wouldn't be able to take the place of reality for long. She shot a knowing look across the table to Rose.

Trying to draw her daughter into the conversation, Rose asked Shelby, "Honey, do you have a dress to wear for tomorrow?"

Shelby was confused, and asked her mother, "What's going on tomorrow?"

John blurted out, "It's Kent's funeral," before realizing what he'd said, and the tone he'd used.

All the blood drained out of Shelby's face, leaving her pale. "Oh yeah," She said quietly, trying to cover up the fact that she forgot her husband's funeral.

The parents looked at each other, at a loss for what they could, or should, do to help Shelby through this.

Chapter 3

The sun was nowhere to be found when Shelby woke up the next morning. The weather matched her mood perfectly. Today would not be easy, it would be hell, and she didn't want to do it.

Her parents offered to stay over the night before, but Shelby told them no. She needed some time to herself to try and get herself together for today. It sounded so crazy, even when she said the words inside her head, 'Kent's funeral.' They didn't make any sense and she didn't want to go. If she didn't go, then it wouldn't be true.

At a little after ten in the morning, there was a knock on the door. A robe wrapped around her, Shelby answered the door. Her hair was up in a towel, her face half smudged with makeup, and she had a toothbrush in her mouth.

Rose Brentman looked at her daughter, and smiled. Partially ready was better than not ready at all. The service was scheduled to begin at 2pm so they had plenty of time. She stepped forward and took her daughter into her arms.

Shelby eagerly accepted her mother's hug. She needed the emotional reinforcement that having her parents brought. "Come in," She mumbled around the toothbrush poking out of her mouth.

As Rose came inside, she saw the house was still unchanged. She had absolutely no idea what Shelby did when she was alone here, but it didn't look like she touched anything. There was a deep sadness in her chest for her daughter, and the frustrating thing was that Rose couldn't figure out what to do to help Shelby during this time. She talked to her husband almost completely about it since they received the awful news about Kent. What could they do? How could they help their daughter? It was an endless merry-go-round of questions and worries.

Shelby turned to go back toward the bedroom so Rose followed her.

The sound of the blow dryer broke the silence in the house, and had Rose jumping. Shelby was standing in the bathroom, with only her robe on, and blow drying her hair. Rose studied her daughter for a few minutes, noting the lack of any emotion in Shelby's features. When the blow dryer shut off, throwing the room back into deafening silence, Rose stepped forward, and asked, "Do you want me to do your hair?"

Nodding, Shelby pulled out a small bench she kept tucked under her vanity, and sat down. Since she had no ambition or clue as to what she'd do with her hair, it was a relief that her mother was willing to take on the task.

"Up or down?" Rose asked Shelby, her fingers loosely playing with her daughter's long hair.

Staring at herself in the mirror, and feeling numb, Shelby told her mother, "Kent liked it down."

With a nod, because her throat was too tight with emotion to speak, Rose began doing Shelby's hair. She curled the long tresses and loved the feel of her daughter's hair in her hands. It was like when Shelby was a little girl and asking her mommy to do something pretty with her hair. The memories of long ago happiness slammed into the tragic reason for today's events.

An hour later, Shelby's hair was done in long curls, the sides pulled back with clips, and her hair finger-brushed until it floated around her shoulders. Her mother helped her with some light makeup, mostly to keep her from looking so pale, and even helped her get into her dress. It was a black evening dress that she'd never worn. It was one she'd bought with "date night" in mind. It was difficult to look at herself in the mirror, knowing she was dressing up for her husband for the very last time.

The two women walked down the hall and stopped at the entrance to the living room. Shelby's father, along with Kent's parents, were there, sitting down and talking quietly.

With a deep breath, Shelby stepped forward as her father stood. She gave him a hug, and a small smile.

Kent's mother, Angelica, commented, "You look beautiful."

With another small smile, Shelby took a few steps and embraced her mother-in-law. "I know he would want me to look my best."

Angelica nodded, and tried to hold back her tears.

Shelby reached out, and took Tony's hand into hers. She looked at all four parents, and said to them, "This is for Kent. We need to be strong for everyone else. I know I haven't been strong up until now, but I know Kent is behind me, pushing me like he always has been, to be better at whatever I'm doing. I mean that in a good way, I just want to make him proud today."

There were sniffles from the mothers, and the fathers were clearly fighting back their own emotions, but all four of them nodded in understanding to Shelby.

Taking one last deep breath, Shelby announced, "Okay, let's get on with it then."

They all filed outside and into a waiting car. No one was emotionally equipped to be behind the wheel driving so it made sense to just get a driver for the day.

When they pulled up to the funeral home, Shelby waited until all of the parents got out before saying quietly, "Kent, honey, I'm going to need you today to keep me up."

The same lady who met them for the preparation meeting met them now. She asked, "Mrs. Forrester, would you like to go in alone first?"

Zoning out, Shelby didn't realize the woman was speaking to her. "Oh," She blushed, "I thought you were talking to Kent's mom." She nodded to the woman, and the two of them walked down the main hall and through some double doors.

Not knowing what to expect, Shelby just tried to breathe. It was difficult because her lungs didn't seem to want to open to accept oxygen. They were tight, and her breathing became shallower as she walked across the large room.

Her first glimpse of Kent, Shelby started crying immediately. He looked wonderful. He'd been wearing his helmet, thank God, and so all of his injuries were to his body from the impact of the accident. Shelby was thankful that she could see his face once more.

The representative from the funeral home seemed to disappear, leaving her with Kent for a few minutes. "Oh, my love," Shelby whispered, "I know you had to go, but I don't want to be here by myself."

There was no answer, only the soft music as it drifted through the room. In her mind though, Shelby could hear Kent saying, *'I'll always be with you.'* Logically she knew he didn't say it, but hearing it in her mind made her feel better. She covered his hand with hers, leaned down to kiss it, and walked out of the room, to meet back up with their parents.

Even though her own time with Kent was filled with a sense of peace, seeing his parents was a painful reminder of the enormous loss they all faced. His mother kept brushing his hair with her fingers, and crying. His father, just kept saying, "My boy," over and over and Shelby's heart ached for their agony. Her own parents were fighting back tears, but were flanking her on either side to give her their support.

Finally, Angelica and Tony kissed their son's forehead, and said their final goodbyes. They walked over to where there were chairs placed for the five of them.

The first people to arrive were Lisa and Jeff, Kent's partners at the gym. They were heartbroken as they gave their condolences to the parents. When they came to Shelby, their hesitation was apparent.

"I'm sorry," Shelby pre-empted anything they were planning to say, "I was angry and bitter, and I took it out on the two of you because I didn't know what else to do."

Lisa was crying, and hugged Shelby tightly, and whispered, "We are so sorry, we miss him so much!"

Shelby nodded, "I know."

Jeff couldn't even speak, his pain was written all over his face. He only nodded and hugged Shelby. She felt his shoulders start to quiver in his battle to hold back from crying. She hugged him tighter, and whispered to him, "You are his best friend."

Shelby stood where she was, after Jeff released her, and watched as they went over to the casket to say their goodbyes. Watching as others had to say goodbye was something Shelby hadn't really considered before now. It wasn't just her who was reeling from Kent's loss, but others were too. She felt shame over her behavior up to now, and looked over to find her mother staring at her.

Rose squeezed her daughter's hand, and said, "You're okay," before turning back to other people who'd come to pay their respects.

The trail of guests went on and on. Someone mentioned that the line went out the doorway of the funeral home and wrapped halfway around the building. Shelby smiled at the thought. Kent would have been humbled that so many people thought enough of him to pay their respects.

A man came through the line, hugged Kent's parents, gave his condolences to her parents, and then stood before her. Shelby thought he looked familiar but couldn't place him.

"Your husband and I went to high school," The man said to Shelby, "he was the biggest pain in the butt, but also the nicest guy you'd want to meet."

Shelby thought the description of Kent was right on. She smiled, and returned, "I would agree with you. I'm thankful that Kent has so many people who wanted to say goodbye."

The man gave her a funny look. His eyes told Shelby he wanted to say more, but he just gave a quick nod, and moved along with the other mourners.

Turning to the next person in line, Shelby heard some whispering about, "Did you see him?" along with, "I didn't know he knew Kent." She had no idea what people were saying, she only knew her feet were aching from standing, and she was tired.

She was about to ask her mom if they could sit down, when she saw Kent's gymnastic students come into her line of sight. This was the part that Shelby was dreading. These young girls looked up to Kent to guide them, and now he was gone. She knew it would be emotional and took a deep breath.

Jeff and Lisa came back over to escort the team, and the gymnasts' parents, through the procession line of mourners.

"Coach was awesome," The first young woman said, tears streaming down her cheeks.

Another student, her name was Olivia, hugged Shelby tight. "I asked him to stay to help me with my floor routine. I just couldn't get my back two and a half punch down, and I begged him to stay and help me."

Shelby hugged Olivia tightly. "It wasn't your fault," She said to the teenager.

Shaking her head, Olivia swiped at her tears, "He told me it was date night and you'd be mad, but then he said that he'd smile and kiss you and you'd forgive him."

Smiling now, through her tears, Shelby replied, "And he was right. I would have."

She hugged the other team members as they came through, making sure she told each of them how important they were to Kent.

Some of the girls were so upset, they couldn't even walk the few feet over to where Kent lay in the casket. Jeff and Lisa didn't force them, neither did their parents, and Shelby was grateful for that. This would be tough enough for them.

Within a half hour, the viewing was over. The pastor who married Kent's parents and baptized Kent stood up and began to speak. "This is not a joyous occasion. There is so much pain in our hearts. But, Kent wouldn't be happy about that...."

Shelby listened as the Pastor went on to talk about Kent's life. He told them about Kent's escapades as an "inquisitive" youngster. Shelby smiled at that, because the Pastor was being kind. Kent himself, along with his parents, always admitted that he was a hellion as a child. She, herself, could attest to seeing some of that during the time they dated.

"I never thought I would be speaking to you all on such a day, but I am comforted by the knowledge that Kent is now with the Lord." The Pastor said with complete resolve.

Sitting down, her parents on one side of her and Kent's on the other side, Shelby wanted desperately to believe the words the Pastor spoke. She knew that Kent was a good man, but they never really discussed faith during their marriage.

He spoke for a few more minutes, announcing that they would be going to the cemetery for a small service.

Since Shelby hadn't been paying attention during the planning of Kent's funeral, she didn't realize that the cemetery his parents wanted him buried at was almost two hours away from where they lived, and closer to Austin, Texas. His grandparents were buried there and his parents had burial plots there as well.

Given the distance, a lot of people declined to go to the service at the cemetery. Shelby was secretly relieved. There were so many at the viewing that she would feel a little less "on display" there.

They drove up a hill to where the cemetery sat. As she got out of the car, Shelby looked around. The view was gorgeous, complete with a valley to look down on. This was hill country, and very rural so there wouldn't be malls and whatnot popping up anytime soon. Knowing Kent would be here, in peace, eased Shelby's pain slightly.

The Pastor got out, and led the processional to the burial site. Both of their fathers, with Jeff, and a few other friends were the pallbearers.

Shelby sat down and stared ahead as they brought Kent's casket over to the burial site. She didn't want to acknowledge anything just yet. Angelica's hand was in hers and it was shaking, so Shelby focused on her mother-in-law for a few minutes.

When they placed the flowers on top of the casket, the breeze picked up, making them not want to stay in their designated spot. Shelby watched, and tried to stifle a little giggle. She swore it was Kent, pulling one last prank on them, forcing his sense of humor on them.

She looked over at her mother-in-law, and recognized the same thoughts in Angelica's eyes. They shared a smile.

Again, the Pastor said some words about Kent, recited a favorite passage of Kent's mother, and then asked if anyone wanted to say anything.

Shelby didn't expect it, but wasn't surprised that Jeff got up and walked over to where the Pastor stood.

"I've known Kent since college," He began, "and he was crazy enough to believe we'd actually make a living at doing something we loved." There were a few chuckles. "I also knew how he felt about his parents," Jeff looked at Angelica and Tony, and said, "He respected you both immensely and wanted to make you proud."

Angelica started to cry, Tony standing behind her, his hands rubbing her shoulders.

Jeff looked at Shelby, and said, "And I know how he felt about his wife, he used to say that Shelby was the only person who could see through the BS," he looked over at the Pastor and whispered, "sorry," before turning back around, and continuing, "He dished out, and loved him anyway."

Shelby couldn't help but smile. That was Kent, cutting to the chase, no matter what.

Finally, Jeff looked at Kent's casket, and told him, "You'll never know the gaping hole you've left in our hearts, but we love you."

Now Shelby started to cry again. It was difficult to see men break down, and Jeff was certainly doing that. Lisa held out her hands to him as he returned to where she stood.

The Pastor spoke a few more words, said one last prayer, and then people began to depart.

Shelby couldn't do it, she couldn't leave just yet. Her mother, and Kent's, sat with her, not saying anything. A few minutes later, Kent's parents got up and walked over to the casket. His father kissed the smooth wood first, said something, and allowed Angelica a final moment with her son. She said something as well, although it was quiet so only she and Kent would know.

Rose was sitting next to her daughter, watching her closely. She hadn't made any attempt to get up and say a final goodbye to her husband. "Honey, you should go up and say something, before the funeral home comes to do their job."

Slowly, Shelby turned her head to look at her mother. "You mean, say goodbye before they come back and lower him into the ground."

Understanding that her daughter was grieving was one thing, but having Shelby be so crass at a time like this wasn't something Rose was ready to accept. "You will not talk like that to me, Shelby," She made sure her words were quiet, but serious.

Her mother's tone hit home quickly and Shelby felt remorse. "I'm sorry, Mom," She said to her mother, "I just don't want it sugar coated, I know what's going to happen, and I want to stay."

Rose gave her daughter a nod, and replied, "Fine, we'll go with Kent's parents back to the Pastor's house, he's invited us there for a bit before we return to Houston." She looked over at Kent's casket, "You can stay here and witness your husband being put in the ground and I hope it brings you some measure of peace."

John overhead the conversation, but didn't comment until his wife stood up and walked away from their daughter. "Rose, are you going to leave her here?" He asked, surprised by the words his wife spoke.

Stopping, Rose looked at her husband, the pain showing in her eyes, "I don't want to torture her, John, I want to be there for her, but she has some strange sense of wanting to see all of this," she pointed to where the cemetery crew was starting to gather, "And I'll let her learn the hard way."

Not sure he agreed with his wife, but not wanting to start an argument, John sighed, and followed his wife to the car. They were met by Angelica and Tony, then got in to leave the cemetery.

Chapter 4

Shelby watched her parents walk away, and knew she couldn't just sit here and watch the cemetery workers like some weirdo.

Getting up, she started to walk up the hill, finding a large elm tree that grew there. She sat down at the base of the huge tree, and looked out over the large cemetery.

The sun was shining here, a far cry from the cloudy Houston weather. There were birds singing and a light breeze blew through the hillside. It was actually very beautiful. Shelby watched as the parents left, the Pastor's car following them. She was, for all intent and purpose, alone.

She did watch, as the cemetery crew took the flowers off of the casket. They handed some things to the representative of the funeral home, and then uncovered the pile of dirt a few yards away. Shelby thought it was strange that they covered it up in the first place. It wasn't like people didn't know how this worked.

One man worked a turning mechanism that lowered the casket into the ground. There was some maneuvering, she assumed was the vault top being set in place. Then, within minutes, there was a backhoe pulling up to backfill the grave with dirt.

It was morbid curiosity, Shelby knew it, and yet she couldn't stop watching. Maybe she just wanted to make sure that Kent was taken care of properly? Maybe it was that this meant that the constant nightmare she'd been stuck in for the last five days was actually real?

Shelby pulled her knees up to her chest, hugging them to try and get herself warm. Even though the temperature was in the low eighties, she was shivering.

Leaning back, Shelby allowed the large tree to be her backrest. She closed her eyes, and tried to see Kent.

He was standing in front of her, smiling. "You know this is it, right?" He asked in a total Kent-smart-ass way. Shelby smiled at him, "I don't know any such thing," She replied in an equally sarcastic tone. He walked up the hill, to where she was sitting, and crouched down in front of her. "Baby, you're going to have to let go, you know that don't you?" He asked her in a soothing tone. Shelby shook her head no, and asked him back, "How can I let go of you, Kent, we haven't said goodbye yet?" Kent leaned forward and kissed her gently, before whispering, "We just did, baby. I love you." And then he was gone.

Shelby woke with a start. Her lips still tingled, so she lifted her fingers to touch them. She could have sworn that Kent was right here, it was so real. "Oh, Kent," She said into the breeze, "I miss you!"

The sun was starting it's decent to the west, and Shelby saw a car pull up a few yards away. A young man got out, walked over to her, and asked, "Are you Mrs. Forrester?"

Nodding to him, Shelby smiled. He couldn't be much more than seventeen.

"I'm Caleb, I'm here to take you back to meet up with the others," The young man told her. He switched from foot to foot, feeling nervous.

Reluctantly, Shelby got up from her seat in front of the tree. She looked down at the place her husband now rested, and said a short prayer for him, and thanked him for helping her.

She followed Caleb down to the car, and got in.

They drove for about ten minutes, past a beautiful church, and to a small house set back from the road. She recognized the car that drove them all up here. They got out and went inside.

Rose was the first to stand and walk over to her daughter. She felt awful for being so stern at the gravesite. "I'm sorry, sweetheart," She said to her daughter.

"Don't be," Shelby reassured her mom, "I needed it."

With a nod, Rose stepped aside to let John, Angelica, and Tony all give Shelby hugs.

The Pastor and his wife asked if she was hungry or thirsty, but Shelby shook her head no.

After a few minutes, the five of them left, with thanks to the Pastor and his family for their hospitality.

They'd been in the car about fifteen minutes, when Shelby turned to Angelica and Tony, to say, "I think it was a wonderful thing, having him here, thank you."

Kent's parents looked at Shelby, and didn't say anything at first. There had been a number of discussions about whether or not this was right, but with Shelby's lack of interest in the arrangements, and their need to have their son in the family cemetery, it seemed like the right thing to do.

Tony spoke a while later, telling them a story, "When I was about six, my grandpop passed on, and we were there, at the service. I swear, I saw him walking across the grass, it was the craziest thing."

Shelby knew that now would be a good time to tell them about her "dream" with Kent, but she wanted to keep it to herself for a while longer. It was her private time with her husband.

The drive back down to Houston was decidedly different than the drive up to the cemetery. The parents made small talk periodically, and tried to include Shelby in their discussions. Although she nodded here and there, Shelby didn't contribute anything verbally.

They were going down the freeway when Rose asked her daughter, "Do you want to come back to our house for a while?"

It wasn't difficult to hear the hope her mother had, and Shelby felt bad because she knew she was going to disappoint her parents. She answered, "No, I think I'd like to go back to our house."

No one missed the use of "our" in the sentence. Shelby wondered if any of them would ever get used to the idea that Kent wasn't going to be there anymore.

After she was dropped off, amidst promises that she would call the parents within the next two days, Shelby sighed as she walked into the house.

The funeral home delivered the flowers to the house, something she apparently hadn't remembered being arranged. The perfume of the flowers drifted throughout the house. Usually flowers made Shelby smile, but these flowers, they just reminded her that her husband was gone.

Without reading any of the cards, or even moving anything, Shelby just went into their bedroom. She flopped down on the bed, pulled Kent's pillow to her, and breathed in the scent of him. Within minutes, she was asleep.

"I want kids, Shelby!" Kent yelled. They'd been in the house almost a year now and he was back on the 'let's have a family' tangent. They'd had this same argument about a half dozen times in their six years of marriage. "I'm not ready yet," She told him, and cringed when he left the room, slamming the door behind him. She sat down in the chair and cried. Why did he want kids so badly? They were still young and had plenty of time for that.

Shelby woke up, tears still fresh on her cheeks. She'd forgotten the argument about children, and had a large pile of guilt heaped on her chest because of it. Why hadn't she wanted to have kids with Kent? She loved him, he loved her, and yet, she didn't want kids yet.

A frown on her face, she turned over and looked at the clock. It was about 4am and she was now wide awake. Turning over, so she was laying on her back, Shelby let out a big sigh. That particular fight had happened only weeks before Kent's death. Did he know something she didn't? Throwing that thought out the proverbial window, Shelby pushed herself up and walked over to her dresser.

She put on her running gear, stretched out, and was running down the street within a half hour. There was music blaring in her headphones, and she was just trying to maintain her breathing as she ran.

It was tough, doing this kind of physical exercise with no food or good sleep in your system. Shelby knew that, being a gymnast, which was that any athlete had to take care of themselves if they wanted to perform well.

By the time she got home, she was beat! It took the rest of her strength to get her clothes off and get in the shower. When she stepped out of the shower, she almost yelled, "Kent," out of habit, but stopped herself.

Wrapping a robe around herself, Shelby went into the kitchen and grabbed an apple out of a fruit basket on the counter. She'd have to read the card and get out the thank you note to whomever had it delivered. Grabbing some bread off of the counter, she popped two slices into the toaster.

Checking her phone, she saw she had a couple dozen voicemails, and over fifty text messages. That wasn't getting dealt with anytime soon. The toast popped up so she put a little butter on the slices before taking the plate, and the remaining uneaten portion of her apple, and sat down at the dining room table.

Quietly, she munched on her makeshift meal. It might've only been an apple and some toast, but it tasted good. By the time she was finished, she felt full.

"When are you coming home?" Shelby asked Kent. She finally called him at the gym when he missed dinner. "I don't know baby," He answered, clearly distracted. She could hear his muffled directions to someone, probably one of the gymnasts. "I'll get there as soon as I can," Kent told her, and added, "I love you." She smiled, despite the fact that she was mad that he missed dinner, "I love you too, you pain in the ass." Kent laughed into the phone, before hanging up.

Shelby snapped out of the memory when there was a knock at the front door.

Pulling her robe tighter around her, she walked down the hall. After pulling the curtain aside, she saw her parents.

Sighing, she unlocked the door, and opened it for them. "Hi mom, hi dad," She said in an overly bright tone.

John didn't even respond, he just snorted. Rose looked at Shelby and asked, "Have you eaten?"

Nodding proudly, Shelby led the way into the kitchen. "I had an apple and not one, but two," she held up two fingers, "pieces of toast."

The look of surprise on her parents' faces was priceless.

Sitting down, John asked, "How about some coffee?"

With a nod, Shelby went over and started to make a pot.

Rose watched her daughter, "Something is different," she announced.

Both John and Shelby looked at her, their faces filled with surprise.

Getting up, Rose walked around the counter toward Shelby, "Don't think I don't notice anything about you, young lady."

Shrugging, Shelby responded, "I went running this morning."

The admission had both of her parents looking at her now. "What?" She asked them, "Am I not supposed to jog as part of a grieving ritual?"

Rose rolled her eyes. "Why must you always be so sarcastic?" She asked her daughter.

Raising her eyebrows, Shelby retorted, "Uh, probably because I've been married to the master of sarcasm and smart mouthing for over six years."

Throwing up her hands, Rose looked at her husband, and mumbled, "Even the response to the sarcasm is sarcasm."

John smiled, a little relieved that he could see some of his daughter again. Not that she was done grieving, that particular thing took a long time, but if she was doing things that she would've done before Kent's death, then perhaps she was at least accepting it. "That's my girl," He said quietly, and winked at Shelby.

"I heard that," Rose told him sternly.

Smiling at her parents, and their word play, Shelby actually felt okay. She wouldn't use the word good, but okay was better than what she'd been feeling like.

After waiting for the coffee to finish filling the carafe, she poured her parents each a cup, and took them over to the table. She sat down, cupping her bottled water and intensely watching the condensation as it poured down the side of the plastic bottle.

Rose asked, "What's on your mind?"

Shelby shouldn't be surprised that her mother asked, the woman could read her like a book and it used to irritate Shelby. Now, it made her feel better. "Well, I had a dream, at least I think it was a dream," She told them.

John frowned, "What do you mean, you think it was a dream?" He asked.

"Well, I was sitting there at the cemetery, and I closed my eyes. I don't know if I actually fell asleep, but Kent was there. He walked up the hill and spoke to me." She was talking, but refusing to look at her parents as she spoke.

Concerned, Rose asked Shelby, "What did he say?"

Sighing, Shelby answered, "He said it was time to let go."

John was curious and asked his daughter, "And what did you say?"

"I told him I couldn't let go because he hadn't said goodbye yet." Shelby knew this sounded crazy and hoped her parents didn't decide to admit her to the nearest psychiatric facility.

After taking a sip of her coffee, Rose put the mug down, and turned to look at her daughter. "Did he say anything back after that?" She asked.

Shelby nodded, and told them, "He kissed me and said he just did, say goodbye I mean."

Rose was crying, she couldn't help it. "I'm so glad he did that. He must've known you needed it."

Looking at his wife, John was thoroughly confused. He'd never heard of such a thing, other than the story Tony related to them in the car. "You believe it?" He asked Rose.

Smiling at her husband, Rose answered, "Yes, I do."

'Well,' Shelby thought to herself, 'maybe they wouldn't commit her as long as one of her parents believed her.

"Not to be sarcastic," John said to the women, "but what makes you think this wasn't just a trick of the mind?"

Rose looked at Shelby, and waited.

Shelby took a deep breath, "He kissed me, and Dad, I swear, my lips were still warm from his touch when I woke up."

John wasn't sure he believed in all that ghost stuff, but if his little girl was this sure that her husband came to her and said goodbye, then he would believe it. "Okay," He answered, and drank his coffee.

They sat there at the table, talking for another hour.

Shelby knew they were checking on her, and probably would for some time. Everyone wanted to make sure she didn't shrivel up. Telling her parents about her "dream" at the cemetery did help her. She felt as if there was some merit to the experience, but only time would tell.

Chapter 5

Three months later, Shelby felt as though she'd hit a kind of plateau, as far as her feelings went anyway.

Getting home from the store, she went over how low she'd sunk since her husband's death……..

Every day she got up, went for a run usually, came home and got ready for work.

At the urging of her parents, Shelby took a job as a temp for the electrical firm her father worked for. One of the office ladies was out on temporary disability so her dad got her "in." It was easy enough work; she filed, answered phones, sent out bills, that sort of stuff. It was enough to keep her from going stir crazy at the house, but didn't fill any kind of emotional void she had.

The nights…..the nights were the most difficult. The house was so quiet, she thought she might go mad sometimes. She'd gotten into the habit of sleeping on the sofa with the television on so she didn't have to listen to the quiet.

Her friends called, emailed, and texted, and Shelby did answer. The problem was that her answers mainly consisted of one or two words and were delayed, sometimes by days. She knew that people were getting tired of her "drama," but to her, it was just her life. She now existed……alone.

With her parents coming over one or two times a week, to check on her, she did have company, it just wasn't Kent, and nothing seemed to make her feel good.

One particularly lonely Friday night, she picked up a bottle of wine on the way home, drank the entire bottle, on an empty stomach, and felt strong enough to look through her and Kent's wedding pictures. Even the numbing from the alcohol couldn't completely block out the pain of seeing herself so happy, with Kent, produced. Finally, her body had enough and she spent the rest of the night throwing up in her bathroom. She hadn't touched a drop of alcohol since.

She didn't dare tell anyone about the humiliating behavior, or consequences. She didn't say much anymore.

Looking at her phone, and seeing that her parents were due to arrive within the hour, Shelby hurried up and went inside the house.

After putting the few groceries away, enough to make it look like she really was eating regularly if her mom checked, Shelby went into her bedroom to change from her daily business attire of slacks and a white shirt.

She walked into the bedroom closet, kicked off her sensible heels, and stood there, staring into space.

Unfortunately, she was still in the exact same spot when her parents showed up for dinner. They found her there, just standing and staring at nothing.

Rose looked at her husband, a worried expression on her face, and asked Shelby, "Honey, what are you doing?"

They knew she was home since the car was in the driveway, and, after knocking, they came in. They even called out, but got no response. Now, their daughter; their once vibrant and loving daughter, stood in the middle of her closet and looked so lost.

Shelby didn't answer her mother. She could see her mom's lips move, but nothing could permeate the static that was filling up her head. It was a dull roar of nothing that threatened to engulf her completely.

John, very worried about his daughter, finally walked over to her and grabbed her arm. The jolt of his movement seemed to startle her.

As if she were coming out of a dense fog, Shelby's mind finally started picking up again. She felt the pressure from her dad's hand on her arm. "I'm sorry, what?" She asked her mom.

"That's it!" Rose shouted, and stalked out of the closet.

Looking at her father, Shelby asked him, "What was that about?"

Trying to remain calm, but sharing his wife's concern for their daughter, John explained, "We knocked, we shouted, we walked in, and you just stood there."

Even though Shelby knew her father didn't mean to, he sounded accusatory, and her anger started to churn up. "It's my house, I can do as I please," She responded sharply.

For the first time, in too many years to count, John wanted to shake some sense into his daughter. "What do you think we worry about?" He asked Shelby.

Confused, Shelby answered, "I don't know."

"We worry about you," John replied sharply, this time intending for her to understand the severity of their pain, "we worry about whether you're eating, sleeping, living, and frankly, we've had enough."

Her anger, now in full swing, took over. She lashed out verbally, "I didn't ask you to, so just leave!" She wanted to be left alone, "Go! See if I care!"

Rose had stood a few feet away, listening to her husband try to reason with Shelby and, in turn, get upset. It was obvious that wasn't going to work. She turned and went back into the closet. Very calmly saying, "I don't give a shit if you want to be left alone young lady," She managed to hang on to her own anger, "you will stop this madness now, you will get your ass into counseling, you will go out and see people, besides us," she pointed to herself and John, "and you will deal with the fact that your husband isn't coming home."

Turning on her mother, Shelby pointed at her, "You don't think that I don't know Kent will never come through that door? You think that I don't realize that he'll never tease me about my cooking, or hug me, or kiss me, or love me? Believe me, mom, I'm reminded every damn second of every damn day!"

The two women stood there, face to face, neither budging.

John couldn't take it. "Shelby, please," He said, his voice breaking, "please listen to your mom. We love you, sweetie."

All the yelling, Shelby could take, but her father breaking down, tears spilling down his cheeks, tore at her heart. "I'm sorry," She said, her own tears coming fast and furious.

Rose caught her daughter, as the weight of her grief buckled her legs. They all sat down, there in the closet, holding their girl while she cried her heart out.

Stroking her daughter's hair, Rose looked over her girl's head to her husband. He gave her a small smile, letting her know they were finally making some progress.

Although she had no idea how, Shelby actually fell asleep with her head on her mother's lap. There was the soothing motion of her mother's hands running through her hair and it lulled her when she didn't think she'd ever relax again.

John got up, went into the kitchen, called Kent's parents on the house phone, and then came back, handing his wife a bottled water. He sat back down, across from her. "I've talked to them, they're waiting for us to call and set up a time."

Rose nodded. It was easy to think that someone's death was the biggest hurdle to get over. It wasn't. The truth was, learning to grieve and still manage to go on living; that was the real struggle. All the immediate stuff, the planning, the "busy" work of laying someone to rest made the initial loss bearable. It was the lonely days afterward that made you feel gutted out, emotionally.

"Are you okay, love?" John asked his wife.

Coming out of her thoughts, Rose smiled, "You always could read me so well, couldn't you?" she asked her husband.

Smiling at her, John replied, "It isn't tough to put this one together."

Wanting to shield her husband from any unpleasantness, Rose shrugged. They had an unspoken rule to not talk about the past, it was something they agreed on when they first met, at Rose's request.

Reaching over their daughter, John took Rose's hand into his. "It's okay, you know," He told his wife softly. "I know we don't talk about it, and now I'm sad that we never did."

Tears were flowing down Rose's cheeks. She whispered, "I thought it would hurt you if we talked about it."

Surprised, John frowned. "Sweetheart, you are my wife, I love you, I think I figured you wanted to file that away and not discuss it again. I'm sorry, I should've been more sensitive."

"It's not that," Rose responded, "I really did put it to rest, until now."

Nodding, John could understand. He sighed, and said, "Then maybe you need to tell Shelby about it, maybe that's why you went through what you did."

Even though what her husband said was true, she wasn't sure how well their daughter would accept the information. For now, at least, they would need to just be there for Shelby. "I'll see," She told John, and prayed she wouldn't need to tell her daughter.

When Shelby woke up, they were still in the closet. Her mother sat, her head leaning against the wall, her eyes closed, and still cradling Shelby's head in her lap. Slowly, Shelby turned her face so she could see her dad. He too, was sleeping while sitting up. A wave of shame slammed into Shelby. She was torturing her parents with her own problems, and they didn't need to suffer because she couldn't cope with losing Kent. She realized, she had to stop acting crazy, and start to figure this out.

Feeling her daughter move, Rose opened her eyes. "Are you okay?" She asked Shelby.

Sighing, Shelby looked up her mother, and answered, "No, but I think I can be if I stop this......whatever this is."

Smiling, Rose nodded, "This is you accepting, and it hurts like hell and it will hurt like hell for a long time."

"Mom," Shelby said, then asked, "How do you know so much about this? I mean," Shelby started to sit up and face her mother, "I know you lost Grandma and Grandpa, but this feels like you know what I'm feeling."

Rose happened to look past her daughter, to see her husband was awake now. He nodded slowly. She took a breath, and answered, "I was married before I married your dad." The admission felt so strange to her, as if it were someone else she was talking about. Her daughter's look of shock made her nod, and add, "He was in the Marines, and oh he was so handsome." Her mind drifted back to a time long ago, "We were high school sweethearts, his name was Charles, and he went off to some Top Secret place and was killed."

The impact of her mother's words were like hammers being slammed into Shelby's chest. This was unbelievable. "Why didn't I know about this before?" She asked her mother, and then turned to visually include her father in the conversation.

"Don't look at your dad, Shelby, he wanted to tell you, I was the one who didn't." Rose told her daughter.

The look of incredulity was written all over Shelby's face. She asked, "Why not?" once again.

Looking around the small room, Rose noticed her son-in-law's clothes still hung there. She wanted to be anywhere but here, opening up this tightly closed jar of feelings. "Because, we were only married for a few months, right out of high school, and when he died, I thought I died too."

That, Shelby could understand. She nodded for her mom to continue.

Rose had to take a few deep breaths before speaking again. "They came to the door of my parents' house, a Major and the Chaplain, that's what they do," She began. "I knew, I knew because I hadn't received a letter in weeks. I was staying at my folks' place so we could save up for a house when he got back stateside." The tears started to spill. "I stood there, with my mother behind me, and listened to these two men tell me my husband was dead."

Instinctively, Shelby started rocking back and forth in an effort to understand and soothe herself. Her mother's recollection was so much like her own experience.

"So, we waited until his body came home, and we buried him near our hometown," Rose explained. "I moved from California to Texas soon after and, a year and a half later, met your dad." Smiling for the first time since she began her story, Rose said, "He was the first man who didn't make me feel bad for loving Charles, and he told me, I'll never forget this, that he knew I had a big enough heart for both of them, Charles and John." Looking over at her husband, she mouthed, 'I love you,' then looked at her daughter and told her, "And I did, I had enough room in there for both of them, and you." She cupped her daughter's face with her hands.

For the first time in three months, Shelby felt a shift. There was someone, right next to her in fact, that knew exactly what she felt. She probably should be upset that her mother didn't tell her sooner, but knowing herself, it wasn't until now that Shelby was willing to listen. "Thank you," She whispered to her mom.

Rose smiled, and asked her daughter, "For what?"

Reaching one hand out to her mother, and the other hand out to her father, Shelby replied, "For being who you both are and not taking my BS anymore."

John chuckled, he liked it when his daughter was headstrong because she reminded him of himself. "Well then, let's get out of the closet and get some dinner."

They all got up, and went into the kitchen. Dinner consisted of a salad with chicken. Even though her dad complained that "a salad didn't actually make up a meal," they ate and talked a lot. By the time they left for the night, Shelby felt some semblance of healing had finally begun.

The next day was her last day working at the company her dad helped her get the job at. The employee she's been filling in for had to quit and the company hired someone else full-time. They offered the position to Shelby, but she knew she wouldn't be happy there so she declined it. The ladies in the office wished her well and even brought in cupcakes for her last day there.

When she got home, the house, even though still empty, didn't feel so lonely anymore. She picked up the mail and waved to her neighbors. They waved back and then practically ran inside whispering because she hadn't so much as acknowledged anyone since Kent's death.

The grief was still with her, still hung on her like a heavy, wet robe, but it seemed a little more bearable now.

After she changed into some yoga pants and a tank top, Shelby went into the kitchen. She made a chicken breast, marinara sauce, a small portion of noodles, and grabbed some provolone cheese out of the refrigerator. It was a real meal and Shelby did eat half of it, which she thought was a good effort.

Flipping through channels on the television helped her mind deal with its restlessness. She picked up the pile of mail and started to go through it. There was the customary junk mail of solicitations, most of them were for Kent. A few bills came, and then a letter from Imperial Gymnastics, the gym Kent and she half owned. Curious, Shelby opened up the envelope. It contained a letter.

Shelby:

We know you didn't want to discuss this when we last met, and then at the funeral, it wasn't the right time. We contacted Kent's parents and got the information from them needed to file with our insurance company. Here's the enclosed check. Know that we're thinking of you and praying for your healing. You're always welcome here, anytime you want.

Love,

Jeff and Lisa

Another wave of guilt swept through Shelby's chest. She was awful to them when they came to the house and she shouldn't have been. There were truly only trying to help. She didn't quite have that in mind when they came by and would have to face them sooner or later. After folding up the letter, she took out the other papers that were in the envelope. There was a form letter from the insurance company stating that they were paying out the claim. What shocked Shelby was the addendum to the policy, which included a payoff for the mortgage on the house. Shelby didn't know anything about that. She wondered, when they bought the house, why Kent didn't put that into the contract, and now she knew why. She said a quick prayer of thanks to Kent and pulled out the check. Only when she'd read the amount several times, did she catch her breath.

Grabbing her phone, Shelby called down to the gym. Lisa picked up, and gave her standard greeting of Imperial Gymnastics, how may I help you?"

"Lisa," Shelby's voice was a croak, "it's Shelby."

Standing up, Lisa went over and shut the door to the office so no one would interrupt their phone call. "Shelby, how are you?" She asked her friend.

Staring at the check, Shelby answered, "Well, I got your letter, thank you, but the amount on the check......well, it's pretty big."

Smiling, Lisa replied, "Well, I guess when Kent and Jeff started up the business they had a clear understanding of the net worth and wanted to make sure we were okay if something like this happened." Trying not to cry, Lisa went on to say, "You know you still own half the gym, just because Kent passed away, you retain your ownership."

Another thing Shelby wasn't aware of, "Oh," was all she could say.

'Obviously Kent didn't keep Shelby in the loop,' Lisa thought to herself. "Yes, and you're welcome to decide if you want us to buy you out, or if you want to be a silent partner, or if you want to come to the gym and work."

There were a lot of things running through Shelby's mind at the moment. The most important thing was that she was not in a stable enough emotional state to go to the gym; not yet anyway. "Thank you for the offer, Lisa," She tried to sound calm, "but I'm not ready for any kind of decisions like that yet."

"Perfectly understandable," Lisa responded, "it's kind of a mad house today, so I'll have to let you go but thanks for calling, Shelby. We miss you!"

Sighing, Shelby returned, "I miss you both too, say hi to Jeff," before she disconnected the call. After putting her phone back on the table, Shelby curled up in a ball and cried herself to sleep.

Chapter 6

A few days after receiving the check, Shelby called and asked her mother to accompany her to the bank. It was time to get things in order, financially, and a little bit emotionally. Kent was still on all of the accounts and still had bills in his name. Shelby paid them, and with the life insurance, could pay off all of their debt, including the house. She would always be grateful to Kent for being so responsible and taking care of things for her.

Her mother pulled up in front of the house and Shelby went out to get into the car. "Thanks," She said to her mom, "I didn't want to do this alone."

Smiling, Rose replied, "You'll never have to do anything alone, Dad and I are here for you."

Knowing it was true, was reassuring, but hearing her mom say it made Shelby feel better.

They drove over to the bank. Even after her mom put the vehicle in park, and shut it off, Shelby had a difficult time moving to get out of it.

Finally, Rose spoke, "You have to do this, it's been overdue for a while already and, although it's painful, it's important to get it taken care of."

Nodding, Shelby opened the door and got out of the car.

There was a receptionist at the bank, and Rose gave the woman Shelby's name and asked if they could speak to someone about accounts. The woman nodded and smiled, and put some information into the computer before asking them to take a seat in the waiting area.

For some reason, Shelby's hands were sweaty. She absently rubbed them down the sides of her skirt, wanting this to be over with.

Rose watched her daughter. Her motherly instinct was telling her to step in and just take care of it, but she knew that wouldn't be the best thing for Shelby in the long run. Her daughter needed to do these little things in order to put her life back together. "How are you doing?" She asked Shelby.

Swallowing hard, Shelby replied, "I'm okay, nervous, but okay."

"Good," Rose said, then added, "the okay part."

Smiling at her mom, Shelby was glad she wasn't alone doing this.

A few minutes later, a smiling lady came out of a hallway and said, "Mrs. Forrester," before leading the way back down the hallway and into an office.

The three of them sat down, Shelby taking out a folder she'd placed all of the documents into before leaving the house.

The woman, her nametag said Elaine, spoke first, asking, "How can I help you today?"

Shelby stared at her for a few seconds, then darted her eyes over to her mom. Her mother just nodded her encouragement, but didn't speak. "Okay, so my husband died a few months ago, and I'm not sure how to go about doing all the necessary paperwork."

Elaine looked at the young woman, and her heart ached. 'Too young to be going through something like this,' she thought to herself, and then offered, "I'm so sorry for your loss, we'll see if we can't help you get all of the documentation and accounts settled for you today."

They began with Elaine asking for the account number. Shelby passed over her little card with the account information on it the bank provided when they opened it. She also pushed the folder across the desk, toward Elaine, as if it was contaminated and she didn't want to touch it.

An hour and a half later, Shelby sighed in relief. Elaine had assisted her in taking Kent's name off of all the accounts and depositing the insurance check. She also called the insurance company to verify the check so they didn't have to hold funds before paying off a credit card she and Kent had through the bank, and their mortgage. It turned out to be much easier than Shelby anticipated.

Rose asked her daughter, "Feel better?" as they were leaving the bank, and smiled when Shelby nodded eagerly. "How about some lunch then?" She asked.

"Yes," Shelby replied, sighing in thanks.

They got back into the car and drove downtown to a little diner. The lunch rush was in full swing so it took a little while to get seated. They each ordered a water, and scanned the menu.

Shelby looked over the menu at her mother, and said, "Thank you again, mom, for going with me."

Putting down her menu, Rose smiled, "Oh, baby, I will do whatever you need to get you through this."

"Why is it so hard?" Shelby asked her mother.

Not an easy question to answer, Rose thought for a few moments then answered her daughter with, "I think it's the finality of it all. When Charles passed away, I didn't want to think of my life without him, truthfully, it was easier to deny he was gone. But, when we had his funeral, I had to say goodbye. I was only nineteen and hadn't even begun to live yet, really."

Still confused as to why her mother never told her about her first husband, Shelby asked, "Were you afraid to tell me?"

"A little, I suppose," Rose admitted. "I think I was afraid that you'd run off and get married right out of high school, like we did, and I wanted more for you. Kent gave you the "more," at least that's the way I saw it."

Nodding, Shelby tried not to cry. It was so difficult when Kent drifted into her mind. He just sort of snuck into her thoughts when she least expected it, and the feeling of overwhelming pain followed. "He did, although he was a pain in the butt a lot."

Laughing, Rose asked, "What man isn't at one time or another?"

Her lips forming an "O," Shelby pointed at her mom, and said, "I'm going to hold onto that and tell dad the next time I'm in trouble."

It was good, so good, to see Shelby joke and laugh, Rose thought it had been far too long. Those little things didn't mean you forgot the loved one you lost, only that you were committing to be alive and continue living.

They ate lunch leisurely, discussing inconsequential things mostly.

Shelby felt like the afternoon was so nice, spending time with her mom out of the house. The last months were mostly home and work. If she ventured anywhere else, it was so quick, she usually forgot where she went. It was if now she realized she didn't need to hide. That thought would need to be explored a little further, but not quite yet.

The following week, Shelby's parents invited her over for dinner. She happily accepted, thinking it would be good to get out. After her outing with her mom, the week before, she'd been slowly going through things at the house. It was still really painful to touch something that was Kent's. Just going through his nightstand in the bedroom was like walking down memory lane. The man had saved every single card or note she gave him. He even dated them so he knew when she'd given each item to him. It was a slow replay of their romance. She actually saw, in writing anyway, herself falling in love with Kent. There were a lot of tears and laughter as she read the funny notes.

When she arrived at her parents' house, a few hours later, Shelby recognized Kent's parents' car in the driveway. She wasn't mad, she just would've preferred her mom told her they'd be coming to dinner too. She'd been horrible and practically avoided them since the funeral. If they called, she would answer, but make some excuse to hang up quickly. It wasn't right, and Shelby knew that, but she couldn't seem to stop the behavior.

Getting out of her car, she took a deep breath, before walking up to her parents' door.

Rose met her daughter at the door, and gave her a look of warning, before inviting her in by opening up the screen door.

They walked into the house and saw Shelby's dad with Kent's parents in the living room.

Without hesitation, Shelby walked over and gave both Kent's mom and dad a hug. It wasn't that she wanted to be distant from them, she just didn't want to be reminded of the hurt.

"Shelby," Angelica looked at her daughter-in-law after they hugged, "you're too skinny."

Everyone laughed and Shelby realized that Kent's parents held no ill will toward her either.

Her dad got her a glass of lemonade, and she sat down in the living room. Her mother sat down next to her and shot her a quick look of pity before saying, "Shelby," her tone light, "Angelica and Tony thought maybe you didn't want to see them but I assured them that we are all still family."

Shelby got her mother's not-so-subtle reprimand, and smiled sheepishly. "I'm sorry," She addressed Kent's parents, "I've been very isolated and basically selfish."

Angelica shook her head no, "Oh, God no!" She told Shelby, and added, "We are lost ourselves, I think we were trying to be helpful but ended up being a nuisance and we're so sorry about that."

Looking from Kent's mom, over to his dad, Shelby felt like she was the most awful person. "You are never a nuisance, I've just had a hard time coming to terms with it all."

Tony nodded, "I have the hardest time when we pass one of his pictures in the hallway. I want my son back in the worst way."

Since Tony was not a man who easily spoke of his feelings, the revelation surprised all of them, including Angelica. She reached over and took her husband's hand into hers.

"We've started to go to grief counseling for other parents who've lost their children," Angelica announced. "It's heart breaking to hear the stories, but it also makes us feel so Blessed that we had Kent for as long as we did."

Several people, including her parents, tried to convince Shelby to go to grief counseling. She just didn't have the patience to listen to other people's stories of loss, not yet anyway. "I'm glad you did too."

John leaned against the wall, on the other side of Rose, and asked, "Have you talked to Jeff and Lisa about the gym?"

Shelby nodded, "I talked to Lisa briefly last month, they did all the preliminary paperwork for Kent's life insurance," she smiled her thanks to Kent's parents since she knew they'd given Lisa a copy of Kent's death certificate. "Anyway, they said I'm still a partner and told me I could go whenever I wanted to. I just can't decide what that is, not yet."

Everyone nodded their understanding and Shelby was relieved. Sometimes she had friends ask her why she wasn't out more, or even dating yet. It was crazy, how people's perspectives on loss varied. She thought it was a good sign that she could get through the day without wanting to hide in her closet and cry. The thoughts of that night, with her parents, ran through her mind. She was so lucky to have such a support system.

When she came back to the present, the parents were talking about something Kent did a few years earlier. Always the consummate showman, Kent couldn't do anything in a quiet way. Even buying a car was a family affair. The laughter from her parents and Kent's was like a soothing balm on her pain. There was a little less every day. Not the pain of loss, that would always be there, it was more like the pain of being alive when someone you loved so much wasn't. That pain could suck the breath right out of you.

"What do you think, Shelby?" Angelica asked, knowing that her daughter-in-law was miles away inside her head.

Looking at her mother-in-law, Shelby asked, "I'm sorry, what did you ask?"

Brushing it off, Angelica told her, "I was just asking about our yearly plan to go to the cabin, I wasn't sure we should go or not."

Hearing Angelica's question, Shelby went with her gut, "I think Kent would be ticked off if you didn't go. He loved that time with you there, and always talked about it with affection."

A tear slipped down Angelica's cheek, "He did, didn't he?" She asked to no one in particular.

John lifted his glass, "I think we should drink a toast to Kent, he could always appreciate a good drink, a good meal, and love."

Everyone nodded and smiled.

A week after the dinner with both hers and Kent's parents, Shelby felt funny. She didn't feel sick really, just really worn down. It took great effort to get out of bed and get dressed. She was thankful that she didn't have to keep a job, because she doubted she could go.

After two weeks, Shelby realized that something was wrong. Her appetite was all but gone, and she was getting weaker. She decided to go to her doctor. It was about time for her annual physical anyway, so it worked out as an explanation to her parents.

Danette Fogarty

Sitting in the doctor's office, Shelby looked around. There were mothers there with their sick kids, older couples, who held hands, and a few individuals, like her, who looked miserable. When the nurse called her back to the examination room, Shelby actually sighed with relief.

The nurse took her weight, vitals, blood pressure, and smiled benignly. Then she asked Shelby, "So, what brings you in today?"

Taking a breath, Shelby explained her symptoms, and feeling a little silly. After all, it wasn't like she was running a fever.

When the nurse went out of the exam room, Shelby thought about just leaving. This whole thing was just her being silly.

Her doctor came in, looking at her chart, and frowning. "Shelby," He said, finally looking directly at her, "What's going on?"

Again, Shelby explained her "symptoms" and again, she waited for the doctor to tell her she was just being worried over nothing.

"Well," The doctor said, "you're very underweight, your blood pressure is high, and frankly, you look sickly."

Being sarcastic, Shelby shot back, "Well, thanks for the support, Doc."

The doctor gave her a stern look, "I'm being honest with you. Has anything happened in your life?" He asked.

Answering him, Shelby frowned, "My husband, Kent, passed away a few months ago," she answered.

Her doctor put down her file, scooted his stool closer to her, and took her hands into his. "Shelby, I'm so sorry," He told her, then explained, "I think you might be showing some signs of depression, but I'd like to draw some blood and get some numbers."

Shelby was quiet through the rest of the exam, having the doctor poke and prod her, checking her eyes, ears, throat, lymph nodes, and asking her to lay down so he could press on her abdomen. Nothing hurt, so she was relieved about that at least.

Walking out, she was directed to the lab room at the end of the hall, and waited for the tech to draw her blood.

An hour later, she was on her way home, and could only think about getting into bed and sleeping.

The next morning, Shelby's phone went off, and she recognized the number as her doctor's office. She picked up and said, "Hello."

Her doctor's receptionist asked if she could come into the office the next morning to speak with the doctor about her labs. The no-nonsense tone of the receptionist put Shelby's nerves on edge for some reason.

The whole day was spent pacing the house, wondering if there really was something wrong with her. That would serve her right for being such a jerk to everyone around her after Kent died. "Stop it Shelby!" She finally said out loud to herself.

Waiting for the doctor to come into his office was interminable for Shelby. She'd arrived the designated fifteen minutes before her appointment time, but he was running behind. When he did finally come into the office, he wore a look of worry.

"Shelby," He said as he sat down in the chair next to hers, "you've got to make some changes."

Nodding, Shelby didn't reply, she just wanted him to tell her what was wrong.

Looking at his patient, the doctor worriedly said, "You're anemic, so I'm going to put you on some vitamins, we need to get your appetite back or you're going to run a risk of developing heart problems, and I'm going to put you on an antidepressant."

Her eyebrows raised, Shelby smiled at her doctor, "Well, I guess I'll listen to you, but just this once." It was something that Kent would say, and struck her as funny.

Smiling back, her doctor shook his head. "Okay," He responded.

Chapter 7

Within days, Shelby was feeling better physically. Her doctor did explain that it would take a while for her emotional wellbeing to return, which was understandable given that Kent passed away. The relief that there wasn't anything "really" wrong with her, like cancer, or something like that, was a mental slap to wake up. She needed to take care of herself, Kent would be furious if he knew she wasn't doing that at least.

Shelby was scrolling through her Facebook feed, for the first time in months, and happened to see her friend, Bridgette, announcing that they were starting an exercise class at her gym. Bridgette ran a gym for kids under ten years old. It was a recreational gym that taught the fundamentals of gymnastics. Because she had the time slots open, Bridgette would sometimes put in other classes, for adults, or lease out the gym space for other groups.

Shelby thought maybe a class, even if it was exercise, might be nice and give her a reason to get out of the house for a little while. She "liked" the post and sent Bridgette a message saying she would be joining the class.

Within a few minutes, Bridgette messaged her back.....

I'm so excited you want to come. I know it's "work" but it will be good to see you. I've been thinking about you.

Shelby smiled and logged off.

The next week, the class began. Shelby was there a few minutes before they were due to start. She didn't want to allot too much time for her and Bridgette to talk beforehand, basically because she didn't want to answer the standard questions about her grief that people asked.

Bridgette was coming out of the small office when Shelby came in the door. Shelby noticed two things, that Bridgette looked extremely happy, and that there were quite a few people here.

"Shelby!" Bridgette exclaimed when she saw her friend. It had been too long.

Hugging her friend, Shelby couldn't help but smile. Bridgette was her friend all through high school and college. After they both got married, they sort of drifted apart for some reason.

Because people were buzzing around, and trying to pay and sign up for the class, Bridgette's time was tight, she whispered, "We'll talk after class," and kissed Shelby's cheek before rushing around to get everyone's information.

The instructor for the class came into the lobby area of the gym and clapped her hands, "Thanks for coming, ladies, but let's get moving."

It was a sizeable group, but everyone fit into the gym's big space. Bridgette and her team moved the equipment to the back of the room, to allow all the exercise participants to be able to stand in front of the wall of mirrors.

Shelby watched as people stretched out. She wasn't in horrible shape, but she was too skinny, and had very little muscle tone. For the first time in her whole life, Shelby was unsure as to whether she could get through an hour of exercise.

Music started playing, and they were off. The class was a mixture of dance and aerobics. Difficult, but Shelby managed to get through it. All her years of doing gymnastics certainly helped. She felt she was about mid-range in the class as far as keeping up with the instructor, but not really knowing what she was doing. She found herself smiling at the comments the other participants made. By the end of the hour, it felt more like she was meeting up with friends rather than actually exercising.

"Thank you," Shelby said to the instructor.

With a nod, the instructor smiled, and then turned to a few of the other ladies to answer questions they had for her.

Shelby walked out into the lobby area and got her purse. She pulled out her credit card, and walked over to the office to pay Bridgette.

Her friend had just hung up the phone and was staring out into space when Shelby stood in the doorway.

Turning to see Shelby, Bridgette smiled, and said, "Oh, we'll get your payment next time. I was wondering if you felt up to grabbing a bite to eat, there's a sub shop at the end of the shopping center so we can just walk over and not worry about our attire."

These days, Shelby would've most definitely declined the invitation, but there was something in Bridgette's tone that gave her pause. She replied, "Sure," and followed her friend out the door.

Luckily, there wasn't much of a line at the sub shop, mainly because it was midafternoon and after the big lunch rush. The two of them ordered salads and found a small table in the corner.

After they were settled down with their food and bottled waters, Bridgette gushed, "Okay, I'm pregnant."

Not expecting that kind of announcement, especially while she was drinking, Shelby was barely able to avoid choking. "Wow," She replied, "that's great news Bridge," she used the nickname she gave Bridgette when they were in school.

"Are you mad?" Bridgette asked Shelby, bursting with the news, but not wanting to offend her friend.

Confused, Shelby asked in return, "Why would I be mad, that's wonderful news. How did Kyle take it when you told him?"

Shaking her head, Bridgette told Shelby, "I haven't told him yet, I just got the phone call at the gym right before you walked in."

Now it really was a surprise. "That's so awesome, honey," Shelby told her friend.

Reaching across the table, Bridgette grabbed Shelby's hands with her own. "I think it's an omen that you were the first one I told, you were the first one I've told about everything important."

The comment made Shelby tear up. "I'm glad, I've missed you."

"Me too," Bridgette returned, "I didn't know what to say to you and didn't want to placate you with all the trifle platitudes people say." She smiled, and squeezed Shelby's hand, "But know that both Kyle and I are praying for you."

Shelby's tears did come then, she was so touched by her friend's ability to see that she needed time alone. "I've been trying, really I have been," Shelby explained.

Bridgette shook her head no, and told her friend, "No explanations, I know you, how strong you are, how much you love Kent, and I know you'll open up if and when you're ready."

It was tough not to feel like a heel when you had such a great friend saying that your self-imposed exile was completely understandable. "I promise," Shelby said, "that I will be there, from morning sickness, to swollen ankles, and even labor, but I'm sure Kyle would prefer to do the honors."

"The man, God love him, may be the one needing help. He practically faints at the sight of blood and I'm the one who has to kill all the bugs in the house," Bridgette confessed with a giggle.

They sat at the shop for almost an hour, catching up with each other, and talking about other friends from high school and college. By the time they left, to walk back to the gym, Shelby was sure that she would come back for more exercise classes and she'd most definitely stay in touch with Bridgette.

After saying goodbye to her friend, Shelby went home. She showered, called her parents to let them know she was okay, as per instructions, and then sat down in the overstuffed chair in her bedroom. Her mind drifted back.......

"I love this chair," Shelby said to Kent as they walked through the store.

Looking at the piece of furniture, Kent looked skeptical, "Why?" He asked, "It doesn't go with anything in the house."

Crooking her head from side to side, Shelby studied the chair. "It would look so awesome in our bedroom."

A frown creasing his brow, Kent shot back, "I guess," he looked at his wife, and smiled, "If you want it, we'll get it."

Shelby loved the chair, she imagined herself sitting in it and holding their children, with Kent lying in bed, watching her.

Drifting out of the memory, Shelby wiped the tears from her cheeks. Even a friggin chair could make her cry these days. She logically knew that it wasn't the chair, or the memory; it was the combination of them along with Bridgette's announcement.

She was truly happy for her friend, and wanted only the best for anyone she loved. But, there were moments, when she resented that the rest of the world was moving on while she was still trying to tread water on a daily basis, emotionally speaking.

Shelby sat in the chair for a long while, trying to examine her own feelings about Kent, herself, and even how she could possibly move on. There was no resolution, she didn't expect to find one, but it was a good sign that she could open up the doors to options.

At the six month anniversary of Kent's death, Shelby hit a wall emotionally. She couldn't believe how quickly the time flew by, and she wanted to make all the pain of losing him go away. Friends posted their regards on Facebook and sent her messages. She was touched that people remembered since she didn't post anything on any social media.

The medication that the doctor started her on did help, she felt less deserted by life. That, combined with the classes at the gym, where she could talk with other women, and seeing Bridgette, helped a lot.

Seven months after Kent's death, she received a message from his parents asking her if she'd like to join them at the cabin for their yearly vacation.

Shelby listened to the message several times. She wasn't sure what to do. She remembered the first time Kent asked her to go……..

"I'd like you to meet my family," Kent said as he walked her back to the dorm after seeing a movie.

Surprised, since they'd only been dating a few months, Shelby wasn't sure what to say at first. "Really?" She asked him.

Kent squeezed her hand, and said, "Shelby, I love you, I've loved you since the moment I walked into that gym and gave you a tough time over your beam routine, I'm not afraid to say it or tell my parents how I feel. We go to this cabin, it's on a lake in West Texas, and we unplug so it's just us and nature. Come with me?"

Smiling to herself, Shelby was trying to comprehend the fact that he was saying he loved her. Now he wanted her to go to a cabin, with his family, and be in nature? That truth was, she loved him; had from the moment he said he liked her ass. "Okay," She told Kent.

He swept her up in his arms, and spun her around. People around them were whistling and cat calling. It was completely embarrassing and totally romantic at the same time.

Dialing Kent's parents' number, Shelby waited for the line to connect. Angelica answered, asking, "Hello, sweetie, how are you?"

Smiling, Shelby answered, "I'm okay," and knew that was the truth, "But, as much as I'd like to see you and Tony, I don't think I can face going out to the cabin."

Angelica was happy that Shelby told the truth, it made it easier than if she made up some excuse as to why she couldn't go. "We understand, but we want you to know that you're always welcome."

Appreciating her mother-in-law's reaction, Shelby said, "Thanks for understanding. I'm doing better, just not great."

Everything that Shelby was telling her, mirrored her own feelings, so Angelica could empathize. The situation was not good for anyone involved. She and Tony were having their own problems dealing with the void left from Kent's death. They would survive it because their marriage was strong, but both of them knew they would never be the same. Their family was forever changed. "I am the same," Angelica sighed. "I wish there was something that switched it all off and made it easier."

Her eyebrows raised, Shelby replied, "That would make it so much better."

They talked for a few more minutes, then hung up. Shelby hoped their trip went well, and helped give them some closure on their grief.

Eight months after Kent's death, Shelby felt like she was back to square one. The antidepressants didn't seem to be helping, she was losing weight again, and didn't want to leave the house.

Four weeks passed before she even answered the door. It was her mother, demanding that she seek professional help and shoving a card in her hand, while dialing a phone number.

The card was for a therapist. Shelby read it, and listened to her mother make an appointment for her. Feeling defeated, she plopped down into the closest chair.

"Tomorrow," Rose told her daughter, "ten in the morning, I will pick you up at nine-thirty. I want you showered, dressed, and ready to go. Do you understand?"

Nodding, Shelby didn't even try to answer. There was no use, even if she wanted to fight her mother on this, she didn't have the energy to do so.

The next morning, Shelby woke up an hour before she had to leave, showered, got dressed, and even put on a bit of makeup. She hoped it would help make her look less sickly, but if the reflection in the mirror was right, it didn't. By the time her mother pulled into the driveway, Shelby was standing there waiting like a sullen child going to detention.

Her daughter got into the car, but didn't say anything. Rose didn't expect her to, but it was just a crazy mess that they were in. Just a few months ago, she would've sworn that her daughter was on her way to being on an even keel. Now, she felt like Shelby was barely hanging on.

They parked in the parking lot of a medical clinic, and walked inside. The halls were brown, with a light tan tile running down the floors.

It was all very much muted, just like the voices of the people standing in the hallway. Shelby didn't care for the feeling….it was like she was being sent to the principal's office.

A door marked Dr. Mitchem was the one her mother stopped at. She motioned for Shelby to lead the way.

Shelby went up to the little window and was greeted by a smiling receptionist. She mumbled, "Shelby Forrester, I have an appointment."

The woman handed Shelby a clipboard and asked her to "fill it out," before shutting the glass door above the desk quietly.

Feeling even less "okay" with this, Shelby walked over to a chair next to her mother, and sat down. She filled out the forms and was going to take them back to the reception desk when her mother snatched the clipboard from her hands.

Rose read over all of the information her daughter put on the forms. Medical history, current symptoms, type of loss, and dates. All of it seemed truthful so she gave the clipboard back to Shelby and gained a nasty look for it. She didn't care, this was her daughter, and Rose wasn't going to just let Shelby waste away from grief.

Quietly knocking on the glass, Shelby waited for the still-smiling receptionist to take her clipboard. She sat back down next to her mom, but didn't say anything.

Within fifteen minutes, Shelby's name was called.

Chapter 8

Being escorted out of the waiting room, Shelby studied the woman who led her down a short hallway and into a large office. She was thin, and wore a fashionable outfit with a pencil skirt and white shirt. Although there was nothing too extravagant about the outfit, the woman wore it very well.

When they parted, inside the office, Shelby had a chance to look around the room. There was a sofa at one end, with a chair next to it, just like you saw on television or the movies. There was also a large desk with chairs across from it. The woman, whom Shelby originally thought was a nurse or front office assistant, walked past her and sat down behind the desk before motioning for Shelby to sit down across from her. "I'm Dr. Mitchem," She introduced herself while looking over Shelby's clipboard of information.

She was younger than Shelby expected. Although, having never seen a therapist before, Shelby didn't have anything but television shows and commercials to go off of.

"So," Dr. Mitchem started, "what brings you in to see me today."

Being honest, Shelby replied, "My mother."

Trying not to laugh, Dr. Mitchem nodded. "Yes, they can be quite persuasive when they want to be." She leaned back in her chair, putting the clipboard on her desk, and asked Shelby, "Why did you listen to her?"

That particular question made Shelby pause. It was a good question. Certainly Shelby could've told her mother no, and just refused to come. But, she hadn't. She did what her mother demanded because she needed help. Looking at the doctor,

Shelby answered, "Because she was right. My husband died nine months ago and I can't seem to get up and go," She motioned pushing up and away.

Dr. Mitchem nodded, "Okay," she leaned forward again, "if we're going to do this, I have to have two things from you."

Two things didn't seem too bad, in Shelby's opinion. She nodded back to Dr. Mitchem in agreement.

"Number one, I need you to be honest, I'm not here to judge you or advise you, I'm here to assess your psychological needs," She smiled at Shelby, "And number two, I need you to be on time because when people are late, it really pisses me off."

Shelby chuckled. The dead pan tone of the last statement was truly funny. "I think I can do those two things," She told Dr. Mitchem.

Sighing, Dr. Mitchem got up from behind her desk and walked over to the chair across from Shelby. She sat down, her trusty pen and paper in hand, and got comfortable. "Tell me about your husband."

For the next hour, Shelby told Dr. Mitchem as much as she could…..about Kent, about their relationship, about how tough it was after he died, about how she seemed to be getting better, and then how she was sliding backwards again into a pit of nothing. It wasn't easy, admitting things like being weak, being depressed, wishing you'd died with your spouse, but Shelby did, she was honest and told Dr. Mitchem what was in her heart and mind.

Sitting back, once again, Dr. Mitchem told Shelby, "I think you are doing better than you think, but I'm going to help you get back on solid ground." She winked, "Now, you get going and we'll make your next appointment, okay?"

Getting up, Shelby was going to turn to leave, but stopped and turned toward the doctor, saying, "Thank you for not thinking that I'm going off the deep end."

"I never said that," Dr. Mitchem replied dryly, "I only said I'd help you."

Laughing felt good, and Shelby was thankful for the doctor's sarcastic sense of humor.

They left the office, walked down the hall to the checkout counter, and Shelby made her next appointment for the following week.

After walking back into the waiting room, Shelby watched her mother get up and meet her with an expectant look. It took all of her willpower, NOT to roll her eyes. Instead, she motioned her head towards the door.

When they were in the car, going back to Shelby's house, Rose asked, "So? What did the doctor say?"

Smiling, Shelby replied, "You know, she said I didn't have to tell anybody what we talked about, not even you." Seeing the fallen look on her mom's face, Shelby felt only slightly bad for teasing. "We talked, Mom, about what was, what is, and what I want things to be."

It wasn't a straight up answer, but Rose would take whatever she could if it meant her daughter would feel better.

Over the next few weeks, Shelby's visits with Dr. Mitchem were directed at how to cope with being alone, triggers that might remind her of her loss, and what she really wanted to do now that Kent was gone.

They talked about the gym, how jealous Shelby was of it at times during her marriage. They talked about Kent and how he called most of the shots in the marriage, how that control was literally given up and how Shelby had to deal with making her own decisions now.

It was easy, telling Dr. Mitchem about her thoughts and feelings. In therapy, Shelby didn't have to worry about offending someone or hurting their feelings, Dr. Mitchem just wanted to support her.

There was a brief discussion about group therapy, but Shelby flat out declined it. Not only did she not want to tell strangers about her loss, but she was pretty sure it would be too tough to hear about someone else's loss. So, Dr. Mitchem prescribed a different antidepressant, and asked Shelby to keep a journal that she could take a peek at during their sessions. It was good to be able to go back and see her progress during the week.

After a month of therapy, Shelby started to understand a few things.

The first, and probably hardest to deal with, was that Kent was gone. Logically, she'd known since the day the police officers came that he was, but her mind wanted to remember, wanted to think about him, about them, and wanted to keep things as they were before. Really understanding, and coming to grips with loss was sincerely difficult. If Shelby thought she'd cried when Kent first died, then now it was like constant waterworks.

The second thing Shelby started to realize was that it would be impossible, given her age, to think in terms of her life being "over" now that Kent was gone. She was still young, still able to have children, not that bearing children would make a difference, but Dr. Mitchem did point it out, and she was still completely capable of living a productive life.

The third, and last, thing that Dr. Mitchem told her over and over again…..grief has absolutely no expiration date. Some part of her would most likely grieve for the rest of her life for Kent. She had to find a way to accept that, before she could truly move on. Not to mention that anyone she may become involved with in the future had to understand that fact.

She was leaving Dr. Mitchem's office and thinking how absurd the thought of "dating" sounded. There was a mixture of guilt, disgust, and just plain exhaustion that ran through her every time she discussed the possibility with her therapist.

Bridgette called her earlier in the week and asked to have lunch with her. Shelby explained she had an appointment but would meet her afterward at the sub sandwich place near the gym.

Pulling up in front of the strip mall, Shelby sighed. She truly did want to see her friends, and laugh, and be happy. It just seemed so far from where she was, right now.

Bridgette waved to her as she got out of her car and Shelby waved back in greeting. She walked into the little restaurant and was astonished at how her friend had changed in the last few months. Gone was the slender, muscled gymnastics teacher and, in her place, was a healthy, happy, and rounded woman. "Oh my Lord," Shelby said, smiling as she hugged Bridgette, "what happened?"

Patting her swelling belly, Bridgette smiled, and answered, "That's why I wanted to meet with you. I'm having twins," She almost screamed, her eyes wide with excitement.

"Twins?" Shelby asked. "Wow!"

Nodding, Bridgette told her, "I know. We were shocked since neither of us thought they ran in our families, but it turns out I have some great uncles who are twins. Go figure."

Still reeling from the news, Shelby tried to be happy for her friend. "Are you excited, or what?" She asked her friend.

The deli manager came over and set down two sandwiches. Bridgette smiled her thanks, and started to eat.

All Shelby could do was watch her friend as she shoved the food into her mouth. It was like she hadn't eaten in days rather than probably just that morning. It was fascinating, watching a pregnant woman eat.

Wiping her mouth, after finishing the first half of her sub, Bridgette came up for air. "I'm sorry, I'm always hungry."

Shelby just nodded her understanding. She was still fixated on how quickly Bridgette devoured the food.

"I wanted to ask you a question," Bridgette explained.

Her curiosity piqued, Shelby raised her eyebrows, but didn't say anything.

Bridgette leaned forward, and grabbed Shelby's hand, saying, "You know we've been friends forever and I love you."

Again, Shelby nodded.

Blowing out a breath, Bridgette asked, "Would you consider taking over the gym?" she put her hands up when Shelby looked shocked, "Just while I'm on maternity leave, I promise."

The only thing Shelby could think was she wished that she'd scheduled her appointment with Dr. Mitchem later, because this would have made a dandy use of their hour. "Uh," Shelby started to say, but was cut off by an anxious looking Bridgette.

"I have someone else who is willing, but you are my first choice. You've always been patient, and you know your way around a business like this." Bridgette was trying to sound convincing since she really wanted Shelby to do this.

Sighing, Shelby took a moment to compose herself, before answering, "Bridge, I would do just about anything for you, but I just don't think I can do this, not yet."

Bridgette nodded, "I figured," she was let down, but she didn't want Shelby to feel the slightest amount of guilt, "it was worth a shot. I'll call the other lady, no problem." She smiled warmly, "So, what's been going on with you?" She asked Shelby.

As if the conversation didn't include Bridgette asking Shelby to run the gym for her, the subject changed and didn't come up again. Shelby told Bridgette about seeing a therapist, and was relieved when she saw no judgement in her friend's eyes. They talked about their parents, and then it was time for Bridgette to go back to the gym for the first of her afternoon classes.

The two friends hugged outside the sub shop, and promised to get together soon.

Shelby got into her car to go home and, without warning, burst into tears. The sobs were gut-wrenching and she couldn't even drive until the first wave abated. The whole way home, the tears fell down her cheeks. She would drive and swipe, drive and swipe. Thank goodness there were a few napkins left over from a restaurant she ordered from months earlier.

When she finally did pull into her driveway, it was like all the time she'd spent with Dr. Mitchem, working on herself, was a big, fat lie. She felt just sucked down into the mire of grief and it was impossible to get out of it.

By the time she got into the door, the tears had dissipated. In their wake was the hiccup/sob that meant you were out of tears, but not out of pain.

Shelby walked through the house and into her bedroom, plopping down on the bed. She pulled Kent's pillow up to her face and tried to smell him. He wasn't there, not even his smell was there anymore. How was she ever going to recover?

The next day, Shelby felt a little better. She'd stopped crying and left the pity party she attended after her lunch with Bridgette. She tried to sort out her feelings, as Dr. Mitchem instructed her to do. Was she jealous of Bridgette's pregnancy? Was she just jealous of Bridgette because she had a husband? When asking herself those questions, Shelby didn't have any negative feelings toward her friend, only love and caring. So, if that was the case, why did Bridgette's happiness upset her so much? Or was it Bridgette's happiness that was the issue? Was it taking over the gym? Was that what sparked the emotions to well up inside of Shelby like an erupting volcano? When she asked herself that question, a whole lot of something came up. But, if THAT were the case, why didn't she just say yes when Bridgette asked? "Because you're not ready," She answered herself out loud. "You're not ready to live again."

She went out to get the mail in the afternoon, waving at her neighbors. They waved back now and didn't run inside like she was a crazy woman, so that was good.

There was a stack of mail, probably because she hadn't collected it in a few days. Sifting through it, Shelby divided up the piles into bills, advertisements, and personal. Even now, almost a year after Kent's death, she'd still receive a condolence card from someone who knew him, but only recently learned about his death. From the stack of cards she had in the spare bedroom, Kent had a lot more friends than he ever thought.

The envelope that she assumed was a card, wasn't. She opened the envelope to find an invitation inside. Frowning, Shelby read it....

This invitation is issued to Mrs. Shelby Forrester.

In this difficult time, you have been invited to spend a week in Galveston, Texas to help you recuperate.

You will meet others who have also suffered loss.

Please contact Ms. Willa Hanson at

713-555-2245

Shelby turned the invitation over, hoping to see some clue as to who issued it, but there was nothing. Hmmmm.

Curious, Shelby called the number on the paper. Within two rings, someone answered, saying, "Galveston Retreat, this is Willa speaking, how may I help you?"

The woman's voice was so.........happy. Shelby smiled despite herself. "Uh, I'm Shelby Forrester," She told the woman.

"Oh, Mrs. Forrester, I was hoping to hear from you," Willa announced brightly. "I do hope you were calling to make your reservation?" She asked.

Still confused, Shelby explained to Willa, "Well, I don't know anything about Galveston Retreat, I just opened the invitation."

Smiling, Willa replied, "We're a beautiful bed and breakfast on Galveston Island and we make reservations based on need. This is a private place for grieving people to come and take the time they need."

Looking around her kitchen, Shelby thought maybe, just maybe, it might do her some good to get away from the house, from her life, just for a while. "Okay," She said to Willa, "what do I do?"

Relieved that Mrs. Forrester chose to accept the invitation, Willa gave her the spiel, "You pick the dates you'd like to come, and you show up. That's it."

It seemed way too easy to Shelby, but she was kind of desperate. It was either do this, or go stark raving mad because she couldn't figure out what to do with her life or how to get over her husband's death. "Let me look," She grabbed a small calendar off of the counter. "Uh, how about next week?"

They talked for a few minutes longer, and settled on a date that worked well.

After hanging up the phone, Shelby stared at the calendar. She'd written "Shelby's vacation" on the dates she was scheduled to go to the retreat. That was the only thing written on the calendar. Before Kent's death, that calendar was filled with gym appointments, or competitions, recruiting schedules, or their personal stuff like dentist or doctor appointments. Seeing it so empty made Shelby want to cower back down. But, she didn't. Instead, she picked up the phone and called her mom.

An hour later, after explaining the trip to her mother, then her father, Shelby felt better about it. It wasn't as if she was going too far, Galveston was less than an hour away, but the change of scenery made it feel like worlds away. And, for some unknown reason, that made Shelby feel a lot better.

Chapter 9

Shelby scheduled her trip for the day after her next appointment with Dr. Mitchem. It only seemed right to let her therapist know about this, and ask her advice.

She sat down in Dr. Mitchem's office feeling a bit nervous.

"So, what's been happening?" Dr. Mitchem asked, starting their session.

Her hands clasped together, Shelby answered, "Well, I received an invitation to go to a retreat for grieving people in Galveston."

With raised eyebrows, Dr. Mitchem asked, "When did you decide this?"

"Last week, after our session, I went to lunch with a friend. She's pregnant and asked me to take over her gym during her maternity leave." Shelby took a deep breath, "I couldn't do it." She smiled at her therapist, "Then, afterward, I just cried and cried. I couldn't figure out what I was so upset over. Truly, I'm happy for my friend, she deserves all the happiness in the world, but I was just crying."

Dr. Mitchem was making notes and nodded for Shelby to continue.

Still confused as to why she had her little "breakdown," Shelby continued. "The day after that, I received this invitation," She pulled the invitation out of her purse and handed it to Dr. Mitchem. "I don't know, but I called the number and spoke with Mrs. Hanson. It sounds so nice, I guess I just need to get away."

Putting the invitation done on the table beside her, Dr. Mitchem smiled, and said, "Well I'm thrilled for you. You made a choice, a choice that could potentially help you. I'm only surprised by the fact that it sounds as though other people who are grieving will be there and you've always been adamant about no groups."

Nodding eagerly, Shelby replied, "I know. It surprised me too."

"Well," Dr. Mitchem's voice was bright, "I think this is a huge step forward for you, Shelby. Why don't you tell me more about your lunch and your, as you call it, breakdown?"

They talked a lot about Shelby's questions to herself about it, about the intensity of her feelings, and what they both thought was the culprit. Dr. Mitchem agreed with Shelby's self-assessment, that it had more to do with the gym than with seeing Bridgette so happy and pregnant. As if it was a missed opportunity for Shelby. They both agreed that maybe Shelby's agreeing to go to the retreat was in direct response to that, and that it was a good thing.

When Shelby left Dr. Mitchem's office, she felt better. It was as if a weight was lifted. The guilt of doing something without Kent wasn't there this time, and that alone, was amazing.

After she got home, Shelby started packing for her trip to Galveston the next day. She got out her suitcase, and started grabbing the things she would need. The act of packing threw her back into another memory.......

"Shelby, we're going to be late," Kent called out from the front entryway.

In their bedroom, Shelby stuck her tongue out. He could wait another five minutes. She zipped up her bag, and grabbed it off the bed before going down the hall to the door. "I'm ready," She said, a big smile on her face.

Kent gave her a questioning look, "What's up? You look sneaky."

Her eyebrows raised, Shelby told him, "My short delay will be something you'll appreciate later."

His smile was slow and sweet, "Oh, well then, I guess I'll just have to be patient," he answered, and took her into his arms for a kiss.

Shelby had been packing up lingerie for a weekend trip they took with Jeff and Lisa a few years ago. She'd ended up not wearing it, but they'd had a good time anyway. Smiling, Shelby started pulling clothes out of the closet to pack her bag.

That night, Shelby dreamt of Kent. He was talking to her, but she couldn't figure out what he was saying. It was like his volume was muted or something. He seemed to be trying to push her too, like he was shooing her out of the house or something.

When she woke up the next morning, Shelby felt anxious. The last time she could think of having this feeling was the last time she competed in a gymnastics meet for college. There was the excitement and nervousness of what was to come.

She didn't get on the road until the afternoon. There were calls to make, to her neighbors just letting them know she was going out of town, and to her parents. Her mother told her, "Don't call us, we want you to focus on yourself while you're there, but text me and let me know you arrived safely." Shelby laughed at her mother's contradictory behavior, but was glad to have such caring parents.

Traffic was starting to get congested when she got on 45 South toward Galveston, but wasn't too bad. It took her a little longer to find the address since she made a wrong turn off of the main road in the resort town. Once she pulled in the driveway, though, all she could think was, 'Wow!'

The retreat was huge! A Victorian styled house with a large front porch and lots of windows. She wondered if the house was old or one of those houses people built nowadays that looked old. She parked next to another car in the gravel area to the left of the house. Grabbing her bags, Shelby went up the stairs to the front door. She was about to knock when the front door opened. There stood the warmest smile, belonging to a very happy looking woman.

"Are you Shelby?" Willa asked, knowing that it was. She'd received a picture of Shelby with the request for the reservation. Although this version of Shelby was much thinner, she was no less enchanting.

Shelby nodded, and asked, "Mrs. Hanson?" in return. The woman stepped aside and gestured for Shelby to enter. They walked through a large foyer and into a huge great room. Another mental, 'Wow,' went off in Shelby's mind.

Still smiling, Willa remarked, "Grand, she is." At Shelby's questioning look, she responded, "The house, it's very grand."

Looking around the room, Shelby added, "I'm not even sure if grand covers it."

Willa chuckled, "Well, let's get you upstairs and settled." She turned toward the large staircase, and grabbed one of Shelby's bags.

Listening to Mrs. Hanson tell her about freshly baked cookies and sweet tea being ready in a little while, Shelby didn't wonder how this place was meant to relax and help people. Just walking in the door was enough to allow Shelby to take the first really deep breaths in months. There were no expectations of her here. They stopped at the top of the stairs. Shelby peeked around Mrs. Hanson and saw a half dozen closed doors. The one at the end of the hall had a small chalkboard sign that read "Hannah" on it.

Willa asked Shelby, "Which one would you like? That room is the only one taken so far," and she pointed to the door marked with Hannah's name.

Deciding to "follow the line," Shelby pointed to the closed door just to the right of Hannah's. It was like when you were a kid filing into a bus, they told you to just go to the back and start filling up seats so everyone was able to fit.

"Great choice," Willa told Shelby. She led the way down the hall and said, "Dinner is promptly at six, so don't be late," then she opened the door.

As they entered the room, Shelby couldn't help but smile. It was so bright in the room. The walls were done in a very pale yellow, but the accents were all in brighter shades of the color. There was a little green thrown in, and that gave the illusion that you'd just walked into a field of sunflowers. "It's so pretty," Shelby whispered.

It never got tiring for Willa to hear the guests' reactions to the rooms. She'd helped pick the color schemes for the house so she understood the need to be awed. Each room had its own beautiful color palette with things that were welcoming and comforting at the same time. It was necessary to put guests at ease when they arrived. There was usually a period of tension so this helped battle that. "I think so," She answered to Shelby's response. "I always think of a springtime bloom when I'm in here, and I can't help but smile."

Shelby nodded. That made sense to her. It was difficult to feel gloomy in a bright room like this. She put down her bags and walked around the bed to a set of windows. They overlooked the side yard mostly, but did provide a partial view of the Gulf of Mexico. She opened them, and allowed the breeze to fill the room.

Willa watched her, and could see that she was thinking. "I'll just go down and get that afternoon snack going," She said quietly, and left the room.

Hearing the soft click of the door closing, Shelby sighed. This was what she needed, a change of scenery to help her make sense of it all.

She stood at the windows for a long while, just listening to the noises from the beach. Somewhere in the distance someone was mowing a lawn, she could hear the hum of the lawnmower. The sun was shining and matched the brightness inside her room.

Finally, Shelby decided she needed to unpack. She walked over to where her bags sat, and put them up on the bed to open them. She moved slowly, leisurely, and making a mental note not to rush through it. Just the process of unpacking should be savored. She was lucky......she was alive and she had people who loved her.

After the unpacking was done, Shelby sat down in a plush chair, just to the right of the windows. It was just tall enough to provide a perfect view outside. She could see the mature trees sway in the afternoon breeze, their leaves almost dancing in response. And before she realized it, Shelby fell asleep.

There was a noise, and Shelby woke up with a start. It took her a few moments to figure out where she was. 'Oh yes, the retreat,' she thought before unfolding herself out of the chair. It was so comfortable that she wasn't even sore from sleeping in it.

She walked over to the nightstand, where she'd placed her phone while unpacking, and noticed three messages from her mother. Feeling chagrined, she typed a quick text to her mom, telling her she'd made it to the retreat and actually fell asleep. Within moments her mother responded with a smiling emoticon. Apparently her mother was going to make good on the "no pressure and no harassing" policy she spoke of before Shelby left.

Looking at the time, Shelby saw it was 5:35pm. Remembering that Mrs. Hanson said dinner was at six sharp, Shelby walked into the adjoining bathroom to freshen up. When she flipped on the light, she stopped and stared. It was a completely modern bathroom, but looked like something out of the Victorian Age. There was a claw-footed tub, a pedestal sink and the tile was retro, but tasteful.

Shelby pulled her brush out of her toiletry bag and brushed her hair. She applied lip gloss, but left her face free from any other makeup. Pleased with the results, Shelby put her brush and lip gloss back in her toiletry bag and placed that in a small basket that was on a chrome metal shelving unit.

Stepping into the hall, Shelby turned to go downstairs when she almost ran into another woman. "I'm sorry," The other woman said, surprised. Shelby assured her, "It's fine, no harm done," and watched her go by. She was beautiful, her long hair flying behind her as she moved.

Going down stairs, Shelby made her way through the grand living room, down a short hallway, and noticed an open doorway that led to the dining room. There was another woman already sitting there, and looking very uncomfortable. Shelby nodded her hello, but didn't say anything. There was something about this woman that made her think words were not welcomed.

They sat there, in pregnant silence, for a few minutes before the other woman, the one Shelby almost ran into, came into the room. She stopped when she saw Shelby and the third guest, as if she were taking in the situation.

"Good evening," The hurried guest said as she sat down.

Shelby was seated in between the other two women and tried not to feel like an intruder.

"I'm Hannah," The woman to her right said lightly.

Replying, Shelby said, "I'm Shelby."

The other woman didn't say anything. Hannah was about to say something when Mrs. Hanson came into the room and announced, "Dinner is served."

Mrs. Hanson placed a large platter down on the table. It looked as though they were being served at a five star restaurant. There was ham, potatoes, carrots, and fresh green beans displayed on the platter. The ham was already sliced so they each only had to take a piece.

Wanting to keep the feeling upbeat, Mrs. Hanson started by introducing everyone. It was fine until she explained why everyone was there. Hannah had lost her father recently and the angry-looking woman lost her daughter a few months prior.

Shelby wanted to pay her respects and told them how sorry she was for their loss.

Even though she wanted to do the beautiful meal justice, Shelby wasn't big on eating anyway these days and the charged atmosphere did little to help her. Looking around, the other two guests seemed to have the same issue.

Mrs. Hanson told them, "You're all here for one reason, and one reason only, to start healing."

As soon as the words left Mrs. Hanson's mouth, Payton, the woman to her left, stood up, and threw her napkin down, demanding, "How can you ask that?" of Mrs. Hanson. She yelled at the older woman about not being able to move on, and left the room.

Sitting there, feeling decidedly uncomfortable, Shelby sighed. Any possible thought of eating was now gone. She told Hannah and Mrs. Hanson, "If you don't mind, I'd like to take a walk on the beach." She didn't even wait for an acknowledgement before getting up to leave.

Moving through the kitchen, which was also spectacular, Shelby went out the back door. There was a small patio complete with a dining set for outdoor entertaining. The yard wasn't very deep, but ran the width of the large house. Shelby slipped off her sandals and dropped them at the edge of the patio. After only a few minutes, Shelby's feet felt sand. She walked down a small embankment that met up with the beach. The sand was still very warm from the day, but not so hot that it hurt.

She walked down to where the water was meeting the sand. The water was rather warm too, and that made it fun to wade through the small waves as they kissed the beach.

Shelby tried to remember when the last time was that she and Kent actually came to the beach, but she couldn't. Once he and Jeff got the gym, the days of impromptu trips or relaxation seemed to fly out the window.

Frowning at her thoughts, Shelby tried to figure out why she had that attitude. Sure, she'd already admitted that she felt like a distant second to the gym and Kent's commitment, so any other thoughts were extensions of that private animosity. The thing was, that she should be glad that Kent had the gym. It made him happy, gave him purpose, and he was successful. If she complained or thought negatively about that, was she basically spitting on all he accomplished?

Walking down the beach, Shelby watched as the sun set. It was a perfect metaphor for her thoughts, and she smiled. As the sun went to bed for the night, she laid her thoughts to rest about the gym and any possible blame she held for it in causing Kent's death.

It was dark when Shelby made her way back toward the retreat house. Luckily, the house was so magnificent, it couldn't possibly be confused with any others. There was a light coming from the back door, a welcoming beacon, but otherwise the house was dark.

She didn't want to go up to bed just yet, so Shelby sat on the edge of the yard and looked out over the water. It was comforting, the consistent sound of the waves as they met the shore. It lulled Shelby's mind into thoughts of her childhood. Vacations with her parents, or spring break with her friends during high school and college.

When she finally got up to go inside, Shelby realized she was hungry. Walking into the kitchen, she went into the refrigerator and pulled out some leftovers from dinner. There were little night lights placed strategically around the large space, so at least she could see without turning on too many lights.

Hearing something behind her, Shelby turned around to find Hannah standing at the kitchen door. "I'm sorry," Shelby asked her, "I didn't wake you, did I?"

Coming further into the room, Hannah sat down on one of the barstools at the island. She answered, "No."

Before she realized it, Shelby was talking to Hannah about Hannah's loss as well as her own. It was easier than she thought it would be, sharing her pain. Hannah was a great listener. And when Shelby heard about Hannah's mother's and father's deaths, it made her feel a little ashamed that she was being so difficult about Kent's death. She had her parents, Hannah didn't.

Hannah's outlook was amazing, and Shelby even commented on it. She wished her own mind would be so positive.

After she ate, the women went upstairs and whispered, "Good night," to one another.

Once in her room, Shelby shut the door quietly, and turned on the bedside lamp. The glow of the light traveled far into the light room. Shelby sighed as she slipped off her clothes. There was a hamper just outside the bathroom door, so she dropped her clothes inside of it, before going into the bathroom to shower.

The water felt good against her skin, calming her just a little more.

She came out of the bathroom and turned down the bed. Grabbing pajamas from the dresser she placed her clothes into.

Within minutes of laying down, sleep claimed her.

Chapter 10

The morning sunlight spread its warmth through the room, waking Shelby up early.

She'd slept well, not long enough, but well. It was the first time in almost a year that she didn't have tormenting dreams involving Kent, and that was a Blessing.

Throwing the covers aside, Shelby got up. She'd showered before going to bed so she just went into the bathroom and washed up before getting dressed. She chose a light sundress that used to look good on her. Now, it almost sagged it fit so loosely. This time of year she was usually tan as well, but with being a hermit for so long, her pale skin looked even more washed out from the light colored fabric.

By the time Shelby got downstairs, she felt like a frumpy old woman. No one else was around, so she decided to sit on the sofa in the living room and picked up a magazine that was laying nearby.

A few minutes later, she heard someone coming downstairs. It was Hannah and Shelby felt kind of silly this morning. Sure they spoke last night, in the darkness, where it was safe to talk about your pain. Things looked really different in the bright light of morning. "Good morning," Shelby said softly.

Hannah smiled and sat down on the sofa across from her.

Within a minute or so, Payton was also coming downstairs. She silently walked to where Shelby and Hannah were sitting, and sat down in an overstuffed chair.

To Shelby, the silence was maddening. She spoke first, saying, "My husband, Kent, was so wonderful. He would be so mad at me right now."

The other two women stared at her.

Hannah responded with saying, "My dad, Frank, was all about me getting on with my life, and now I just feel lost."

Payton looked like she wanted to say something, but only sat there, staring into space.

A minute or so later, Shelby started talking about Kent, about how funny he was. Hannah told them that her father thought he was funny, but he really wasn't, which prompted a chuckle from Shelby.

Payton asked a question about Hannah's dad, and off they went, talking. It was nice, to have someone to talk to. Before they knew it, Mrs. Hanson was announcing that breakfast was ready.

The three women walked into the dining room and sat in exactly the same seats they picked for dinner the night before. It was like everyone had their own place staked out.

It was noticeably easier this morning, during the meal, and Shelby was relieved. She wasn't sure she could take another outburst so soon.

Mrs. Hanson asked, "What's on everyone's agenda for today?"

Shelby was the first to answer, "I think I'm going to Moody Gardens," there was an article done on the tourist attraction in the magazine she was reading before Hannah came downstairs earlier. It seemed interesting. Payton didn't answer, only shrugged and Hannah announced she was meeting up with some people.

Surprised that someone in the midst of grief actually had a social life, Shelby was curious. Mrs. Hanson explained that they were a father and daughter that Hannah helped out yesterday.

The meal was over within minutes. No one really ate a lot, but it was a better effort than the dinner the night before. Mrs. Hanson asked Shelby, "Would you mind helping me clean up this morning since Hannah helped last night?"

Wanting to be courteous to the innkeeper, Shelby smiled and nodded. They got up and started clearing dishes. Payton went upstairs and Hannah remained sitting while they carried the plates into the kitchen.

Shelby started rinsing off the plates and serving dishes as Mrs. Hanson emptied the uneaten contents on the plates into the trash and the leftovers into containers.

Placing the dishes into the dishwasher, was a task that helped Shelby process the morning's events so far. She cried when she talked about Kent, but it was more because she felt like she was a disappointment to her husband, in her current state.

She heard voices from the dining room and smiled at the sound of Mrs. Hanson shooing Hannah out. She made a mental note to avoid getting on Mrs. Hanson's bad side.

All the dishes were in the dishwasher when Mrs. Hanson returned to the kitchen, a smile on her face. It wasn't difficult to see that the innkeeper thrived when there were guests around. Even if those guests were surly, emotional wrecks.

Wiping her hands on a nearby dish towel, Shelby said to Mrs. Hanson, "Well, I'm off," and waved quickly as she left the kitchen.

She went upstairs and grabbed her purse and keys before coming back down to leave for her sightseeing. Just after she closed the front door behind her, it opened and Mrs. Hanson called out, "Have a good time."

The drive to Moody Gardens only took about ten minutes and Shelby was excited to be out. That was, until she saw the line of cars in front of her. There was a large sign that read, Special Event. Her hopes dashing, Shelby decided to make a u-turn and see if there was someplace else she could go. She remembered that there was Moody Mansion here on the island as well.

Picking up her phone, while she was stopped at a red light, Shelby pulled up directions to the mansion. It was only minutes away and she smiled. Maybe today wouldn't be a total loss.

Moody Mansion was located right off of Broadway, the main street into Galveston. The house was old and stood the test of time, just like the island. Although it was hit from time to time with hurricanes, the people of Galveston still thrived.

After parking in the small parking lot, Shelby walked over to where the visitor center was located. She walked in and was transported back in time. There were old, restored cars in the building. She walked forward and bought her ticket, with the counter person telling her the next tour would be in about fifteen minutes.

Shelby meandered around the cars, peeking into them. There was a timeline on the walls showing the development of Galveston, which was very interesting. She was still reading when an older woman spoke loudly, "All the people for the 11 o'clock tour, please come with me."

The group, comprised mainly of couples or families, walked a short distance to another building. There were benches for people to sit on and they were shown a movie. It detailed the history of the Moody family. Shelby was fascinated by it, all the history and hard work. The fact that the house was sold for pennies on the dollar to the Moody family was an interesting fact as well.

When the video ended, the group was led around the building and up a wide staircase. The guide described it with such detail that Shelby could picture the horse carriages as they arrived under the portico for a local celebration.

They went around a wide front porch until they were at the front doors.

The romance of it all was overwhelming. Shelby listened to the knowledgeable guide as she talked about the family's day-to-day activities. How wonderful it must have been to live in such a grand house.

An hour and a half later, Shelby was back in the parking lot, and trying to picture herself in that time period. Impossible, but worth the daydream.

Shelby wandered around Galveston for the rest of the afternoon, popping into shops or walking along the boardwalk. She made her way back to the house just before dinner.

The others were there too, she could hear Hannah talking to Mrs. Hanson in the kitchen. She noticed Payton sitting in her room, across the hall from Shelby's own room, staring into space.

Not wanting to dwell on the pain that seemed to seep into each of them, Shelby went into the bathroom and washed up. She felt a little salty from walking along the boardwalk, but felt her day was good. Her skin even looked a little pink so she'd have to remember to use sunscreen the next time she went out.

Dinner was good, still tense, but it seemed that the three of them were starting to understand each other better. Mrs. Hanson provided most of the conversation, and that was fine with Shelby. Lord knew she probably couldn't carry on a conversation that lasted more than five minutes these days.

After dinner, she let Mrs. Hanson know she was going for a walk again.

The sun was still up and shining brightly. Shelby remembered her purse and walked down the beach until she came to a little souvenir shop. She bought sunscreen and put it on as she was leaving the shop. A nasty sunburn wouldn't do her any good.

Walking back down the beach, Shelby came across a group of kids who were building an enormous sand castle. Sitting some distance away, since she didn't want to be labelled weird for watching some kids, Shelby observed their efforts. It wasn't bad, and it certainly was one of the biggest sand castles she'd ever seen. Too bad, it would be washed away by morning..... She wished that would happen to her grief, that it would be washed away as well.

Shelby made her way back to the retreat house after dark. She repeated her routine from the night before, sitting on the edge of the lawn, where it met the sand from the beach. Every so often she heard a noise coming from the house. It took her a little while, but she eventually figured out that it was someone crying. She couldn't tell whether it was Hannah or Payton, but her heart ached for them.

Not long after, Shelby quietly made her way inside, and up to bed.

Sleep came easily once again, and Shelby was grateful for it.

The next morning, Shelby was up early again. There was something about the morning light, as it came into her room, that made her want to get up and face the day.

She was the first one down, and again sat on the sofa and read a magazine.

Hannah came down next, and sat down saying, "Good morning."

Looking up from an article on gymnasts, her mind was preoccupied with Kent and his current students. She finally gave a reply of, "Good morning," and smiled at her new friend.

"I saw you sitting out last night," Hannah mentioned.

Afraid that she'd done something wrong, Shelby asked, "Did I disturb you?"

Quickly shaking her head no, Hannah said, "Not at all, I was sitting out on my balcony last night."

"Me too," Came from Payton, who was standing at the bottom of the stairs. Neither Hannah nor Shelby heard her come down.

Hannah motioned for Payton to join them, and mentioned that she heard Payton crying. That solved the mystery Shelby wondered about. She looked at the young mother, trying so desperately to hold on and not give in to the misery of grief.

Wanting to comfort the other two women, as well as herself, Shelby blurted out, "I feel better, being around the two of you." It was the truth.

Joining in, Hannah talked about how Shelby and Payton helped her. Payton talked about being angry, and Hannah comforted her with her words. Shelby was amazed at Hannah's poise and compassion when her father just died a week earlier.

Mrs. Hanson came in to break up the chit chat, telling them, "They'd better eat the food she made."

The joke broke the tension and everyone laughed or, for Payton, at least smiled.

Breakfast was good, Shelby ate more than she had the previous night, so she felt like she was making progress. Payton was chosen to assist with clean up duties and Shelby told them that she had to go pick up something from the store. Hannah was off to spend time with her new friends, Asher and Skyler.

Going to the store was something of a cover. Shelby thought a lot about what Payton said about being angry. In that feeling, Shelby could relate. She'd had her fair share of yelling, screaming, pitching fits, and altogether losing it in the name of anger. She came across a book shop the day before, and wondered if they had some books on grief. She wanted to find one for Payton.

The shop was open, just barely, and the shop owner smiled warmly at Shelby when she entered.

Walking along the rows of books, it would be easy to get distracted by a biography here, or a travel book there, but Shelby was on a mission. She found a small section, only having about ten books, on grief. Luckily, the one she had in mind was in stock. She quickly took it up to the counter and made her purchase.

When she got back to the house, she saw Mrs. Hanson. The retreat manager was doing some cleaning, looking as content as could be. Shelby waved hello and went upstairs. She knocked on Payton's door and waited. A minute later, Payton opened up the door and stood looking at her. It was clear that she'd been crying, and Shelby just wanted to hug her. For some reason, that didn't seem like the wisest thing to do, so instead, Shelby handed Payton the book, with the directions to, "Read this and come to my room when you're done." She turned around to go into her own room, but turned back when she heard a noise come from Payton, probably an excuse. Shelby cut her off saying, "Read!"

In her own room, Shelby went over to the windows, and opened them up. The breezes off the Gulf filled the room, making the curtains dance with their ebbs and flows. She sat down in the same comfy chair she'd slept in the day she arrived, and pulled out her phone.

There was a message from her mom, and one from Bridgette.

She listened to her mother's first, smiling as her mother recorded, "Don't call me, I just wanted you to know we love you and we're proud of you."

It was hard to be sad when your parents made you laugh. She sent her mom a quick text saying.....

Everything is going well. Met two other women, also grieving. I think we're helping each other. It was good that I came.

After sending the text to her mom, Shelby listened to the message from Bridgette, her face contorting into numerous emotions as the words her friend was speaking hit her full force. She listened to the message one more time before putting the phone down.

This was something she would need to think long and hard about. It was ironic that Kent wasn't here because he was the one person she could go to in this case and ask advice from. Of course, he was the reason she was here in the first place. He wasn't here any longer, and he wouldn't be back. She was on her own this time and had to make her own decision.

She sat in the chair for a long time, until there was a knock on her door. Getting up, Shelby crossed the room and opened the door. It was Payton, her eyes swollen from crying. She held out the book Shelby gave her earlier, and said, "I read it."

This time, hugging Payton didn't feel awkward or unwelcomed. She gathered the other woman into her arms, and whispered in Payton's ear, "I'm proud of you."

Chapter 11

Payton and Shelby went downstairs. They ended up meeting up with Mrs. Hanson, who announced that lunch was set up in the dining room.

Shelby asked, "Where's Hannah?"

Mrs. Hanson replied, "She's off with that handsome dad, and his adorable daughter."

Payton shot her a look of surprise, but Shelby just smiled in return. It seemed as though Mrs. Hanson was as smitten with Asher Kelley as Hannah was.

They ate lunch, casually, this time. There were the fixings for sandwiches, and homemade cookies. Simple comfort food that made everyone happy.

Trying to fill up the lapses in conversation, Mrs. Hanson asked both Shelby and Payton what their plans were for the rest of the day. Not looking at Payton, Shelby answered, "We're going to walk on the beach later, maybe grab a quick bite; so if Hannah is out, we'll give you a free night off of cooking duty." Even though she hadn't discussed any of this with Payton, she was relieved when Payton added, "Yep."

Quickly, they helped Mrs. Hanson clean up the lunch fixings and left the house.

As they walked, Shelby had her own crazy thoughts to contend with so she didn't instigate any conversation with Payton. Not that Payton was talkative on a good day anyway. The only thing that Shelby thought rivaled Payton's grief, was her obvious anger. Understandable, but at some point, you had to let it go. She tried to understand that losing a child was the worst thing that could happen, so Payton's responses were valid.

They walked up to the boardwalk, and wandered slowly through the shops. One of them would comment on something, and the other would nod, but there wasn't any real communication.

Not talking didn't bother Shelby. She just wished she could find some words to help Payton.

"You know," Payton said as they were walking along the sidewalk, "I didn't know how much I was missing, just closing myself up in the house."

Surprised by the statement, Shelby looked over, and asked Payton, "Really?"

Nodding, Payton added, "I'm trying, Shelby, I really am. This is just something I can't seem to get over."

Shelby wrapped her arm around Payton, gave her a quick squeeze, and then released her. "I know," Was the only thing she could think to say. It was true.

"It's been almost a year since your husband died, right?" Payton asked a few minutes later.

With a sigh, Shelby nodded. "Yes, and there are some days when it feels like much longer and some days when it feels like just yesterday."

Payton was quiet, as if she were processing the information. "So, do people ask you when you'll start dating again?" She asked.

A smile formed on Shelby's face, "Actually, yes," she answered.

"Someone actually told me, at my Joey's funeral, that it was okay because I was young and could have more children. Can you believe that?" Payton's voice cracked with emotion.

Her face contorted into a confused look of disgust, "I actually can, believe it or not, and I'm sorry they said that. It was unfeeling and stupid."

They walked a short distance in quiet, each of them thinking about the unintended cruelty of people.

Cocking her head, Shelby asked, "You said Joey, but I thought you had a daughter?"

Smiling, Payton answered, "She was named after where her father and I met. Her father asked if we could name her after his grandmother as well so her full name is Raleigh Josephine. He called her Joey."

Shelby couldn't help but be touched by the love that tinged Payton's voice as she spoke about her daughter. "Why don't we head back?" She suggested to Payton.

They stopped at a local pizzeria and ordered takeout so they could eat it back at the retreat.

Within the hour they were coming back up the back yard to the retreat house. Looking up, Shelby noticed Hannah up on her patio, waving to them. She nudged Payton and they both waved back.

Shelby dropped the pizza off on the kitchen counter, planning to eat it a little later. Right now, she was tired. She excused herself to go upstairs.

After she shut the door to her room, Shelby sat in the chair and listened to Bridgette's voicemail again. She wasn't any closer to an answer than she was the day before, but something was niggling her insides. It was almost like when Kent would nag her until she gave in. Only, Kent wasn't here now.

Leaning her head back against the chair, she let her eyes drift shut.........

She was leaning against the elm tree at the cemetery. Kent stood in front of her telling her goodbye. She shook her head no, as if she could undo his leaving. "Baby," He said as he leaned closer, "you're okay now, it's time to go back and start again."

When she woke up, the sun was low in the sky, and her stomach growled. It was a new sensation and made Shelby smile. She went downstairs to find Payton in the kitchen talking to Mrs. Hanson. It was strange because Payton seemed so antagonistic toward Mrs. Hanson when she first arrived.

Payton noticed Shelby first, and smiled. "Come on in," She said, "Mrs. Hanson is teaching me the fine art of baking."

With a strange look on her face, Mrs. Hanson shook her head, and said, "This young woman has never baked a cake, can you believe it?"

Shelby bit her lip, she was trying not to laugh at Mrs. Hanson's incredulousness.

After Mrs. Hanson got the cake into the oven to bake, the three of them went out to the back patio. Mrs. Hanson brought out a pitcher of lemonade, so Shelby ran inside to throw a couple of pieces of pizza into the microwave.

She brought out a large piece for both her and Payton. She gestured to Mrs. Hanson, who looked at the pizza as if it was evil. Smiling, Shelby sat down, and took a bite. It was soooo good.

The sun was set now, darkness making the atmosphere quiet. There were lights on downstairs so the back of the house provided a lot of light. They sat there, chatting, and trying to coax Payton into eating something.

Mrs. Hanson was pouring refills of lemonade when she hollered out, "Hey, you two, come on up!"

Shelby turned to see Hannah and Asher walking toward them and could see the steam permeating around them. Oh, she remembered those days....

Hannah asked, "What are you up to?"

Still frustrated with Payton, for not eating, she said, "We're trying to get Payton to eat something."

Hannah gave Payton a look, and then introduced them to Asher. Shelby smiled, thinking he was a handsome man, and totally enamored with Hannah. Willa had her own crush going on him too, and Shelby thought that was sweet.

There was a little bickering because of her comment about Payton eating, so Asher was a wise man, and excused himself. Hannah walked him back to the end of the lawn. Shelby turned around, wanting to give them a few minutes of privacy, and saw Payton making a run for it inside the house. Mrs. Hanson had a look of defeat on her face, and grabbed the pitcher of lemonade and glasses to take inside, she commented, "I'm going to send out some emails, goodnight."

By the time Shelby watched Mrs. Hanson go inside, Hannah was making her way back up to the patio and asked where everyone went.

Shelby explained that Payton went to her room and Mrs. Hanson went inside to answer emails.

Hannah asked Shelby, "So how was your evening?"

That was a pretty potent question for Shelby, she replied, "Very interesting."

Hannah's eyebrows rose in interest. "Do tell," She urged Shelby.

Shelby explained the call from Bridgette. How her friend was forced to go on maternity leave earlier than expected and how the lady she originally had in place to take over the gym wasn't available yet. It helped for Shelby to get it off of her chest.

After she was done, Hannah asked her questions, and then apologized for asking them. That was funny to Shelby. She now considered Hannah a friend and friends were allowed to ask questions. Shelby answered all the questions, and as she was explaining it to Hannah, she realized that she'd already made up her mind. Her dream of Kent helped her in that too.

Hannah told her, "Maybe this is what you need then, to sort of "dip your toes in" as it were. Maybe this is what you need to get some footing for yourself."

It was funny how some people thought exactly the same things. Shelby answered, "I think you might be right."

They went upstairs a while later, and Shelby went right to sleep, almost excited about the next day.

When she came downstairs the next morning, she saw that Hannah was already gone with Asher and his daughter. Payton hadn't come down yet, and Mrs. Hanson just set out some homemade pastries that they could grab at their leisure.

Danette Fogarty

"Good morning," Shelby said when she saw Mrs. Hanson come into the kitchen. She was pouring herself a cup of coffee, another indulgence she hadn't allowed herself in way too long.

Mrs. Hanson smiled at Shelby, noticing something different in the young woman's face. "You're going to do something extraordinary today, aren't you?" She asked Shelby with a smile.

Well, if the woman couldn't make it work running a B&B, then she could become a mind reader. "Yes, I'm going to do something I didn't think I could before today."

Not wanting to pry, Willa said, "Good for you," and walked over to give Shelby a quick hug.

Shelby welcomed the praise, and the hug, she needed all the reinforcement she could get right now. "Okay, I'm off," She said as she put a lid on the to-go cup for her coffee.

"Good luck," Willa shouted after her, and said a quick prayer. It never hurt.

Shelby got into her car. She'd texted Bridgette as soon as she got up this morning, and asked if they could meet at the gym.

The drive was bearable, but took a long while because the gym was in downtown Pearland, and there were, what seemed like, a million stop lights.

When Shelby finally pulled up in front of the small gym, she had to take several deep breaths before she got up the nerve to get out of the car.

Walking into the gym, Shelby saw a few moms sitting on the chairs of the waiting area. She turned to the left, and went into the office. It hadn't even been a week since she saw Bridgette, but the woman certainly had grown. Her belly was even more pronounced now. When she saw Shelby, her eyes lit up, "You're here!"

"I'm here," Shelby said quietly.

Giving her friend a dry look, Bridgette replied, "Stop it, you are a life saver if you're here to tell me you'll do it."

Trying hard not to grin, Shelby answered, "I'm here to tell you I'll do it."

Bridgette clapped her hands together in excitement. "Thank you, thank you, thank you," She said to Shelby.

Feeling overwhelmed already, Shelby replied, "You can thank me if you have any students left when you come off of maternity leave."

Not buying Shelby's sarcasm for one second, Bridgette just beamed at her. "Well, let's go over everything, then."

They spent the next two hours going over all parts of the business, from the payments to the classes. Bridgette gave Shelby copious amounts of notes on her students. Mostly observations, and ways for Shelby to remember who was who. Shelby looked over the lists while Bridgette took a phone call, and her brow furrowed. When Bridgette finally hung up, Shelby asked her, "Why did you put two stars after this little girl's name?"

Peeking at the paper, Bridgette nodded in understanding, and told Shelby, "That's Kendall. She's a dynamo, and not her personality, although that's bigger too, but Shelby, this little girl, she has real, raw talent."

The way Bridgette described the little girl, Shelby was curious to see her in action. There were mostly the little kids who came into gymnastics for something to occupy their time, give their parents some time off, or get help with physical conditioning. But, once in a while, there was a student who showed an amazing aptitude toward gymnastics. It got coaches excited because they could see what the potential was. On more than a few occasions, Kent came home to go on and on about one of his more talented gymnasts.

Shelby tried not to let thoughts of Kent intrude on her interest in what Bridgette was saying. She needed to pay attention so the changeover went off without a hitch. Mentally, clearing her brain, Shelby listened as Bridgette listed the basics that were taught in each class, how some students needed a little more attention.

They went back down to the sub deli to get a bite, Shelby watching Bridgette out of the corner of her eye to make sure she was alright.

"Stop watching me like I'm going to explode," Bridgette said as they went inside the deli, "I'm pregnant, that's it."

If pregnancy made people this jittery, Shelby was a little relieved that she hadn't gone through it as of yet. "Okay," She replied, feeling chastised.

The two friends had sandwiches, and discussed Bridgette's pregnancy. She felt good, the doctor just said that with multiples that bed rest started sooner. It was precautionary to make sure the babies stayed inside as long as possible.

Just hearing Bridgette explaining it made Shelby nervous. How did people have more than one baby? The thought seemed so foreign to her. She'd have to ask her mom about her pregnancy, just out of curiosity.

After lunch, they went back to the gym and Shelby observed a class taught by Bridgette and her assistant, Carrie.

It was fun to watch the kids, just two and three years old, going through the paces. They stretched out, their little hands reaching, and their faces focused.

Bridgette had these little plastic dots that were in different colors. Each child had one assigned to them for the day, and that was where they were supposed to sit until it was their turn. To get two and three year olds to sit, for any amount of time over thirty seconds seemed an enormous feat. Yet, Bridgette did it. She was "tough" on them but calm and patient. Basically, she didn't let the kids get away with anything they weren't supposed to. Watching her friend, Shelby thought she was going to make a great mother.

When the class was over, Shelby walked into the office with Bridgette, asked a few questions, and sat with her until her next class showed up. They talked about the kids, with Shelby commenting here and there about them.

"The most difficult thing is not to laugh," Bridgette told her. "I have a few who think clowning around is fun, and it is, but it distracts everyone from what we're working on."

Shelby thought that was a good point.

By the time Shelby left, she felt really good about her decision to take over the gym.

The drive back to Galveston was spent singing to music on the radio. Another thing Shelby hadn't done in a year. She missed some things, and didn't even know she'd missed them. Living life seemed to be like riding a bike, once you got back on, it all came back to you.

A song came on, one that Kent particularly liked. Instead of turning the radio off, or crying, Shelby simply smiled while it played and hoped her husband could hear it up in Heaven.

Chapter 12

Shelby parked in the parking area in front of the retreat. She felt good, really good, and was hoping that Hannah and Payton were there so she could tell them about her day.

Walking in the front door, Shelby stopped to listen. She didn't hear anything downstairs, so went upstairs. There were voices, but they were distant. She peeked her head inside the open doorway of Payton's room. Hannah noticed her first, and waved her inside.

They were out on the patio, so Shelby walked through the room. It was done in varying shades of purple and, even though she didn't know Payton very well, the room suited her.

"Hey," Hannah said to her as she stepped out onto the patio.

Smiling, Shelby replied, "Hey to you, how are you both?"

Payton spoke first, saying, "Hannah has been helping me."

Surprised, but glad, Shelby commented, "Well, she is wise beyond her years."

Wanting to divert attention from herself, Hannah asked Shelby, "So, where have you been?"

Leaning against the door frame, Shelby looked out over the water, "I've been visiting with a friend."

Her eyebrows raised, Hannah gave her a questioning look.

Shelby shrugged, realizing it implied that she hadn't made a decision yet.

"Good for you," Payton said.

That comment, coming from Payton, had both Shelby and Hannah standing in shock.

Payton looked between her new friends, "What?" She asked.

Before anyone could say anything else, Mrs. Hanson showed up to announce dinner.

The feeling as they went down to dinner, was upbeat. Shelby was content and hoping that they would all make a decent dent in the wonderful food that Mrs. Hanson took so much time and effort to make.

Within minutes, however, things went downhill quickly. It all started with Mrs. Hanson asking about Asher Kelley and his little girl. She issued an invitation to the handsome man and his little girl for dinner. Payton was, understandably, upset by this. Although Mrs. Hanson explained why she wanted them to come over, Payton had an outburst. It was then that things really got emotional. Mrs. Hanson, in an effort to counter Payton's accusations that she didn't know what losing a child was, told the three of them about her own son's death.

Even now, hours later, Shelby couldn't shake the look of devastation in Mrs. Hanson's eyes. Was this how it was to be for them? This pain lingering inside of them for the rest of their lives? It was overwhelming to think of it in those terms. Shelby missed Kent like hell, she loved him so much, but she didn't want to find herself, years later, stuck in the agony of grief so intense that it cocooned her and made her keep herself apart. She didn't think that Mrs. Hanson was keeping herself apart, she was helping other people who were going through the same thing. It was generous of her, but not something that just anyone could do.

In the middle of her thoughts, Shelby heard a door open and close in the hallway. Getting up, she walked over and peeked her head out her own door. Speaking to Hannah about her "rendezvous" with Asher and offering to cover for her in the morning made Shelby feel like they were sorority sisters.

Sitting back down, Shelby thought that they were, in a matter of speaking, sorority sisters; her, Hannah, and Payton had all known the pain of loss. Shelby swore that she would do everything she could to help them, and herself, get back on track.

The next morning, Shelby got up and started getting ready. It was her last day here at the retreat, and she had to say, that being here helped. Mostly, it was having Hannah, Payton, and Mrs. Hanson; their understanding and support.

When she got downstairs, she found Mrs. Hanson in the kitchen, humming nicely as she pulled muffins out of the oven. When she noticed Shelby, she said, "Good morning," in a bright tone.

Grabbing a seat at the kitchen bar, Shelby watched as Mrs. Hanson put the muffins into a wicker basket, lined with a cloth napkin, and folded the fabric over to keep the warmth in. Shelby had never been that good of a cook, she hadn't given anyone food poisoning, but she couldn't make a four course meal either. "How are you this morning?" Shelby asked, a little worried that last night's admission may have upset Mrs. Hanson.

Stopping what she was doing, Mrs. Hanson looked up at Shelby, and replied, "I won't say that I'm my best, but I understand that sometimes you need to open up your own wounds, just a little, in order to help others."

Shelby was in awe of Mrs. Hanson. She was an amazing woman! Trying to get their minds off of the night before, Shelby asked, "Am I the first one up?"

Smiling, Mrs. Hanson commented, "That depends on what your opinion on "up" is."

Intrigued, Shelby gave Mrs. Hanson a quizzical look.

"I caught Hannah sneaking in about 6:30am," Mrs. Hanson couldn't keep the smile off of her face.

Ooooohhhhh, very interesting. "So, she did stay over," Shelby said quietly, but apparently not quietly enough because Mrs. Hanson gave her one of those motherly looks. Smiling back at the innkeeper, Shelby admitted, "I caught her sneaking out last night and told her I'd cover for her this morning."

Shaking her head, Mrs. Hanson sighed. "You realize that you are all adults, I'm not your mother, or your priest, and you can do as you please."

Now it was Shelby's turn to sigh. "Well, I don't really think we look at you that way, more like a sorority mom, I'd say."

Mrs. Hanson laughed. "That's a new one," She said to Shelby. She turned around to grab something off the counter, and when she turned around, Payton was standing in the doorway.

Shelby noted that Payton looked like she slept very little. The poor woman didn't know which way was up, a feeling Shelby was only now losing, thankfully. "Good morning," She said to Payton, wanting to break the ice.

"Morning," Payton mumbled, and proceeded to go over and pour herself a cup of coffee. She sat on the stool next to Shelby.

Mrs. Hanson, sensing what her guests needed, walked around the bar and gave Payton a quick hug, saying, "All is forgotten."

Shelby smiled as she watched relief flood Payton's face. The younger woman really needed a break to figure out what to do in the wake of her daughter's death. Shelby ached for her, but had no idea how to help.

They ended up staying in the kitchen, nibbling on muffins and drinking coffee. It seemed more comfortable than the formality of the dining room.

After breakfast, Shelby asked Payton if she wanted to go for a walk. Payton declined, so Shelby went off on her own. She walked along the beach, enjoying the smell of the air, the breeze against her skin, the feel of the sun on her skin, and even the noise from the other beachgoers made her smile.

There was a shift inside of her. She started to feel it yesterday, and was glad that it carried over into today. It was a long time coming and, if she was honest, she would admit that Kent himself helped her get to this point.

By the time she got back to the retreat house, Shelby was famished.

As luck would have it, Mrs. Hanson was getting lunch ready when she came in through the back door.

"Just in time," Mrs. Hanson said, handing Shelby a plate, "you can help me take the food in."

Happy to help, especially if it helped fill her belly, Shelby dutifully did as she was asked.

Payton was coming into the dining room as they were putting the plates down, she smiled at Shelby and sat down. Shelby had just joined her when Hannah came into the room.

Lunch was a happy event, Payton and Shelby were ribbing Hannah about texting with Asher. It was all in good fun. Payton revealed some more about her life, which surprised Shelby. The woman kept things private for sure. Although, Payton did ask that they keep in touch after they left the retreat. Shelby didn't think there was any other option. These women were her friends now.

Later, at dinner, she received a text from Hannah saying she was staying over with Asher. The tone of the text was meant to be private, but Shelby happily announced it to both Payton and Mrs. Hanson. She texted Hannah back, telling her that everyone knew.

After dinner, Shelby went upstairs to pack. She sighed as she looked out the window. The sun was setting, leaving streaks of colors in its wake. It was beautiful, to see such a thing. It had been a long time since she noticed something like that.

When she finally fell asleep, Shelby dreamt of Kent. He was telling her, "You're ready, baby."

The next morning, there was a ruckus in the kitchen when Shelby walked in. Mrs. Hanson was trying to hold a crying Hannah in her arms. "What did he do?" Shelby demanded, knowing that only a man could produce such tears.

After a somewhat confusing answer from Hannah, Shelby tried to step back and allow Mrs. Hanson to take over. It probably would've been fine had Payton not come into the room and decided to let her anger and grief play into her words. She basically accused Hannah of just clinging to Asher because Asher was alive and provided a band aid for her grief.

It was then, that Shelby decided to intercede, and spoke up, "No, Payton, that's not it. Kent has been gone a year now, and I haven't gone and found someone to make me feel "alive" yet. I know what it's like to love someone, and Hannah had that look when she talked about Asher."

"Look?" Payton shot back, raising her voice. "What man is ever there for you?" She was angry, and lashing out, but she couldn't stop it, "Hell, your husband went and died on you!"

In that few seconds, the anger inside of Shelby burst out. She couldn't help it, she turned and slapped Payton right across her face, leaving a red mark from the contact. She got in Payton's face and, with forced calm, told her, "My husband loved me and I have to believe that he didn't leave me because he wanted to. Now you quit being a bitch and support Hannah."

The silence that followed was crazy. Even Mrs. Hanson just stood there, her jaw slack from shock. It was only when Hannah got up, made an effort to straighten her clothes, and commented dryly, "Good talk, thanks girls," that they all realized how ridiculous they were being. Shelby cracked first, a small laugh coming from her mouth. She covered her hand over it, in an effort to keep from going on, but she couldn't. Payton was smiling, and they all just sort of burst out together.

Payton came over and hugged Shelby. "You know," She said as she stepped back, "all I could think of was that scene from Steel Magnolias, where they talk about taking a whack at Weezer."

Mrs. Hanson was laughing now so Shelby knew they were all okay.

Shelby, Payton, and Mrs. Hanson sat down at the dining room table, and talked until Hannah finally came back down. Shelby was relieved when their friend showed up, "Thank goodness," she played up the dramatic tone, "Mrs. Hanson wouldn't let us start until you came back down." She received a play slap from Mrs. Hanson for her sassiness.

It was plain that Hannah was more composed, but still unsure about what to do about her budding relationship. She talked to Payton, who told her how Shelby had set her straight.

She should probably feel badly about slapping Payton, but Shelby didn't. She meant what she said. There was no way Kent would've gone unless he had no choice. He loved her, she knew that too. Payton's mentioning her daughter's name pulled Shelby out of her thoughts.

"Is that your daughter's name, Raleigh?" Hannah asked.

Nodding, Payton pulled out a picture and showed it to Hannah, then Shelby, and finally, Mrs. Hanson.

The little girl was adorable. What surprised Shelby so much was the difference in Payton. In the photograph she was so happy, hugging her little girl, her smile big. Shelby watched Hannah start to cry and couldn't help but tear up herself.

Then, when Payton said that she'd been responsible for Raleigh's father not being a bigger part of her life, and the agony she carried for that, both Hannah and Shelby got up to hug her.

After breakfast, they all helped Mrs. Hanson clean up the dishes and then went out onto the back patio.

The discussion merged from topic to topic, mostly focusing on their regular lives. The others knew that Shelby was going to cover for Bridgette at the gym, but neither Hannah nor Payton knew what they were going to do when they returned to their homes.

Hannah received a text from Asher's daughter, to which both Shelby and Payton gave their two cents about. In the end, Hannah went to see Asher and Skyler before she left the island.

While Hannah was gone, Shelby helped Mrs. Hanson with some laundry. She took her bags out to the car and came back in to find Mrs. Hanson tidying up their rooms, probably for the next guests.

Curious, Shelby asked her, "How busy are you normally?"

Mrs. Hanson was putting clean linens on the bed in the blue room, and answered, "Not as busy as I'd like, but not everyone is open to this," she gestured around the room, "way of grieving."

Without being told, Shelby picked up the other end of the sheet and helped Mrs. Hanson make the bed. "Well, if you need a testimonial, I'll be happy to give one," She told the older woman.

Smiling, Mrs. Hanson winked at Shelby, before saying, "I'll hold you to that."

They made up the beds in the blue room and the yellow room. Shelby hoped whomever got her room next enjoyed it as much as she had.

By the time they went back downstairs, Hannah was walking up the backyard to the house. Everyone started saying their goodbyes, and putting phone numbers into each other's phones. Both Hannah and Payton promised that the three of them would get together soon.

Hannah pulled out first, and then Shelby backed her car up. She watched Mrs. Hanson and Payton in her rearview mirror and tried not to cry.

Back at home, later in the day, Shelby texted her mom to let her know she made it safely. Her mother asked when they could see her, and Shelby texted back telling her the next day.

The house felt different now. It wasn't as empty as she thought it was before she left. It was a house, a space that she lived in.

Walking down the hallway, she glanced at the pictures she'd hung when they moved into the house. The first one was taken just after she and Kent started dating in college. Another one was from their engagement, the marching band members all gathered behind them, yet another one was of them at the gym. These were beautiful memories of happy days. Shelby refused to see them as anything else anymore.

Feeling braver than she had in a year, Shelby started going through the closet. She packed up most of Kent's things, leaving out anything she thought his parents would want or Jeff would want for the gym. Her husband had a lot of t-shirts and gym pants.

What she didn't think anyone would want, was packed into boxes to be donated. Kent was meticulous in how he kept his clothes so anything in there was in great condition.

After coming out of the closet, Shelby decided that she needed to get some food. Mrs. Hanson spoiled them with preparing 3 meals a day.

Chapter 13

She was making something to eat when she got a text from Hannah....

(From Hannah) House is lonely. Got some financial stuff out of the way, but it's still weird not having my dad here. How are things there?

Shelby smiled as she texted her reply....

Decided to take the job filling in at my friend's gym. You were right, I need to step out and start living again. It's been a year and I know Kent would want me to be happy. Miss you, Ms. Hanson, and hell, even Payton.

It was easier to say it in a text, Shelby felt less likely to encounter judgement that way. She shouldn't have worried....

(From Hannah) Keep me posted and send pics. I want to see you hopping around with all those little kids. ☺

After replying with an LOL, Shelby put her phone aside. She didn't want to be interrupted during her meal. Not that her friends were interruptions, but she needed to get used to focusing on one thing at a time, she'd need it when she started to teach classes at Bridgette's gym.

She ate pretty well, a half of turkey sandwich, and a salad. As far as eating went, it was a gourmet meal.

She cleaned up the few dishes she'd created, and sat down in the living room. This call would be difficult, but it was necessary. She dialed Kent's mom's number.

Angelica answered on the second ring, "Hello, there," she greeted her daughter-in-law.

Shelby smiled, "Hello, there yourself."

It was apparent to Angelica that the retreat did Shelby some real good, she sounded so much better. "How was the retreat?" She asked her.

Surprised, although she shouldn't be, her mom probably told Rose and Tony about her going. "It was good," She answered, "I made some friends and I'm going to work."

Now it was Angelica's turn to be surprised, "Work?" She asked Shelby.

"It's just filling in for my friend, Bridgette, while she's on maternity leave. She owns a small recreational gym, just down the road actually from Imperial."

Another surprise, Angelica smiled widely. "I'm so glad for you, you sound good."

With a sigh, Shelby said, "I feel good."

Tony gave her a hand signal, saying silently to ask her a question. Angelica rolled her eyes at him and mouthed, 'I am,' and asked Shelby, "Did you want to get together soon?"

Smiling into the phone, Shelby replied, "Funny you should ask that, I was calling to say that I went through Kent's closet, I put aside some clothes I thought you and Tony would want to keep," she swallowed hard, "we could get together at your place and I could give them to you."

It was difficult for Angelica to keep her emotions under control. She knew this would be something they would all face sooner or later; moving on. She understood it as a person, but as a mother, it was painful.

Shelby got worried when Angelica didn't comment. Had she hurt Kent's mother's feelings? She certainly didn't want to do that. Rose and Tony were her parents too, for as long as she'd been with Kent. They always treated her with respect and love. "I'm sorry," She rushed to apologize.

Clearing her throat, Angelica interjected, "Oh, sweetie, you have no reason to apologize. None whatsoever. I know this is something you have to do."

Relief washed over Shelby's skin, but she started to tear up. "It is," She croaked.

Nodding, Angelica added, "Then we'll do it, and we'll do it soon."

They hung up without actually setting a date to have dinner. Shelby wanted her parents there too. It would be good for all of them to talk about Kent and remember the good things.

That night, when Shelby was in bed, she felt like it was the first time she'd slept without Kent. After a year, it wasn't their house anymore, but hers. She turned out the bedside lamp, kissed her fingers, pressed them to a picture of Kent on the nightstand, and then laid down to go to sleep.

The next morning, Shelby was getting caught up on her emails when she saw one from Mrs. Hanson. It was so sweet, inviting her, along with Hannah and Payton, back anytime. She cried just reading it. Sure enough, she received a text from Hannah about it not long after.

They group texted, all of them confirming that they'd each read the email and how they'd cried. It was a lovely reminder of their time at the retreat and their new friendships. She texted

Hannah and Payton letting them know she started teaching at the gym tomorrow and admitted she was nervous.

The big news was Payton's, she texted them saying she'd gone into her daughter's room, something she hadn't done since her little girl passed away. Shelby thought it was very brave of her.

Today was a prep day for Shelby. She was starting classes tomorrow and had workout gear, but not gear that a coach/teacher would wear.

After doing all the stuff around the house, she headed out to the local athletic store. She wandered around for over an hour, getting distracted by other things besides clothes. Finally, she got down to business and picked out some gym pants, coordinating shirts, and even a new pair of tennis shoes.

When she got home, she practiced French braiding her hair, something she hadn't done in quite some time as well. She used to do it all the time when she was active in the sport, but got out of the habit once she left, preferring to keep her hair a little shorter since then.

It took a while, but she found she still had the knack, and smiled at her reflection in the mirror. She was tanned from her time at the beach, and she looked, not exactly happy, but better. Certainly healthier.

She jumped when the doorbell rang. She lost track of time and forgot she promised her parents they'd get together today.

Her parents were already inside when she walked around the corner from the hallway. She wanted to laugh at the look her parents both wore on their faces. "Hey, mom and dad," She said, smiling.

Rose and John talked about what they expected to find when they got to Shelby's house. What they saw in front of them, a younger looking version of Shelby, from her gymnastics days, was not it. "Hi," Rose said to her daughter, and walked over to give her a big hug.

John was less subtle, he didn't even hide his surprise, "Shelby, you look so different."

Shelby couldn't help but laugh at her parents' reactions. "I shouldn't," she said, and then remembered her hair was back in the braid, "oh yeah," she laughed, "I am going to wear it up for classes tomorrow."

"What classes?" Rose asked her daughter, confused.

Closing her eyes for a second, Shelby realized that she hadn't even told her parents about her agreement with Bridgette. She squeezed her mom's hand and asked, "You remember Bridgette, right?"

Rose nodded, but still looked confused.

They all walked into the kitchen, Shelby took the bags her father held and put them on the table. It was funny to her that her parents knew she wouldn't have anything cooked. She started to explain, "Well, Bridgette asked me to take over at her gym while she went on maternity leave. I couldn't do it, not before I went to the retreat, but after being there, I figured out that I could do it."

Her parents just stood there, staring at her.

"Okay, I realize this is weird, but I guess you could say that I've come out of the fog," She wanted them to understand. "Kent helped me too, he loved me, I know it, and he wouldn't want me to just waste away."

Still dumbfounded, Rose wasn't sure if she was dreaming or if Shelby had some sort of breakdown. It all seemed so rash. She asked her daughter, "Have you seen Dr. Mitchem since you got back?"

Shelby smiled, "I have an appointment with her tomorrow afternoon, between classes."

All of Rose's arguments seemed to vanish. Her daughter had a grasp on things, to be sure. It all seemed so sudden, and that was what Rose was afraid of. She decided to be supportive and just answered, "Good," she hugged Shelby again, "good for you sweetie."

John joined in with the hugging, shooting his wife a shocked look over Shelby's shoulder. They supported their daughter one hundred percent. If all of this seemed sudden, well, they'd deal with any aftermath as it came.

Dinner consisted of baked chicken and potato salad. It was good and Shelby ate a piece of chicken and a dollop of potato salad. Even her eating habits seemed to amaze her parents, which kept her on the verge of giggling.

Her parents said goodnight soon after dinner ended, saying they wanted her to get some good rest before her first day. Shelby was glad that she surprised them, it meant that she'd made good progress in her grief.

She locked the door behind them, smiling as she went around the house, securing it for the night. She thought that maybe she should get a dog for company, but immediately nixed the idea. She never had animals growing up and didn't know the slightest thing about taking care of one. Maybe later on, when she was really back on track, she'd revisit the idea.

Sleep was an elusive part of the night. Shelby chalked it up to nerves. She wasn't due at the gym until ten, so she had time to sleep in a little bit. A far cry from Kent's five am practice sessions with his gymnasts before they went to school.

When she finally settled into a deep sleep, she found herself in a peaceful place. Kent was there, but he was far away, almost as if he were watching over her.

The morning was a bit hectic, with Shelby running around the house trying to get organized. She couldn't find the folder with information Bridgette gave her, so that was a good fifteen minutes of frustration. When she finally got everything together she was running a little behind. Luckily, traffic was easy and she made it to the gym with ten minutes to spare.

Bridgette's assistant, Carrie walked up to her as she was unlocking the door, a smile on her face. "Good morning," Shelby said to the young woman.

"Mornin," Carrie responded, chomping on gum and earbuds in.

They walked inside, Shelby disarmed the alarm, and then went into the office. Carrie had her own routine of checking the bathroom, the water cooler, and making sure they were set up for their first class. From what Bridgette told her, Carrie knew her stuff and didn't need a lot of supervision.

Shelby was in the office, turning on the computer when she heard the music. Walking out of the office, she watched as Carrie went through some warm ups. She watched as Carrie did a couple of tucks and round offs. It was fun to watch someone who clearly enjoyed gymnastics.

The door opened and in walked her first group of students, along with their parents. Carrie was shutting off the music and coming out to greet the kids. Shelby could tell that Carrie loved them and enjoyed her job.

All the parents were told about Shelby, and they seemed rather welcoming. Bridgette mentioned that Shelby's husband was an owner at Imperial Gymnastics, and that seemed to impress some of them, from what she was told anyway.

The first class was 2-4 year-olds. It was easy, fun, and Carrie did the majority of the work. It wasn't easy to hold their attention but Carrie did a great job.

Some of the parents stayed, and made small talk amongst themselves, while others went next door to an adult gym for their own workout.

Shelby managed to get all the payments done for this class, she thought Bridgette would be proud of her for that. She also took some notes and fielded phone calls. For such a small gym, Bridgette ran quite a brisk business.

As the kids filed out, she realized that she could do this. It would take some getting used to, and she wasn't the one teaching yet, but she was trying to be positive.

The next group came in, a junior tumblers group. This was a fun way for kids to learn skills while moms helped out. Carrie also took the helm on this one, with Shelby observing.

It was fun to watch the kids, excitement in their eyes, when they mastered a skill.

An hour later, they were filing out too. Carrie packed up her stuff and said goodbye. She was off to her classes for college.

Being left alone was a little tense for the first few minutes, but once the kids started coming in, it wasn't bad. These were the five year olds. They were a little more attentive and knew what they were supposed to be doing. Without Shelby even having to say anything, they each went into the gym, got their plastic dots, and sat down.

Smiling, and introducing herself to the parents, Shelby then went into the gym and sat down in front of them. "Good afternoon," She said to the girls.

From what Bridgette said, this was one of her favorite classes. The kids weren't in school yet because their birthdays were too late in the year, but they were old enough to understand what was expected of them. "Let's get started," Shelby said in a bright voice.

Stretching was very specific, according to Bridgette's notes. There were six kids in the class and they all knew what they were doing. There was a star after a little girl named Kendall's name and Shelby remembered their discussion about Kendall when Shelby first came to observe at the gym. Pushing the thoughts away, Shelby jumped right in and started class.

Gannon Riley was cursing under his breath. Why his sister constantly called him to chauffeur her children around was beyond him. Not to mention, if she didn't have these kids in activities almost twelve hours a day, there would be no need to traipse all over town taking them to this practice or that class.

He pulled up in front of the little gym his niece, Kendall, went to, and went inside. He'd been here a couple of times, and knew that Ms. Bridgette, as Kendall described her, was nice. Only, once he walked in, it wasn't Ms. Bridgette that he saw.

There, on the floor with the kids, was a beautiful woman with brown hair that was pulled back into a French braid. She wore a pink shirt, gym pants, and those little slipper things that gymnasts wore.

Not caring that it was rude, he asked one of the moms sitting there, "Who's that?"

She answered, preoccupied with her phone, "That's the new teacher filling in while Ms. Bridgette is on maternity leave."

The fact that Gannon didn't even know Ms. Bridgette was pregnant meant he hadn't been here in a while. He gave a quiet, "Oh," for an answer, and continued to watch the class. His eyes never left the teacher though.

As the class was going through their balance skills, Shelby noticed that Kendall went over to the uneven bars in the far corner. Not understanding, she called over, "Kendall."

Another student spoke up, saying, "She does that," and pointed to the uneven bars, "she's really good and it intests her," the little girl named Bethany said.

Shelby smiled at the little girl's mispronunciation, but got the gist of what she meant. Even with the other five kids doing their beam work, Shelby kept looking over at Kendall on the uneven bars and was shocked at the skill level the little girl displayed.

Class ended, the other kids filing out of the gym. Shelby walked over to the bars and asked, "What are you working on, Kendall?"

The little girl, concentrating on her body position, answered, "Pullover."

Two things surprised Shelby. The first was that the little girl knew what a pullover was and did it well, and the second thing was the level of concentration Kendall displayed while doing it. Not something one saw right away from a five year-old.

"Cool," Shelby commented, trying to be relaxed. "What other skills do you like to do?" She asked Kendall.

Hopping down off the bar, Kendall answered, "I love the floor routine, and I can do a bridge back kickover."

Her eyebrows raised, Shelby asked Kendall, "Can you show me?"

Sure enough, the little girl walked over to the main space of the gym and did the skill. Not only did it, but did it flawlessly.

Standing there, Shelby was shell shocked. Why was this little girl in a little recreational class? She made a mental note to ask Bridgette.

Kendall was waving at a man Shelby assumed was her father. Her mother said someone else would be picking her daughter up, that Shelby remembered.

They walked out of the gym and into the waiting area. Kendall ran into the man's arms and laughed as he lifted her up high in the air.

"Mr. Dunst," Shelby said, sticking her hand out and introducing herself. He gave her a funny look.

Kendall rolled her eyes, "Ms. Shelby," she said, "this isn't my daddy, this is my Uncle Gannon."

Feeling silly, Shelby replied, "Oh, I'm so sorry, I'm Shelby Forrester, and you are?"

Without missing a beat, Gannon offered, "The man who's going to take you to dinner."

Suddenly, the other parents weren't in such a hurry to leave. Shelby could see them milling around. The man spoke loud enough so everyone in the room heard him. Her cheeks were flushed, and Shelby didn't quite know what to say.

Kendall laughed, and said, "You're silly, Uncle Gannon!"

Thank goodness the five year-old could keep her composure because Shelby certainly couldn't.

He was handsome, she'd give him that. Well over six feet, with light brown hair that was short, but curled a little at the ends, he had green eyes, which Shelby found unusual for a man, for some reason. His frame was solid, so he obviously worked out. Trying not to focus on his redeeming physical qualities, Shelby replied, "I'm sorry, I don't go out to dinner." It was lame, she knew, but it was the only thing she could think of to say.

Giving Kendall a squeeze, Gannon smiled, and told Shelby. "I'll ask again, so be prepared," Shot her a wink, and then took his niece outside, making her giggle as they went.

The other parents filed out as well, and Shelby found herself just standing there, staring at nothing for a few minutes longer. When she did get her bearings, she realized she needed to lock up and get over to Dr. Mitchem's office for her appointment.

Chapter 14

The ten minute drive to her therapist's office was spent going over what the charming Uncle Gannon said to her.

Certainly, it was just the shock of him being forward that made her cheeks feel flushed. It couldn't have been the fact that he held his niece like she was a treasure, or that he looked like a billboard ad for men's jeans or men's cologne.

By the time she walked into Dr. Mitchem's office, she was fanning herself.

Looking up, Dr. Mitchem's face was neutral, but Shelby felt as though her therapist was taking in everything about her.

"Well, I see that the retreat helped," Dr. Mitchem said with assuredness.

Nodding, Shelby replied, "It did, thank you."

Standing up, Dr. Mitchem walked around the desk and sat down in the chair adjacent to Shelby, "Well, tell me what you can" she started.

Diving into her experience at the retreat, Shelby told her therapist about meeting Hannah, Payton, and Mrs. Hanson. She went over the highlights, and even told Dr. Mitchem about slapping Payton. She also told the doctor about her seeing Kent, and him telling her that she was ready. Getting into explaining the gym was easy enough, but when Shelby came to the part when she met the fascinating Gannon, she stopped.

Dr. Mitchem studied Shelby for a minute or so, writing down some notes, before saying, "There's something else you're not telling me." It wasn't a tactic she used often, it usually put patients on the defensive, but Shelby was making progress, so Dr. Mitchem felt it was okay to address it.

"There was this man today," Shelby started, letting her words sort of drift off.

A knowing smile on her face, Dr. Mitchem asked, "Can you describe him for me?"

The question was a little odd to Shelby, but she closed her eyes and began, "He's tall, about six inches over me I suppose. His hair is this light brown, it's short, but the ends kind of flip so I know it would be curly if he grew it out, his eyes were green, and I don't remember meeting too many men with green eyes so they stood out. His shoulders were broad, he held his niece, one of my students, as if she were a little feather he picked up. His arms look so strong. He's trim, but not thin, if you get my meaning."

Taking more notes, Dr. Mitchem couldn't quit smiling. "And when did you meet him?" She asked Shelby.

"Just before I came over here, for about three minutes I suppose," Shelby explained.

Finally looking up, Dr. Mitchem asked, "Did he say anything to you?"

Now, Shelby's cheeks felt warm, and she was sure she was blushing, "He said that he was the man who was going to take me to dinner."

Dr. Mitchem's mouth formed an "O" and she sighed. "Well, he sounds like a force to be reckoned with then."

Smiling, Shelby replied, "He's something alright. And, just so you know, I told him I didn't eat dinner." She rushed to explain herself, "I know that sounded lame or crazy, but he made me feel so cornered."

Jotting down more notes, Dr. Mitchem mumbled, "Interesting."

Her forehead set in a frown, Shelby asked, "What's interesting?"

Putting down her pad of paper and pen, Dr. Mitchem answered, "Well, that you described him in such detail and that you were blushing the whole time."

Luckily, their session time was up, and Shelby didn't have to delve into her insights regarding the forward Gannon.

Back at the gym, Shelby took her last class of the day, it was a class that had 4-6 year-olds. It was a lot of fun, and they were working on the beam skills currently.

Shelby decided to go grocery shopping. It was time that she started eating right and on a regular basis. She was exhausted from working at the gym, but it was a good kind of exhausted. She texted Bridgette as she walked through the grocery store, telling her about the day.

Unfortunately for Shelby, Bridgette was rather good friends with a few of the parents, so she already was up to speed on the impromptu invitation that Kendall's Uncle Gannon had given. She texted Shelby......

I heard you met Gannon Riley, Kendall's uncle, and that he asked you out. You go girl!

Shelby rolled her eyes, 'oh great,' she thought, and responded.....

He's irritating. He just asked me to embarrass me in front of the other parents and he knew they'd all talk.

Feeling as if the subject was dropped, Shelby continued walking. She'd gotten to the produce department when her phone went off. It was from Bridgette…..

He is the quietest man I've ever seen at the gym. He's a cop, so he keeps to himself. Kendall's mom, Peggy, says he's single and rarely dates.

Grabbing a head of lettuce and pitching it into the basket, Shelby was getting upset. She didn't appreciate one single conversation she had, that wasn't even a real conversation, becoming fodder for others.

Gannon dropped Kendall off at his sister's house. He walked his niece inside, opening the back door, and calling out, "Peggy, we're here."

His sister came rushing into the room. "Where were you?" She asked her brother.

Looking over at his niece, who shrugged, Gannon felt like he needed to come clean, "Okay, Kendall and I grabbed lunch before we came home."

Peggy stepped forward, and looked closely at her daughter, before frowning. With a quick jerk of her finger, over her shoulder, she silently told Kendall to go to her room. Kendall didn't hesitate, and left, waving at her uncle. After her daughter left the room, Peggy shook her head, saying, "You could have at least made sure all the chocolate ice cream was wiped off of her face."

He was busted! There were two women in his life that could make Gannon feel uncomfortable. The first was his mother, and the second was his older sister, Peggy. These two women had an uncanny way of making you feel pegged with only a look. Frankly, it scared the hell out of him. "I'll try better next time," He said as he turned to go, "see ya." He tried to make a break for it, but his sister's next words stopped him in his tracks.

"So, you asked Kendall's gymnastics teacher out on a date?" Peggy asked her brother. Watching him look so caught gave Peggy an absurd amount of satisfaction. It was a hobby of sorts, making the big, bad Gannon squirm. Her husband cautioned her often about it, but it had become such habit over the years, she couldn't help it.

Turning back around slowly, he explained, "Technically no, I said I was the man who was going to take her to dinner. There was no real question in that."

Peggy had her hands perched on her hips, "We're going to split hairs on this?" She asked her brother.

His smile smug, Gannon answered, "Yep," before turning around to leave. He yelled out, "I'll pick up Kendall after her next class too."

Standing in her living room, Peggy just chuckled. If she would've known that having a pretty, unmarried gymnastics coach was all it took to get her brother to help her keep the kids in their activities, she might've looked for one sooner.

Shelby was at home, getting her stuff ready for the next morning when her phone went off. It was a group text from Hannah, to her and Payton, saying that she had a fight with

Asher and wanted to know if they could get together. Shelby checked her class schedule for the next day and replied....

I'm free after 3pm, that's when my last class lets out. I'm in Friendswood so we can meet in that area, or elsewhere if you would like. Payton?

She waited to see if Payton responded, and she did quickly, texting.....

(From Payton) I'm open. I was going to call you both to ask if you wanted to get together anyway. A few things I wanted to run by you both and get your take on them. How about Pearland? I'm in Sugarland so that would be about central to all of us.

Shelby hoped that this would help. It wouldn't do her any harm either to get out and catch up with them. It had only been a few days since they left the retreat, but she needed to talk. She read Hannah's text.....

(From Hannah) How about that new restaurant at the Pearland Town Center, 5pm?

Smiling, because she appreciated her friend's attempt to make it better for all of them. Shelby texted her back....

I'm there.

(From Payton) I'll see you both then.

Setting her phone back down, Shelby sighed.

She didn't envy Hannah in her confusion. It had to be tough, wanting to start this new relationship, but still being caught up in a complete lifestyle change after your father's passing.

Because she was thinking of families, a vision of Kendall and her Uncle Gannon popped into Shelby's mind. She wondered if he meant it, his comment about taking her out to dinner.

She walked into the bedroom and stripped out of her clothes and into her pajamas. The house was quiet so she walked into the living room and plopped down on the sofa. After she turned on the television, she channel surfed until she came across a cooking channel. 'It probably wouldn't hurt to learn something,' she thought to herself.

The next morning, Shelby showed up at the gym to a smiling Carrie. It seemed like the young woman had something to say, but Shelby just let it go.

They had four classes today, all in a row. Some of the students from yesterday were in a class today, but normally the students only had class two days a week. As Shelby scanned down her class list, she saw Kendall's name on it.

A feeling washed over her and she couldn't put a name to it. It was like she couldn't wait to see the little girl, she had some more questions after yesterday's demonstration, but she was also leery about running into Kendall's uncle.

As the first class of the day filed in, Shelby put her thoughts away into an imaginary box. Right now, she was a teacher and these little kids needed her to be in the moment, with them. Instead of just watching Carrie, she participated, running the kids through their warm ups. They were required to stand on their plastic dots, to try and learn balance. They went through the beam, walking across it, each student had three times. And then they did a few somersaults and tried cartwheels.

Since this was so basic, Shelby actually found it fun. She wasn't in the spotlight, she didn't have to worry about competing, and wasn't comparing herself to anyone else. It was as if she'd stepped back in time to when she first learned gymnastics, and fell in love with it.

The kids waved goodbye as they all filed out of the gym, to where their parents were waiting. Shelby waved goodbye, then greeted the new class with a bright smile.

Two hours later, it was her last class of the day, and Shelby was once again amazed at what appeared to be, Kendall's natural talent for gymnastics. Today they worked on handstands. There was a big mat that was shaped like a ramp. When you tipped it up on the wider end, it was perfect to help novice gymnasts learn to balance on their hands.

When it was Kendall's turn to do her handstand, she did it a few feet away from the mat, and without any help from Shelby. An idea started forming in Shelby's mind, but she didn't want to talk about it just yet, at least not until she spoke to Bridgette and Kendall's parents.

They were finishing up with the handstands when Shelby felt the hairs on the back of her neck stand up. Looking over to the large window that separated the main gym from the waiting area, Shelby saw him. Kendall's uncle stood there, watching her. It was fine, except for the way he was watching her made her feel as if she were in public, naked. "Okay," She turned away, and smiled to the class, "you did really well today, and we'll see you at next class."

The kids filed out.

Shelby stayed in the gym, pretending to straighten things that didn't need straightening. She figured that if she didn't come out right away, Gannon would leave with Kendall and she could take a deep breath once again.

Five minutes later, she walked out of the gym and into the waiting area, only to find him standing in the doorway of the office. He knew she wouldn't see him from the gym. It was a sneaky move and irritated Shelby. Without the buffer of the other parents around, she felt exposed. "Yes?" She asked in a curt voice.

Gannon stood there, smiling. Oh, she was beautiful even when she was mad. His father always told him, "If a woman drives you crazy, even when she's in the foulest of moods, then you need to snatch her up quick." Thinking of his father's words, Gannon blushed and pushed them aside. "I wanted to know if you had changed your mind about having dinner with me." He blurted the words out to her.

Looking around her, Shelby asked, "Where's Kendall?" in return.

"She's in the car," Gannon answered.

Trying to grasp onto anything, except answering his question, Shelby tried to act righteous, "You let her go to the car alone?" She asked in an accusatory tone.

Pointing out the window, Gannon replied, "She's right there."

Shelby looked out the window, and sure enough, there was Kendall, waving at her. Sighing, Shelby felt silly. "Why?" She asked quietly.

"Why, what?" Gannon inquired.

Almost pleading, Shelby asked him, "Why do you want to go to dinner with me?"

As if he anticipated the question, Gannon held up two fingers, and answered, "Two reasons," he explained, "one, my niece adores you, and two, I think you're beautiful and I want to see you in a setting away from here where I can talk to you, and hear you talk about whatever we want."

Listening to his voice, how low it was, how…...seductive it sounded, Shelby's hairs stood up again. He put her on edge that was for sure. "I don't think so," She finally answered, wringing her hands together.

"Why?" Gannon asked, taking a step closer. He could see her response to his nearness, her pulse was beating hard, her breath was shallow, and she was swallowing a lot.

All Shelby could do was stare up into his eyes. Before she realized what she was going to say, the words just poured out, "My husband died, I'm not ready."

It took a few seconds for her words to register in Gannon's mind, but when they did, he was doused with a huge 55 gallon drum of reality. "Oh," He muttered, "I'm sorry."

With a quick nod, Shelby stepped back, and he walked past her and out the door as fast as his long legs could take him. Shelby stood where she was, watching him get into his SUV quickly and pull out. Kendall looked confused by her uncle's behavior as well, and gave Shelby one last wave before the vehicle pulled out.

Standing there, a few minutes later, Shelby realized that she'd done something that she should never do. She used Kent as a protective weapon against someone else. Pulling out her phone, she dialed Dr. Mitchem's number and asked to make an appointment for the following day.

She locked up the front door to the gym and went into the bathroom to change. She'd brought clothes to change into for her dinner with Hannah and Payton. When she finished changing and looked in the mirror, the only thing she wanted to do was cry.

Chapter 15

Shelby pulled up in front of the restaurant. She saw Hannah as she found a parking spot, and smiled. Hannah looked upset, but good.

As Shelby got out of her vehicle, Hannah was walking over. They hugged, squeezing tight, and letting each other know they were there. "How are you?" Shelby asked.

Shrugging, Hannah replied, "Let's wait until Payton gets here and I'll explain."

Nodding, Shelby followed Hannah inside the restaurant. They were still standing at the hostess station when Payton arrived. The three of them hugged, and then were shown to their table.

Once they were seated, Hannah and Shelby interrogated Payton. She looked different than she did just days before at the retreat. She explained to them that she was in touch with Raleigh's dad, who Hannah and Shelby mistakenly thought Payton was married to. Payton corrected them and explained that she and Raleigh's dad were leaning on one another to get through their grief. Shelby was relieved to hear it because Payton needed someone to help her.

Hearing the story, Shelby thought about Kent and a quick flash of hurt seared through her. She wondered if that would ever go away.

Hannah started in on why she'd asked them to dinner. Both Shelby and Payton asked questions and provided feedback. It was easy to see how much Hannah cared about Asher, but she was still trying to get her feet under her from losing her dad. Everything was jumbled up in her mind.

Shelby was happy to talk to Hannah about Asher or Payton about her grief, but then Hannah turned it around and put Shelby in the spotlight by asking, "How have your classes been going?"

Not wanting to dwell on thoughts of Gannon that popped up as soon as she thought about the gym, Shelby gave a fast, "Fine," trying to keep the focus off of herself.

"Oh, there is so much more to that word," Shelby felt Hannah nudge her with her elbow while Payton chuckled.

"Fine," Shelby said more forcefully, "I met an uncle of one of the students, and he asked me out."

Her eyebrows raised, Hannah asked her, "So, what did you say?"

A half smile on her face, Shelby replied, "I said no, but..." her voice trailed off.

Payton picked up the words with, "But....." and looked at Shelby eagerly.

"But, I'm not sure," Shelby replied. "I know it's been a year now, but he's still here," She pointed at her heart.

Hannah nodded, "He always will be, Shelby, that won't change." Then asked Shelby, "But, do you think Kent would be upset if you went out?"

Smiling, Shelby answered, "He'd be the first one to demand I go on living." A tear slipped down her cheek.

Payton leaned back in the booth, and commented, "I think you just got your answer."

Shelby nodded, but the fear didn't abate one bit.

Leaning forward, Payton whispered, "He's right," she held up her hands to her friends' looks of surprise, "I'm certainly in no position to judge, I'm the worst person probably," she smiled at Shelby, "but there comes a time when it's our responsibility to live."

They did eventually order, and even ate some dinner, before parting ways two hours later.

Tears were shed, but they were mostly happy tears.

The next couple of days were busy. Bridgette had a heavy class load a couple of days a week, between her own classes, and allowing an aerobics instructor to come in and teach adult classes, it seemed that the gym was a revolving door of people. By the time Shelby got home, she fell into bed, exhausted.

Dr. Mitchem's office wasn't able to fit her in, and it was for the better because she was so busy.

At the end of the week, she was relieved that the class times were minimal, giving her time to catch up on paperwork and calls to parents who were interested in getting their kids registered into the next session of classes.

She spoke with Bridgette at the end of the week, and went over any questions Shelby had.

"I'm very impressed with you," Bridgette told Shelby.

Not sure why, Shelby responded, "You gave me detailed notes and gave me play-by-play instructions. If I blew this, I would have to be stupid." She couldn't help the sarcasm that crept into her words.

Bridgette snorted, "You've always underestimated yourself, do you know that?"

Surprised that her friend would make such a statement, Shelby didn't know how to reply. "Maybe I do."

Another snort, followed by a sarcastic, "Maybe you do," and Bridgette chuckled, "Shelby, you are beautiful, talented, and smart, how about you cut yourself some slack. I think you were in Kent's shadow so long that you forgot your own importance."

Even though Shelby knew her friend's comment was meant as a compliment, the reference to Kent caused a quick jab of pain. "Maybe, but I never thought I lived in Kent's shadow."

Bridgette realized her observation hurt her friend. "I'm sorry if I hurt you or offended you. I just always thought you needed to give yourself more credit. Kent may have kept the gym going, but you, my dear, kept Kent going."

That comment, Shelby couldn't argue with. "You are right."

And what's the deal with Gannon Riley asking you to dinner?" Bridgette asked Shelby, her voice laced with curiosity.

Rolling her eyes, Shelby sighed. She did not want to open up that can of worms, but word must've travelled. "Well, he didn't ask, he was kind of cocky about it and I said no."

Pouting, Bridgette told her friend. "There are single moms tripping over themselves trying to get him to notice them. I've seen it all, some subtle, some not, and he hits on you the first day you're there, I'm impressed."

Still feeling bad about what she said, Shelby relayed her last conversation with Gannon to Bridgette, and then waited for her friend's response.

Bridgette could understand Shelby's predicament, "You just had a knee-jerk response to him pressuring you. I sense that you might feel bad about saying no to him now, is that it?"

Not sure, Shelby just mumbled, "Maybe."

Smiling at Shelby's tone, Bridgette advised, "Give it a few days, if he asks again, or if you still feel that "awareness" you spoke of, then you ask him."

Easy for Bridgette to say, in Shelby's mind. She was married with twins on the way, she didn't have to worry about the dating pool.

"So, anything else?" Bridgette asked, trying to get her friend's mind to rest.

The question made Shelby snap back into "gym" mode and comment, "About Kendall, I'd like to have her go to Imperial and show Jeff and Lisa what she can do." The silence that followed made Shelby feel uncomfortable. "Um, Bridgette?" She asked, hoping her friend hadn't hung up.

Bridgette cleared her throat, "I'm here, as I told you before, I think she's got a lot of talent, but Imperial? Isn't it expensive?"

Brushing off the argument, Shelby said, "Don't worry about that, I just want to show them and get their opinion. I'll talk to Kendall's mom tomorrow and see if it's okay."

"Sounds good," Bridgette replied, "Please keep me posted."

They hung up and Shelby sat back in the chair, satisfied. There was something about Kendall that spoke to her, artistically, and Shelby really felt that it would be a waste to not say something about it. If her parents didn't agree, well, that was something else.

The next morning, Shelby got up and called Imperial Gymnastics. She knew the coaches got a break for a few hours after early morning practice, but usually stayed at the gym. Lisa answered the phone, "Imperial, how may I help you?"

"Lisa," Shelby started, "how are you?"

A smile spread across Lisa's face, "Shelby," she waved Jeff over, "I'm good, how are you?" She asked.

This was the part that Shelby was unsure about. "Well, I'm good." She dove in, "I am helping out a friend at a little recreational gym just down the road, and there's a little girl there that I'd like you and Jeff to take a look at."

Surprised, Lisa's eyebrows rose. "Of course, you know you don't have to ask, you're a partner over here."

Frowning, Shelby didn't want to think about that. She told Lisa, "I know, but I've just got a gut feeling about her, but it's been so long, I don't know how accurate my radar is. I don't want special favors, I want you guys to look at her like you would any other kid who comes in."

That sounded fair to Lisa, "Okay, bring her in anytime."

Smiling now, Shelby said, "I'll talk to her mom today and hopefully we can get her in tomorrow."

"Sounds good, you take care now," Lisa said, and hung up the phone. She looked at her husband, and tried to contain her excitement while she explained what Shelby said.

Jeff was smiling by the end of the conversation, saying, "I'd trust Shelby's gut before a lot of other people's eyes."

Lisa nodded, "Me too."

When Shelby arrived at the gym, she was alone. Carrie was off for the day, so it was up to Shelby to get the classes done.

The first class was her 2-4 year olds and was fun. They worked on balance and used the little trampoline with the bar to have some fun jumping.

As the second class of the day started to arrive, Shelby saw Kendall and her mom. She asked Kendall to go into the gym and start the warm ups with the other members of the class, and asked her mom, Peggy, to come into the office.

"I paid for this month, right?" Peggy asked, panicked because she'd be mortified if she forgot.

Smiling, Shelby told her, "Yes, you're all paid up. I wanted to talk to you about Kendall."

Shifting her eyes toward the gym, then back to Shelby, Peggy asked, "Did Kendall do something wrong?"

Again, Shelby smiled, "No, not at all, actually," she took a deep breath, "I'd like Kendall to go over to Imperial Gymnastics and show the coaches there what she can do."

Not understanding, Peggy asked, "For what?"

"Mrs. Dunst," Shelby started to explain, "Kendall is naturally talented, she's years ahead in skills, and is working on new ones all the time. I'd like them to see if she's good enough to take on for competition."

Peggy chewed on her lip, unsure. She asked, "If she's competing doesn't that mean that we have to pay a lot more? I don't think we can afford that."

Trying to reassure Kendall's mom, Shelby added, "Don't worry about that side of it, they have scholarships."

Peggy nodded, shot a look toward her daughter, full of pride, then left. Shelby walked into the gym and asked, "Are we all warmed up?"

Almost an hour later, Shelby felt the unmistakable nervous feeling that only meant one thing, Gannon Riley was watching her. She looked over to the viewing window and, sure enough, he was standing there, his arms crossed. She supposed he was trying to look disinterested since she shot him down, but his eyes gave him away. They scanned her, she felt it as sure as if he were only inches away instead of thirty feet. "Okay, class, we're done," she announced, then said, "Kendall."

The little girl stopped and turned around, "Yes, Miss Shelby?" She asked her instructor.

Shelby crouched down so they were eye to eye, "I spoke with your mom and asked her if you could go to Imperial Gymnastics and try out for Coach Jeff. It's a competitive gym so, if you're good enough, you get placed on a team and you work your skills so you can compete against other teams."

Kendall's eyes got big and she asked, "Is it bigger than this gym?"

Smiling, Shelby told the little five year old, "A lot bigger!"

The little girl took a minute to think about it, and said, "Okay."

They walked toward the door that led to the waiting area, Shelby was impressed at the ease in which Kendall decided to take on this test. A child had so much more bravery than an adult.

It was inevitable that Shelby was going to run into Gannon. He was here to pick up Kendall, after all, but Shelby was nervous about seeing him.

Gannon smiled when his niece came out of the gym, she ran to him, expecting him to lift her up, which he did. Then his eyes fell on Shelby and he stopped smiling. She literally took his breath away. He didn't want to impose where he obviously wasn't wanted, but Lord, she was a sight. Her hair pulled back into that braid made him want to pull the strands loose and run his fingers through it.

Trying to be professional, Shelby greeted Gannon with, "Mr. Riley, Kendall did very well."

Kendall said excitedly, "I'm going to go and try out for a bigger gym," she spread her arms out wide to emphasize it.

Frowning, Gannon looked from his niece to Shelby. "Is that so?" He asked, looking directly at Shelby.

Shelby didn't like feeling so uncomfortable, and Gannon Riley brought that out. Maybe uncomfortable wasn't the right word, maybe it was more like being "exposed." She nodded, but didn't say anything because her mouth was dry.

"Oh yes," Kendall provided the words, "Miss Shelby says that if I do good, that Coach Jeff may want me to go to his gym instead."

Looking back to his niece, Gannon told her, "That's great, why don't you go get in the car, I brought a water bottle for you."

Kendall gave him a kiss on the cheek and then went out to the car.

Gannon waited for his niece to leave before he turned back to face Shelby. His eyes narrowed before he asked, "What does she mean, go to another gym?"

He was trying to be imposing again, and doing a fine job. Unfortunately for him, Shelby was upset by his tone and her attitude backed it up. She replied, "It's just what it sounds like, an opportunity for Kendall to advance to a competitive gym."

Stepping forward, Gannon looked at Shelby, his voice low and calm, totally opposite of what he was feeling, "And who is going to pay for that?" He asked Shelby. "Peggy and Kip can barely afford her going here."

Swallowing hard, Shelby stood straighter, that's how you faced a bully, by standing up to them. "I explained to Kendall's MOTHER that Imperial has scholarships. If Kendall is good enough, she can apply for one."

"So, you're just going to dangle it in front of her, like a bone in front of a dog, and then watch if she crumbles because she's not good enough," Gannon said accusingly.

Her face contorting into anger, Shelby pursed her lips before snapping back, "Listen here, you tyrant," she tried to reign in her anger but it was too late. "First of all, I don't "dangle" anything. I've spoken to one of the coaches over at Imperial and I wouldn't have even recommended Kendall if I wasn't very sure she was talented enough to go there." She stepped forward, forcing Gannon to take a step back. "Secondly, it's none of your concern since her MOTHER said it was okay."

Even knowing he wasn't going to win this fight, Gannon didn't want to back down. "Don't hurt my niece," He warned, before turning to leave.

After Gannon left, Shelby had to clench and unclench her fists several times to get her anger under control. What an ass! How did he come off thinking that she would just dangle anything in front of anyone? All he was really pissed about was the fact that she wouldn't go out with him. If she had said sure, they wouldn't have even had the argument.

Shelby ended up leaving the gym about an hour later, wanting to let her nerves settle before she got behind the wheel of a car. She called Peggy, Kendall's mom, to make sure that Kendall could go with her to Imperial the next day. She texted her mom to see if her parents wanted to do something over the weekend, and then she texted Lisa and said that she would try to bring Kendall in tomorrow morning.

Everything was going well, except Shelby not being able to get the feelings Gannon Riley evoked from her out of her system.

Chapter 16

Shelby slept in bits and pieces that night. She was used to lack of sleep because she missed Kent, now she lacked sleep because of whatever it was that Gannon made her feel. Men! They caused insomnia! She should take out a billboard saying as much.

She got out of bed and padded into the bathroom. After switching on the light, she glared at herself in the mirror, and thought about what Bridgette told her yesterday. Although she didn't view herself as beautiful, she thought she had nice physical qualities. She didn't consider herself that talented, although she did well in college and probably could've been on the U.S. team if she hadn't been so preoccupied with Kent and his successes. Not that she was complaining, she was happy with the choices she made. Smart? Well, she did handle a lot of stuff for Imperial. It was a good thing she went over it all with Lisa long before Kent's death otherwise they wouldn't have known what was what for a while.

'Sometimes it took someone else's description to see who we are.' Shelby thought. With her first smile of the day, she set to work getting ready.

They planned on meeting at the gym, with Kendall's parents bringing her. Peggy explained that her father, Kip, wanted to see what was going on and discuss any decisions.

As Shelby got into her car, she wondered if Gannon would be there, then closed her eyes, praying he wouldn't. She didn't think she could handle another go round with him this soon.

Pulling up in front of Imperial Gymnastics, Shelby sat in her car for a few minutes. This was the first time she'd been back since before Kent's death. It felt weird. With a deep breath, she metaphorically pulled up her pants, and got out of the car.

The inside hadn't changed, the walls were lined with pictures of the different teams coached by Imperial. There was an office to the right, and Shelby turned to peek her head around the corner. A young girl, in a gym suit, was sitting at the desk, manning the phones. "Can I help you?" She asked Shelby.

Before Shelby could answer, Jeff came out of the gym. "Well, there you are," He said loudly before walking over and giving Shelby a hug. She forgot that Jeff was a hugger, and a good one. She hugged him back tightly, and whispered, "Good to see you."

Setting Shelby back a step, Jeff looked at her, "Damn girl, you look good," he said with a smile.

Shelby blushed, and returned, "Thank you, I think."

He's right," Came a voice from Shelby's left. It was Lisa. She also came over and hugged Shelby.

It was difficult not to cry. Shelby had such fond memories of being with Jeff, Lisa, and Kent. They were flooding into her mind at blinding speed. Taking a deep breath, she tried to hold them back, at least for now.

Behind them, the door opened, and in walked Kendall, her mom, Peggy, a man Shelby assumed was her father, Kip, and…..Gannon.

'Crap!' Shelby screamed inside her head when her eyes settled on Kendall's uncle.

He stared at her, his gaze very intense. Gannon insisted he be here with Peggy and Kip today. He told his sister that he was concerned about any undue influence this gym might place on Kendall for her to "join." Peggy told him he was being paranoid, but Gannon didn't think so.

Introductions were made and Shelby could see that Kendall was nervous. She leaned over, and whispered, "You got this, but if you want to stop at any time, you only need to say so."

Kendall nodded, and gave Shelby a smile.

The group walked through the entryway, through the parents' waiting area, where Jeff asked Kendall's parents and Gannon to sit and watch. He allowed Shelby to go into the gym with them, and Gannon secretly seethed because of it. He was still mad; mad that she stood up to him yesterday and mad that she was right. He was trying to be a tyrant, but he didn't need her pointing that out to him and making him even more attracted to her. He was a hairs breath away from kissing her yesterday, and that scared him. Control was a regular part of his job and losing it wasn't something he was used to. With Shelby Forrester, he was at risk of it every second he was within a mile of her.

Peggy chatted nervously as they sat down. The viewing window was huge, and allowed them to see every part of the gym.

Inside the gym, Lisa, Jeff, Shelby, and Kendall walked over to where the beam was located. Shelby asked Kendall to get up on it and perform a few basic steps, turning, balancing, and even a roundoff that she saw Kendall do at Bridgette's gym. Without blinking, Kendall performed each skill flawlessly.

They went over to the bars, and Shelby asked her to do a pullover and a cast. She did the pullover great, and although she struggled a bit with the cast (holding your body weight on your arms), she did it.

Shelby watched Kendall, smiling. The little girl was even better than she hoped. Lisa and Jeff kept a straight face, barking out orders when they wanted to see something else.

Lastly, they went over to the mat where floor exercises were practiced.

"I have a pass I want to show you," Kendall said.

When Jeff and Lisa looked at Shelby, she shrugged, she didn't even know that the little girl had been working on anything.

The three of them watched as Kendall started in the corner, did some elegant dance moves, and then did a handstand that flowed into a backward roll. After a turn, she performed a bridge back kick over, and finished with a round off.

A smirk on her face, Shelby looked over at Gannon, and winked. It was meant as a "Ha ha, I told you so," but when he winked back, she was thrown off balance mentally. Darn it! Why did he have to have that effect on her?

Lisa smiled at Kendall, and asked, "Kendall, can you go out by your parents so Coach Jeff, Coach Shelby, and I can talk?"

Kendall nodded and ran over to the door. Shelby watched as her parents hugged her, and Gannon leaned over to kiss the top of her head.

Jeff looked at Shelby, "She's good," was all he said. Lisa asked Shelby, "So, what's the financial end?"

By that, Lisa was asking if Kendall's parents could afford to pay for their daughter to be coached. It was a business after all, so if the parents couldn't pay, the kids couldn't be coached, it was that simple.

Clearing her throat, Shelby turned so her back was to Kendall and her family. She didn't want any of them to read her lips. "They can't afford it, so I was thinking you could just pull her fees out of my monthly partnership money." She gave Jeff a look when he was about to object, "Kent took care of me, of us," she told her partners, "I believe in this little girl and her abilities. I believe in the two of you and your abilities as coaches. She can go all the way if we encourage it." She smiled sweetly, "Besides, I told her mom and uncle that we offered scholarships so they don't even need to know how it's being paid for."

Lisa raised her eyebrows in surprise. "Well, I trust you," She said to Shelby. "If you believe that strongly, I say we go for it."

Jeff wasn't about to go up against two of the women he respected most. "I'm in, but she's gotta work Shelby, no short cuts."

Putting up her hands, Shelby assured them, "I'm not pulling strings here; all I'm doing is showing you raw talent that you can develop. You're the coaches."

Looking over at Lisa, Jeff said, "She's good."

In "Jeff Speak" that meant that Kendall was really good. She was mastering level 2 skills that a lot of girls her age wouldn't begin for another year or so.

They started to walk back toward the waiting room. Shelby smiled as they went through the door. She didn't say anything, preferring that Jeff and Lisa take it from here. They were the coaches after all.

"Mr. and Mrs. Dunst, we'd like to coach your daughter, she has a natural talent and we think we can develop it," Jeff started, "however, it will take a commitment from Kendall and from the both of you."

Peggy clapped, trying not to burst with pride. Kip smiled down at his daughter, then asked the coaches, "What will this cost?"

Lisa smiled, she was used to this question. It used to be awkward, but now she just said it straight. "During the competitive season, it will be $400 a month, on the off season, the fees run $200 a month. That doesn't include uniforms and travel expenses."

Shelby cringed as she saw the light go out of Peggy and Kip's eyes. Before they could tell their daughter no, she interjected, "But there are scholarships, and I'm pretty sure Kendall will get one."

Jumping on board, Lisa said, "Yes, we have benefactors that will support gymnasts with scholarships and we've got one open. I'll put Kendall's name on it if you're okay with it."

Tears streaming down her cheeks, Peggy looked over to her husband, and then nodded. "Yes, if that's what Kendall wants."

Kendall clapped her hands together and gave an emphatic, "Yes!"

Everyone laughed. Lisa asked Kendall's parents to come with them so they could sign some contracts. Jeff instructed

Kendall to see the receptionist, Danielle, so she could be fitted for her Imperial practice leotard and competition leotard.

The only two left in the waiting area were Gannon and Shelby.

Gannon stood there, watching the others walk out before turning to Shelby. "You're paying for it, aren't you?" He asked, already knowing the answer.

"You think you know everything," Shelby said, a tight tone gripping her voice.

Stepping closer, Gannon smiled, "Yes, I'm a cop."

Shelby squared her shoulders, he was trying to act all bad ass on her again and she wasn't going to take it. "So?" She asked sarcastically, "What if I am?"

They were only a foot apart now, each of them staring at the other, unwilling to budge. Before she could step away, Gannon brought up his hands, cupped her face, and pulled her to him for a kiss.

Almost buckling, because of the shock of Gannon's actions combined with the sensations that were spewing through her from his lips touching hers, Shelby tried to get her balance. Physically and mentally, she was gone, there was no going back. After a few seconds, she covered Gannon's hands with hers and kissed him in return. It was just lips, but the erotic pressure mixed with their hands touching was enough to take both of their breaths.

Gannon released her, gave her an intense look, said, "Thank you," and walked out of the gym.

When Shelby's eyes followed him, she saw Peggy, Kip, Kendall, Jeff, Lisa, and even Denise, all staring at her, their eyes wide.

Shelby left the gym a few minutes later, refusing to answer any of the unspoken questions from the others, she drove directly to her parents' house. She prayed they were home, and sighed in relief when their cars were both parked in the driveway.

Skidding her car to a halt, she got out, and ran inside, not even bothering to knock. "Mom, Dad," She called out as she shut the door behind her.

Rose came out of the kitchen, took one look at her daughter, and asked, "What happened?"

"He kissed me and I kissed him back, and it's a mess. I don't even like him, he's a complete bully." Shelby began pacing in the entryway of her parents' home. "I mean, really? I'm not trying to take advantage of Kendall. He's just being sooooooo.......I don't know!" Shelby threw her hands up in frustration.

John walked in, saw the look on his wife's face, gave a short wave, and walked back out of the room.

Having a pretty strong idea of what was going on, Rose told Shelby, "Okay, take a deep breath," when her daughter did that, she led her into the living room and sat down on the sofa next to her. "Now, who is he?" She asked.

Shelby blew out a breath. "Okay, HE, is an uncle of one of the students from Bridgette's gym. His name is Gannon Riley, and he infuriates me." She couldn't help that her voice was getting higher with every word.

Trying not to laugh, Rose nodded in understanding. "You mentioned a kiss?" She asked her daughter.

Now, Shelby realized that she'd just admitted something she would have to explain. Crap! "Uh," She started, "Well, we were at Imperial," she put up her hands at her mother's surprised look, "Another story," Shelby told her. "Well, afterwards he was in my face basically saying that I was paying for his niece's training, which I am, and then he just puts my face between his hands and kisses me." She stood up and started pacing again. "It was a good kiss too, darn it, I mean not a *kiss kiss*, but a kiss that made me feel like the ground just opened up and swallowed me whole."

Rose took in the information, as fragmentary as it was, and tried to make sense of it. She felt as if she got the gist of it, and summed it up by saying, "So, basically, a man, other than Kent kissed you, you liked it, and now you are freaking out."

"Exactly!" Shelby exclaimed and plopped down next to her mom.

John peeked his head around the corner and yelled, "Is it okay to come in now?"

Laughing, Rose told her husband, "Come on in, Dad, I think our daughter needs a hug."

Walking into the living room, John smiled at Shelby, and told her, "I'm always up for a hug." He waited for Shelby to stand up and he hugged her tight. When he released her, he sat down in a chair to the side of the sofa. "So what's up?" He asked.

Shelby stared at her father, her mouth slack.

Trying not to take something that truly disturbed Shelby, lightly, Rose explained, "Our daughter had a kiss today. A man kissed her and she liked it. Do you have any words of advice?"

Getting up as quickly as he sat down, John wiped his hands down the sides of his pants, "Uh, no," he turned to leave, "I'll just leave you two to sort this out."

They stared after him and, once he was out of the room, broke into laughter.

Once they stopped, Rose looked at her daughter, "All kidding aside, you need to figure out how you want to handle this."

The advice was welcomed, but didn't give Shelby any clear-cut answers. "I have absolutely no idea," Shelby told her mom.

Reaching over, Rose squeezed Shelby's hand, saying, "I know you didn't plan for this scenario," she put a hand up when Shelby looked as if she were going to speak, "I know you, and I know you honestly thought that you wouldn't find a man you were attracted to, or who was attracted to you again."

As much as Shelby hated to admit it, her mom was right. She nodded to her mother, and mumbled, "You're right."

"Of course I am, I'm your mother," Rose said sarcastically. "I know," She reiterated, "but I didn't see your father coming either and then suddenly, there he was, taking up the space in my mind I reserved for Charles." She pulled up memories that she hadn't had in decades, "I was scared, of disappointing Charles' family, of somehow not doing justice to Charles' memory, and I was all torn up." She let a tear slip down her cheek, before adding, "And I almost lost your dad because I was too afraid to make the choice to love again. Please learn from my mistakes."

Shelby nodded. Her mother gave her a lot to think about. If she was honest, and she should be, the kiss blew her socks off and it was only their lips touching. She wondered what more would be like, and that thought in itself scared her too.

Sitting there, Shelby and her mom talked for another hour or so. They talked about her mom's first husband, about Gannon, about her father, and about Kent. The points her mom made; not to compare one man to the other, and just let yourself be open to experiencing whatever comes, were good.

Shelby drove home and kept asking herself, 'what would Kent think of Gannon?' It was a legitimate question. Only time would tell. That was, if she even saw Gannon again.

Chapter 17

Shelby was off the next day so she decided to go grocery shopping and do errands. It wasn't long before she found herself on the freeway going north. Before it even permeated her consciousness, she knew she was going up to visit Kent's grave. His mother sent her a text saying that the headstone was in place now, they'd just been up there, on their way back from the cabin.

She followed the directions to the cemetery and arrived mid-afternoon. The sun was shining, it was hot, but the breeze blowing through made the heat bearable.

Getting out of the car, where Angelica told her to, Shelby made her way past headstones that read Forrester. She thought Kent would've appreciated this, being with his ancestors, and eventually, his parents.

When Shelby finally found Kent's grave, she smiled. There were fresh flowers, no doubt from his parents. The stone looked lovely, reading......

Kent Franklin Forrester

August 13, 1987 – June 1, 2014

Beloved Son and Husband

Shelby smiled again because she knew that Kent hated his middle name. He always said it made him feel old.

She stood there for a while, lost in thoughts of him, of them, and didn't realize how much time passed.

The sun was starting to make its dive to the west when she finally walked up, kissed her fingers, and then lay them on the headstone. "Goodbye," She whispered, and turned to go. She was walking back to the car when she could've sworn she heard

Kent say, "Goodbye." The word passed her on the breeze so she was sure she'd just imagined it.

Driving back down through Houston, Shelby listened to music on the radio and just tuned out thoughts of anything in particular.

By the time she arrived home, it was almost dark. She pulled out her phone and texted her mom, letting her know she'd gotten home from the cemetery. Then she called Bridgette.

Bridgette connected the call with, "How are you today?"

Smiling, Shelby asked in return, "How are you today?"

"I feel like I'm a walking ad for the Goodyear Blimp, and these kids are practicing their soccer skills on my bladder, but otherwise, I'm great," Bridgette provided, in a dry tone.

Laughing, Shelby commented, "Sounds like a hoot."

Not being deterred from the phone call, Bridgette asked, "So, why are you calling me on a Sunday?"

'She's smart,' Shelby thought. "Well, I lost you a gymnast," She told Bridgette, using an upbeat tone that she hoped would lessen the blow.

"You mean Kendall?" Bridgette asked. "I know about that already, Peggy called me yesterday to make sure I wouldn't be upset if they switched over to Imperial."

Shelby grimaced, and asked, "Are you upset?"

Bridgette chuckled, "No! I'm proud of Kendall and a little ticked at myself for being so distracted that I didn't think of referring her to Imperial myself. But, I know they don't do scholarships at those gyms so my question is, are you her benefactor?"

Biting her lip, Shelby didn't want to lie to her friend, so she answered, "Yes, I am, but I don't want her parents to know. It's bad enough that her uncle figured it out."

"Oh, you mean Gannon Riley, as in the Gannon Riley you were kissing yesterday?" Bridgette asked in a sarcastic tone.

Shelby felt her cheeks warm from embarrassment. "Yes," She mumbled, "but he kissed me first," she shot out, as if that point made it better to say.

With a snort, Bridgette returned, "Does it matter who kissed who, I want details! I'm pregnant, my husband is afraid that if he kisses me too hard I'll explode, I want to know, how was it?"

Shaking her head, Shelby couldn't believe her friend. "It was earth-shattering," She replied.

"That good?" Bridgette asked, and added, "I knew it, you know with men who look like he does, you just know they'll be awesome kissers." She sighed, and asked, "So when do you see him again?"

That last question surprised Shelby. She answered, "I don't know if I'll see him again since I'm at your gym and Kendall is going to Imperial."

Frowning, Bridgette commented, "That's a shame to let such a hot guy go like that."

"Keep your pants on Don Juan," Shelby retorted. "We'll see what happens."

Mumbling, "Nothing if he waits for you," Bridgette got quiet, and said, "I'm sorry, I'm so mouthy these days."

Shelby might have been upset, if what her friend said wasn't the exact truth. "You're fine," She told Bridgette, "and right."

They hung up a few minutes later and Shelby was left with thoughts of Gannon Riley and that kiss. What did she do now?

Her second week at the gym started out well. She'd actually registered a couple of new students for the next session, for which Bridgette was very pleased. The classes went pretty well, but Shelby kept finding herself looking up to see if Gannon was standing there, looking at her with those green eyes.

By the middle of the week, Shelby was becoming impatient. She actually wanted to see the infuriating man. After her last class of the day done, she went to her next therapy appointment with Dr. Mitchem.

With her usual, "What's been going on?" Dr. Mitchem sat down opposite of Shelby; her trusty pen and paper in hand.

"I kissed someone," Shelby rushed the words out, "or I should say, he kissed me, but I kissed him back."

If her parents' responses didn't make her laugh, Dr. Mitchem's would have. She looked dumbfounded, and asked Shelby, "I'm sorry?"

Shelby launched into the story of how she met Gannon Riley and then ended the story with the kiss. She half expected her therapist to tell her that it was too soon for her to be starting another relationship, instead, Dr. Mitchem asked, "And how do you feel?"

Shelby shrugged, and replied, "Very confused."

Dr. Mitchem did smile then. "I'm sure you do," She told Shelby. "And from your expressions and tone, I'm assuming that the kiss was pleasant."

"Pleasant?" Shelby asked her therapist, "Dr. Mitchem, I don't think pleasant is even remotely adequate and there wasn't even any tongue involved." The last blurb wasn't something Shelby planned on saying and she blushed.

Smiling, Dr. Mitchem, nodded, "Okay, I think it's good that you're allowing yourself to enjoy things physically, and hopefully, emotionally."

Thoughts of Gannon and her, naked, started filling Shelby's mind. 'Great!' She thought. Even a visit with her therapist made her think of that man.

They talked the rest of the session about Shelby moving on. If she felt that Kent was okay with her decisions up to now. Shelby did think Kent would be okay with her finding happiness. The big question was if Gannon was the man who could provide said happiness for her.

That evening, Shelby decided to text Hannah and Payton, to see what they were up to and if they wanted to get together. Payton responded, saying she was open, but Hannah didn't answer. They both tried to reach her, through calling and texting for the rest of the day. Payton mentioned in her texts that she'd tried for a few days to get ahold of Hannah but just thought maybe she was too busy to answer.

After her last class the next day, Shelby drove over to Hannah's house. Neither she nor Payton was able to reach Hannah and Shelby felt like something might be wrong.

She got out of her car and walked up to the door to ring the doorbell. No answer. She rang it again and knocked with her hand as well. A few seconds passed and then there was a sound from inside. The curtain on the window to the left of the door moved slightly. 'Good girl,' Shelby thought. Then the door opened and Shelby got a good look at Hannah. "Oh my God, what happened?" She demanded of Hannah.

Hannah knew she didn't look good, but the look on Shelby's face spoke volumes, none of it good. "I'm fine," She returned, quietly.

"You are most definitely not fine, Hannah, what's going on?" Shelby walked inside as Hannah stepped aside.

The house was tidy and neat, so that was something in Shelby's mind. She walked over to the sofa, sat down, and motioned for Hannah to join her. When Hannah was seated, Shelby asked again, "What happened?"

Hannah started telling her a horrible story about a man, who used to provide Hospice for her father, had come over, forced his way in, and was going to rape her. The words were hazy and filled with emotion, because Hannah was still in shock over it. "I was just so scared."

Hugging her friend, Shelby returned, "I'll bet," she ran her fingers over Hannah's hair, "but why haven't you been returning our texts or calls?" she asked.

Confused, Hannah stared at her friend blankly, before saying, "I didn't get any."

"What?" Shelby asked, "Where's your phone?"

Hannah looked around, as if she were in a fog, and answered, "I don't know where my phone is."

They started looking for the phone and Shelby finally found it almost an hour later, under the chair in the living room. They deduced that it slid under there when Hannah was fighting off Chris, her attacker.

Shooing her friend upstairs to shower, and suggesting they go out afterward to get a late lunch, Shelby looked at the phone. There were a lot of texts and missed calls. Hannah told her it was okay for her to field the calls and texts, but Shelby still felt funny about it.

Hearing the voicemails from Asher, Shelby understood why he didn't show up for his date with Hannah, and subsequently why she opened the door up to Chris; she thought he was Asher.

She deleted all the texts and calls from her and Payton, not wanting Hannah to feel bad for not returning them. She texted Payton and explained….

I'm here with Hannah. Turns out, a guy who used to take care of her dad thought she was "his" and he attacked her. She's okay, but shaken up pretty badly. Lost her phone in the ruckus, but we found it.

(From Payton) Oh, my Lord, tell her I'm thinking of her. If you need anything, call me!

Shelby smiled, and texted back…..

I will.

Finishing up listening to the messages, Shelby heard one she thought Hannah would want to hear. She left the phone to charge on the counter and walked around the house opening up the curtains. Obviously Hannah was in bad shape, emotionally, and they would need to help her.

When Hannah did come downstairs, Shelby smiled, and said, "You look great!"

She could tell that Hannah felt better. Before she forgot, she told Hannah, "Oh, there was a call from a Ms. Jasper about tomorrow night, your dad's dedication. She left a voicemail."

Rolling her eyes, Hannah remembered, "I'm donating money to the high school for new baseball equipment, and they wanted to do something special for Dad."

Proud of her friend, Shelby asked, "Do you want Payton and I to come with you?"

Hannah's eyes widened, and she asked, "Would you?" She hugged Shelby, saying, "That would be great."

After they parted, Shelby called Payton and explained the situation. Payton said sure and suggested they help Hannah with her hair and makeup.

With that settled, the two friends went to lunch.

Hannah spent most of the time apologizing and feeling awful because she didn't feel like she was making any progress in getting through her grief.

Shelby assured her, "I know, Hannah, we're all doing it here and there. We want to be done with it, but the truth is, it's damn hard."

After they finished lunch, Shelby took Hannah home and made her friend promise to try and contact Asher to resolve things between him and let her and Payton know she was okay.

Driving home, Shelby thought a lot about Hannah's situation. There was Asher, a man who obviously made Hannah happy but she was fighting it because she felt bad about her father's death being so recent. Then her mother's words about almost losing her father because she was too afraid to move on past Charles' death ran through her mind. Shelby seriously wondered if she in danger of doing the same thing?

The next evening, Shelby and Payton showed up early at Hannah's house to get her ready for the tribute to her dad. It wasn't easy due to Hannah's long hair, but Hannah was naturally pretty so there wasn't that much to do in the makeup department.

Shelby drove them to the tribute, and it was amazing! The auditorium at the high school where Hannah's father taught was packed. They even gave Hannah a special parking space.

There was some last minute wavering, but they went inside and were shocked. The school commemorated the event with a slide show of Hannah's father's years of teaching. There were tears in Shelby's eyes, and she hadn't even known Hannah's father. Knowing Hannah, though, Shelby felt that the daughter was quite a bit like the father.

Hannah was supposed to say something and Shelby was a little worried that she would chicken out. Once Hannah was at the podium, though, she spoke eloquently and touchingly. Shelby doubted there were many dry eyes in the auditorium.

The three friends were happy by the end of the evening and both Shelby and Payton felt as if Hannah had just gotten over a huge emotional hurdle.

Her class load was light the day after she went to the tribute so Shelby decided she would pop into Imperial and check with Lisa and Jeff about Kendall's first week there.

Secretly, she might have been hoping that Gannon would be there. She knew that the class Kendall was in was an afternoon session and wondered if she might just "run into him."

Her heart practically skipped a beat when she saw an SUV parked in the parking lot that looked like his.

When she got inside, and looked in the waiting area, Shelby's stomach sank when she didn't see him.

Lisa was walking out of the gym, and noticed her, saying, "Shelby!"

Smiling, Shelby told her friend, "Hi, I'm just here to follow up on Kendall, you know, to see how her first week went."

Pointing toward the gym, Lisa said, "Her class is working right now, see for yourself."

Stepping forward, Shelby watched through the glass. The group was working on the uneven bars, doing different skills. When it was Kendall's turn, Shelby found herself holding her breath, and finally releasing it when the little girl finished.

"She's very good, you were right," Shelby heard the words from behind her, and knew Gannon was standing there. She turned around slowly, and started smiling when her eyes met his. "Of course I was right," She said in her best smart ass tone.

Grinning, Gannon took in the sight of her. She must've come from the gym because she still had on her "coach" outfit, but her hair was released from the ever-present braid. His hands itched to feel it; to ensure it was as soft as he imagined it was. "Are you here to see Kendall, or to see me?" He asked.

It was time to see if she was brave or chicken. Shelby had a choice here and she hoped she chose the right thing. She answered with, "A little of both, I suppose."

Her answer didn't surprise Gannon. She wouldn't give up ground easily, he'd learned that from the few times they verbally sparred. "Are you going to go out to dinner with me now?" He asked her, making it sound like a dare.

Out of the corner of Shelby's eye, she could see a few moms down the row of chairs from where she and Gannon stood. They no longer observed their kids, instead they seemed very interested in the conversation between her and Gannon. 'Oh, who cares!' She told herself mentally. "Yes," She whispered to Gannon before walking out of the gym.

When she got home, she was able to watch the news blurb about the tribute since it made the local news stations. She texted Hannah…..

Just saw you on the news, you looked stunning. Really, Payton and I should do your hair and makeup more often.

She waited a minute, and saw Hannah's response……

Anytime.

Knowing that she had to tell someone about Gannon, Shelby texted her friend……

I said yes.

Shelby actually giggled as she waited for Hannah's reaction. She wondered if her friend understood the text. By her answer, Hannah did, she texted…..

You did? When, where, what are you going to wear?

Laughing, because her friend thought of more details in twenty seconds than Shelby had in the last couple of hours. She typed back.....

Don't know, don't know, and for crying out loud, don't know

That should give Hannah something to laugh about. Her friend's response was quick....

When you get the time and place, text Payton and me and we'll go shopping with you to find a new outfit.

Shelby nodded as she read the text. She would definitely need her friends to help her out. But, it would help if she actually knew when she was supposed to go to dinner with Gannon.

After a few texts, Shelby managed to get Gannon's number through Bridgette, who got it from Peggy, Gannon's sister. She felt kind of silly for needing to go through two people to get a phone number, but she did technically need it.

She went into the kitchen and poured herself a glass of wine. Normally Shelby didn't drink, especially since that night not long after Kent's death when she'd gotten so sick, but she needed the liquid courage now. She downed the glass within minutes and then sent the text.....

Hi, it's Shelby. I got your number from Peggy, I hope that's okay. Obviously this is my number. I wanted to know when this "dinner" is supposed to happen.

Expecting a quick answer, Shelby was shocked that she hadn't received a response by the time she was supposed to go to bed. Getting upset at what she perceived as rudeness, she deleted the number from her phone.

Chapter 18

The next morning, Shelby woke up to the sound of her phone pinging from incoming texts. She groggily looked at the screen and was shocked. She had about six texts from Gannon.

She started reading them when her eyes could focus…..

1:00 am It's Gannon. I'm sorry I didn't answer when you sent your text, I was at work and we're not allowed to have our phones on us for personal use

1:03 am I'd love to have dinner with you, the sooner the better because I'm afraid you'll chicken out

1:05 am I just looked at the clock and realized how late/early it is. I'll text you in the morning

7:01 am I waited until 7am thinking that was late enough, I need to know that you'll go out with me

7:10 am Kendall would probably be okay to chaperone if that made you feel better

7:15 am I am assuming you're still asleep and will answer all of the previous questions when you wake up (Pls don't be mad that I'm texting so much)

Shelby started chuckling when she read the one about Kendall chaperoning. She figured she might as well put him out of his misery and responded……

I'm up now, thank you very much! You're lucky your texts were cute, I was mad that you didn't respond last night. I'll go whenever you have the time.

Not knowing if he was going to respond right away, Shelby got out of bed and went into the bathroom. She was washing her hands when she heard her phone go off again. Picking it up, she read Gannon's text....

Tonight

One word. One word was all it took to get Shelby's heart racing. Tonight? She wondered if she could pull it off. There would be no shopping excursion with Hannah and Payton, but she had dresses she could wear. Maybe if she called her mom and asked for advice...... "No," She said aloud, "time to stand on your own Shelby."

She texted Gannon back......

When and where?

On her way to the gym, she called her mom and told her what was going on.

Rose smiled, "Oh, that's nice," she answered, but sensed her daughter wanted permission, so she offered, "I think it's about time you started getting out there again."

Shelby spoke with her mom for a few more minutes before hanging up. She was relieved that her parents were okay with her dating again. As she pulled into the parking lot of the gym, Shelby wondered if Kent's parents would be so supportive.

On a whim, since class wasn't due to start for another fifteen minutes, Shelby called Angelica. Her palms were sweaty as she waited for her mother-in-law to answer.

Angelica smiled, and connected the call, "Hello, Shelby, how are you?" She asked.

195

Kent's mom sounded good, so Shelby dove in. "Um, I'm calling for," she paused, "you see I've been asked," Another pause, "I met someone who," and she couldn't go on because it all sounded ridiculous.

If Angelica hadn't already received a call from Rose, she might've been more surprised by Shelby's news. But, the truth was, she and Tony knew there would come a day, sooner or later, when Shelby started seeing people. "We know, and we're okay with it. We're proud of you for getting out, and I am touched that you would call and ask our permission, which you most definitely do not need."

Shelby loved her mother-in-law. Mostly because Angelica was just so big-hearted. "Thank you," Shelby replied in an emotionally charged whisper.

"No thanks necessary, now you get to class," Angelica tried to sound funny. After she hung up, she sighed. Tony came over and rubbed her shoulders. Looking up at her husband, Angelica smiled.

The rest of the day was like sitting on a very uncomfortable chair for Shelby. She couldn't seem to sit still, and was always moving. Her classes were a test of patience, not because of her students, because of her own excitement.

When the last child was out the door, Shelby sent Bridgette a text saying......

I'll call you tomorrow, going out to dinner with Gannon tonight so I'm going home to get ready

She locked the doors to the gym and got into her car when her phone pinged with Bridgette's returned text......

You better have some good details or I'm going to be really depressed

Shelby laughed at her friend's desperation for some excitement. It probably wasn't a whole lot of fun lying in bed when you were used to being as active as Bridgette was.

Getting ready took over an hour. They were meeting at a local BBQ place that was very casual so Shelby didn't even need to worry about wearing a dress. She wore some skinny jeans, a cute blouse, and flats. Because her attire didn't need as much tending, she was able to do a little more with her hair, curling it and pinning it back to make it look fuller. Her makeup was light, she didn't think anymore was necessary for where they were eating.

As a precaution, Shelby texted her mother with the name of the restaurant she and Gannon were meeting at. This wasn't college, and even if it was, Shelby heard far too many horror stories about women over the years.

She arrived at the restaurant a few minutes early, her stomach fluttering. As soon as she pulled her keys out, and looked over to open her driver's side door, she saw Gannon. He was standing at the front of her car, a smile on his face. And what that smile did to her insides should have been illegal!

Gannon was tired, he worked second shift all this week and didn't get much sleep the night before, mainly because of the nervousness he had about Shelby's text. Once he saw her, his exhaustion was history, and his mind was focused on her.

She got out of the car, and absently fussed with her blouse.

Taking a few steps, to meet up with Shelby, Gannon said, "You look beautiful."

In Shelby's experience, when a man looked at you the way Gannon was looking at her right now, he was definitely pleased with the way you looked. "Thank you," She returned with a shy smile.

They walked inside the BBQ place and the smells were heavenly.

Shelby had been here before, but it had been ages. She turned to Gannon while they waited to place their orders, and asked him, "Is this place a favorite of yours?"

Nodding, Gannon found himself being more nervous than he anticipated. "They have a good selection and large portions," His answer sounded as if he were doing a commercial for the place and he cringed inwardly at how stupid he sounded.

The line moved forward. Shelby was standing in front of him, so she could feel him behind her. He wasn't so close that they were touching, but she was just "aware" of him. She could feel his eyes on her and she liked the way it made her feel. Too tempted, she baited him, "Do you like what you see?"

A feeling of panic rushed over Gannon for a few seconds, before Shelby turned around and winked at him. "Yes, and yes," He answered.

'Touché!' Shelby thought to herself.

It was their turn to order so they were busy with that for a few minutes. The restaurant was a la carte and you walked through a line, much like one in a cafeteria, to order your food. By the time you got to your table though, your tray was loaded down with food and drink.

They found a corner booth, and slid in opposite one another.

Gannon handed her a paper towel from the roll on the table. She smiled and took it from him.

The food provided each of them some time to just get used to one another.

Shelby asked him, "How often do you come here?"

Smiling, Gannon felt a little embarrassed as he answered, "Once a week."

Her eyebrows raised, Shelby appreciated his honesty. "And why did you pick it for our first date?"

He studied her for a few minutes, a silly grin on his face, before he answered, "Well, first of all, I knew you'd be expecting some fancy place, and I didn't want to be that clichéd, and secondly, I like the food and knew I wouldn't have to wear a suit and tie."

Well, Gannon got points for his honesty. "You did surprise me," Shelby admitted.

"I like that you said first date," Gannon told her, "It makes me think that I have a chance of getting more."

A blush flew into Shelby's cheeks. He was very astute. Putting down her fork, she decided that the interrogation should start, "Bridgette tells me you're a police officer."

Not sure how to read her comment, Gannon tried to be relaxed. Some women were okay with his occupation, and some weren't. "Yes," He answered, "I told you too," he reminded her of their conversation at the gym, before the kiss. "I work for Harris County Sheriff's Department."

Feeling a little sassy, Shelby said, "So, you're a Deputy."

"Yes, ma'am," He returned, making a gesture that looked as though he was tipping the brim of his non-existent hat to her.

Curious, Shelby inquired, "What made you choose that career?"

The answer to that question was complex, but he compressed it to the basics, and told her, "I was always trying to save the other kids from the bullies in grade school, punched out a few jerks in high school for doing the same thing, so I figured protecting people was kind of my thing." Now he turned the tables on her, "And what made you get into teaching gymnastics?"

Pursing her lips, Shelby was pretty sure he knew the answer to the question, but she replied, "I'm sure that Peggy and Bridgette have spoken to you about me filling in while Bridgette is on maternity leave. Bridgette and I were on the same gymnastics teams in high school and college."

His sister tried to tell him information about Shelby, but he refused to hear it. He wanted to learn about Shelby from Shelby herself, not gossip from others. "I didn't know that, so thank you for telling me."

For the second time today, Gannon Riley surprised her. She found she kind of liked it. "Have you ever been shot at?" She asked out of a morbid curiosity, and then followed up with, "I'm sorry, that was a ridiculous question."

Cocking his head, Gannon studied her. She was worried about making a misstep. That meant that she was interested in him, and that meant that he didn't mind answering her questions. "Yes, I have been shot at, but never hit, thank God."

Nodding eagerly, Shelby said, "Yes!"

"I'm not going to lie to you, Shelby," Gannon wanted to lay it all out there for her. "The line of work I'm in isn't easy, it can be dangerous, but it's more often very fulfilling and I don't think I'd be happy doing anything else."

'There it was,' Shelby thought, 'he knows what I've been through and he's telling me that he won't change careers.' In essence, Gannon was giving her an out. She admired that about him, "I appreciate your honesty about it."

After that, the conversation turned more personal. They talked about their families. Gannon told her all sorts of stories about Kendall. He loved all of his nieces and nephews, but he was especially close with Kendall; probably because she was the first one.

They were lingering over their sodas after dinner, when Gannon asked her, "So, why are you paying for Kendall's training?"

Smiling, Shelby looked a little dreamy. "I think," She explained, "that I see something in her that you don't see very often with athletes, a drive that is stronger than what the rest of us have."

It was tough for Gannon to completely understand what she was saying. He did compare it to his time in the Academy before becoming a police officer, how some of the cadets just knew it was for them, him being one of them, while others just sort of struggled. "I think I know what you mean." He was curious so he asked Shelby, "Is she really that good?"

"Kendall is more talented than any other gymnast I know, who's her age," She told him with complete conviction. "She is so good, she doesn't even know how good she is, if that makes any sense."

For some strange reason, Gannon followed her, and nodded his understanding.

Shelby looked at him closely, and noticed he had some BBQ sauce on his lip. Without thinking, she took her paper towel and dabbed at his lip, removing the sauce.

Gannon didn't move as she wiped his lip. He couldn't because if he did, he'd pull her across the table and kiss her until she was breathless.

An employee came by there table, offering to take their plates, and popped the bubble of intimacy that they were enclosed into.

With a nod, Gannon threw some bills on the table for a tip and asked Shelby, "Do you want to go over to the bar area," he thought quickly, "or to a movie?"

Pretending to give it some serious thought, but smiling with contradicted that, Shelby finally told him, "You're a cop so I'm not going to drink and drive, and I don't really feel like seeing a movie," she smiled, "but we can go over to the bar area. I noticed a couple of pool tables and I'd like to see if I can kick your butt."

Oh, there was no way he was going to turn down a challenge at pool from a gymnastics instructor. "Hell, yeah," He replied, and tipped his head, saying, "Let's go."

With a quick smile, Shelby nodded.

They walked through a doorway that separated the restaurant from the bar area. Sure enough there were three pool tables and one was vacant. They walked over to it, Shelby putting her purse underneath one end and grabbing a pool cue.

Gannon was putting chalk on the end of his pool cue when Shelby asked him, "What are we playing for?"

"How about," He thought for a few moments, "whoever wins gets to pick where we go on our second date."

Her eyebrows raised, Shelby commented, "So you think there will actually be a second date."

The look he shot her was one that dared her to contradict him. He knew there would be a second date. There was no way he wasn't going to see her again.

"Fine," Shelby said lightly. "I'll even let you break."

Shaking his head, Gannon replied, "No way, my mother raised a gentleman, ladies first."

Shelby wasn't going to dispute his moral compass and just nodded in acknowledgement. She leaned over, taking aim, and sent the ball flying across the felt top. The cue ball hit the other balls with a thwack and scattered them. Two balls fell into the pockets, the first one was a stripe, the second one a solid. "Ooooh, I inadvertently helped you out," She told Gannon with a fake look of pity. "I guess I'll take stripes and leave you with solids," She said in a completely soft tone.

Within minutes, Gannon knew she was a pool shark. Beautiful, yes. Smart, yes. A con artist, hell yes. He stood by, watching her put ball after ball in the pockets. She finally missed with only two stripes left on the table.

Not willing to look at Gannon, because he knew she was good and didn't bother to tell him how good she was. Shelby just circled the table and watched him take his shot. He was competitive; she could tell by the way he focused on his shot. He got three solids in before missing.

Shelby made quick work of sinking her last two balls and standing there, looking smug.

"Clearly," Gannon said sarcastically, "I should have run a background check on you. Do you have a rap sheet, perhaps as a con artist?"

His sore loser attitude only made the win feel better. "I have no criminal record," She told him, very proud of the fact. "Walk me out to my car please," Shelby directed as she grabbed her purse.

Frowning, Gannon asked her, "No rematch?"

Chuckling, Shelby rubbed her palm along his cheek and told him, "No sense in creaming you twice in one night."

If Gannon thought Shelby was in any way meek or mild, the last twenty minutes convinced him otherwise. She was a force to be reckoned with, and the challenge made him crazy. He did as he was told and walked her out to her car. She unlocked it and was about to get in, when he asked, "Can I kiss you again, Shelby?"

Not answering, Shelby tossed her purse inside the car, leaned against the car door, and brought her lips up to his. This kiss, although chaste like the first one, made awareness thunder through her body like a stampede of elephants. Her heart was beating so fast, she thought it would leave her body. When she finally pulled away, she swore that Gannon had the same experience. She whispered, "Goodnight," and got into the car.

Chapter 19

When she got home, Shelby sent a quick text to her mom, saying she was alright and would call the next day with details. Then she sent a text to Gannon…..

Had a great time. 3. Conversation 2. Getting to know you 1. The kiss

Gannon read the text as he was walking into his house, and stopped when he got to the part about the kiss. Oh, that woman sure did know how to turn a man's head. His father would say, "She's got a bit of the wee folk in her blood," and Gannon laughed. His father always did have a penchant for the folklore of his Irish ancestry.

He unlocked the door and went inside. His house, or bungalow, as the realtor described it, was small, but neat. He didn't plan on having a big family like Peggy or his other siblings. Gannon had always been the reliable brother who helped others out, no one really thought he had his own dreams. And the truth of it was, he didn't, not until the day he walked into that gym and saw Shelby Forrester standing there. His mind went blank, his heart went into triple time, and there was something deep inside of him that just clicked into place.

When he was a boy, his father told him almost the exact same thing about when he met Gannon's mother. "Ah, she was the sweetest thing, she was. I was sitting in a pub with some mates and in walks this girl, oh the loveliest girl I'd ever seen."

Remembering the story, which he'd been told a thousand times, Gannon always thought it was a bunch of malarkey. Until now, until he met Shelby.

He re-read the text, then texted her back……

I have off of work tomorrow, let's do something

If a text was ever open-ended, it was this one. Shelby read it and wondered what "something" meant. Did she text him back flirting or did she just ask what? She didn't know, it'd been a long time since she was in the dating scene. Her fingers typed, and she sent back…..

It depends on what your version of "something" is. I have classes in the morning, but I'm free after that. How about around 2pm you meet me at the gym?

Her words turned Gannon's insides into jelly, they provoked such images that came under the heading of "something" alright. He was a gentleman, at least that's what his mother thought of him so he'd have to try to uphold that. He texted her…..

My idea of something is walking through a park with a beautiful woman next to me (that's you, by the way) and finding out a way to get her to kiss me again. Is that too daring or are you up to the challenge?

'Oh, he was good,' Shelby thought as she read the text. Calling her beautiful and all but daring her to go out with him. He knew what buttons to push with her and they barely knew each other. She was walking into the bedroom, and glanced up to see the picture of Kent she kept next to her bed. Sitting down, she picked it up, and asked it, "Kent, I know I shouldn't be asking you what to do, but I guess that's what I'm asking." There was no response, only a memory…..

When Kent came home to their little apartment and announced, "Jeff and I are going to buy a gym and train gymnasts. Lisa is on board and I want you on board too."

Shocked by his idea, Shelby shrugged, "I don't know, Kent. Do you and Jeff have a business plan, do you have gymnasts lined up to train, and do you have a facility?"

Sitting down beside his wife, Kent leaned in and kissed her hard. When he pulled away, he told Shelby, "I've always thought that living life should be 'taking what comes and making the best of it' and the rest will just fall into place. We'll make it a success, I promise." And he kissed Shelby again.

Floating out of the memory, Shelby guessed that this was going to be the best answer she would get from Kent. She would 'take what comes and make the best of it.' She typed quickly......

Considering I kicked your tail at pool tonight, I'm not sure the best approach is daring me to do anything. However, you did get a lot of brownie points for texting that I was beautiful (thank you, by the way) and my lips are still tingling from that kiss so I'll see you tomorrow. Goodnight.

Gannon read the text and smiled big. Her lips still tingled, eh? He liked that. Maybe tomorrow she'd let him give her a real kiss. He sent his reply quickly.....

It's a date, goodnight

When Shelby slept that night, she dreamed of Kent and Gannon. Her dreams were a mix of memories of then and now and made her feel uneasy. How could she compartmentalize the two men?

Waking up early, Shelby groaned when she looked at the clock. It was way too early to be up and get ready for classes. Instead, she pulled out her phone and started to text.....

You invaded my dreams last night and I didn't appreciate it

Gannon turned over, after hearing his phone go off. He was still half asleep when he read the text, and found himself waking up quickly. He had to blink a few times to clear his vision before texting her his reply.....

I take it as a good sign if I'm in a beautiful woman's dreams

A smile crossed Shelby's face as she read the text. He called her beautiful first thing in the morning. That was something a girl liked.

She didn't text him back, instead, Shelby felt herself drift back off to sleep.

Waiting for her reply, Gannon found his eyes were closing, but he held the phone in his hand so he could feel it and see it right away.

Shelby woke up two hours later, when her alarm went off. When she fell back asleep, she slept deep and restful. Probably, in large part to Gannon's text. She made a mental note to ask him where his name came from because it was so different.

She showered, got dressed, and braided her hair, thinking the whole time how much Gannon like to see it down.

Before she left for the gym, Shelby called her mom. "Hey, mom," She greeted her mother when she answered.

"Hey, you," Rose began, "How did the date go?"

Smiling, Shelby told her about the date, "As you know, we went to that BBQ place in Pearland, then we played a game of pool, and then I came home."

Rose's eyebrows were raised, "He didn't know you played really good pool did he?" She asked her daughter.

"Nope," Shelby replied, and then she laughed.

The sound of her daughter's laughter was like music to Rose's ears. She hadn't heard a genuine laugh from Shelby in far too long. It gave her hope. "And did he kiss you goodnight?" Rose asked, even though she thought her daughter probably didn't want to discuss any physical things with her mother.

Again, Shelby said, "Nope," then followed it up with, "I kissed him."

Proud of her daughter, Rose said, "That's my girl."

They talked a bit longer about the date, and then changed to the subject of Angelica and Tony, Kent's parents. Shelby explained to her mother that she called Angelica and they were okay with her dating again.

Rose listened, but didn't tell Shelby that she herself had already spoken to Angelica. Kent's parents were still, and always would be, good friends. There was no need to keep secrets. Although, she was proud of Shelby for speaking to Kent's mom on her own, Rose took that as a sign that Shelby was ready to move on.

After hanging up with her mom, Shelby grabbed a snack and her water, and went out the door.

The drive to the gym was easy on the weekends, the traffic was less and Shelby didn't even seem to notice the red lights and other drivers who cut her off.

When Shelby was prepping the gym, her phone went off. It was a missed call from Mrs. Hanson. Worried, Shelby called her back, saying, "I'm sorry I missed your call. How are you?"

A worried, Mrs. Hanson said, "I think it's time for an intervention….."

Worried, Shelby said, "I'm listening. The story that Mrs. Hanson gave her made her cringe, because it was sneaky, but if it worked, then maybe one of them could find happiness.

Her first class today was the Toddlers and Mommies. It was done to music to help the kids learn coordination and allow them to have some one-on-one time with their mothers. Shelby chuckled at the antics and rubbery legs the little toddlers had as they did the routines.

There was an hour between the classes so Shelby took the time to give Bridgette a call as soon as she said goodbye to the first set of "students."

"Hello," Bridgette picked up on the first ring. "Please tell me something other than that my feet are swelling and I look like I could be a stand in for an Orca whale at Sea World."

It was that bad? "Well, the first class today went well," Shelby told her friend.

Rolling her eyes, Bridgette's tone got testy, "You know darn well I don't care about a class, I want details woman! How did the date go?"

Bridgette was making it difficult not to laugh. Shelby gave her the rundown of the date complete with the goodbye kiss and the texts afterwards.

"That's more like it," Bridgette said slowly. "I can at least pretend that someone is getting lucky."

Feeling sassy, Shelby asked her friend, "Isn't "getting lucky" what put you into your current situation?"

Laughing Bridgette replied, "That's beside the point."

Now Shelby laughed. "I don't think so, but we'll let it drop, for now."

"So, you're seeing him today?" Bridgette asked, confirmed what she understood from Shelby's explanation.

Sighing, Shelby answered, "No, we were supposed to, but something came up that I have to do so I'm going to reschedule later in the week."

'Ahhh,' Bridgette thought, 'the beginnings were always so dreamy.' "Well, I'll expect a full report then." She saw her husband coming into their room, carrying a tray with brunch. "Gotta go, the hubby is spoiling me." She told Shelby and hung up.

Shelby shook her head as she disconnected the line.

Calling Gannon, Shelby sighed, and hoped he understood.

"Hello," Gannon crooned into the phone when he saw it was Shelby on the line.

Smiling, and feeling guilty, Shelby told him, "I have to reschedule our date, a friend from my grief group really needs my help."

Understanding, but still very disappointed, Gannon replied, "Uh, sure," he calculated his schedule, "I'm on third shifts this next week so I probably won't be able to get together until next Saturday, does that work for you?"

Relieved that Gannon was okay with her doing this, Shelby responded, "Sure, and thank you, Gannon."

Luckily, her second class was the 4-6 year olds and Carrie was willing to come in and take it over.

When Shelby pulled into the parking area of Galveston Retreat, she saw Payton's car, but not Hannah's. Good, she wasn't late. This all had to go according to plan or it could blow up in their faces.

She walked in and found Payton and Mrs. Hanson sitting in the kitchen.

"Good, you're here," Mrs. Hanson told Shelby. "You call Asher and I'll call Hannah. Without waiting for a reply, Mrs. Hanson walked into her room to call Hannah.

Shelby looked at Payton, who said, "You're more personable than I am, plus you know what was going on."

Giving Payton a dry look, Shelby took the paper with Asher's name and cell phone number on it, and called him. She hoped that Asher was the man Hannah deserved. When she hung up with him five minutes later, she believed he was.

A couple of minutes later, Mrs. Hanson came into the room and announced, "Hannah will be getting ready and coming over as soon as she can."

The three of them took a collective breath and hoped for the best. They spoke about Hannah and Asher and Shelby reassured both Mrs. Hanson and Payton that Hannah felt as much love for Asher as he did for her.

An hour later, Asher, who parked in the next parking area over, came up to the back door. Mrs. Hanson asked him to come inside for some tea.

Shelby felt bad for him that he was put on the spot here, but none of them believed Hannah would budge without a little help.

He didn't touch his tea, instead he stood up, looked at the three women, and told them, "I love her, I do," and walked out the back door to go sit on the beach.

"We'd better go upstairs," Payton said to Shelby, and they had just gotten into the room Hannah stayed in when they heard Mrs. Hanson yell up the stairs, "She's here!"

Knowing they would need help, Shelby prayed this worked and gave Payton a tight hug before stepping over to the side of the patio.

Within minutes Hannah was at the doorway to the patio. "What's going on?" She asked of Shelby and Payton, "Ms. Hanson called me to say that Payton was here and very hurt and going crazy."

Sighing, Payton answered, "I am very hurt and upset, let's face it, we all are."

Taking her turn, Shelby piped up, "And we're all just trying to make our way through the feelings we have about losing our loved ones. You knew, Hannah, you knew he was going to die long before it happened." Tears started streaming down her face, as she said the words to her friend. "Neither of us knew, but you did."

Hannah's chest tightened with emotion. She knew what Shelby meant. "He told me," She choked out, "when I came home from college, he told me he was going to die from that stupid disease."

Payton added, "And you stayed, you stayed to take care of him because you loved him so much."

Nodding, Hannah whispered, and plopped down into a nearby chair, "Yes, he was my dad, my hero."

They were all crying now, and they knew it was necessary for them to move forward.

"I called Asher," Shelby admitted. "I told him about what happened with Chris."

Emotions danced across Hannah's face, she didn't know whether to be mad or glad because she didn't think she could ever tell him. "Why?" She asked.

Shelby stepped forward, and took Hannah's hand, "Because, my friend, you weren't going to." When Hannah started to shake her head in denial, but Shelby interrupted her, "We all know you wouldn't. You were ashamed and you were hurt that he didn't show up, even though we all know his reason was valid."

Hannah hated it when her own shortcomings were exposed. "You're right," She said defiantly, "but he could've called me too."

Now Payton stepped forward, "How was he to know?" She asked Hannah. "People can't read your mind, you know, he is just as confused as you are."

Denying it, Hannah retorted, "He doesn't understand."

"How can you say that?" Shelby asked, "His wife CHOSE to leave him, and that adorable little girl. She didn't even look back, from what you told me. None of us," She choked up, trying to get the words out, "none of us chose to have our loved ones leave us. At least we can understand that they didn't want to leave us, it was not their choice."

Now that Shelby explained it, Hannah felt so awful! She knew what her friends were saying, but it was still difficult to just pick up the phone and call him. "What do you want me to do?" She asked, and plopped down in the chair behind her.

Now Shelby smiled, "We want you to go down there," she pointed down to the beach, "and tell him everything that's in your heart."

Looking to her right, Hannah saw a person sitting down on the beach, alone. Her eyes widened and she looked back at her friends, "Is that him?"

Payton nodded, "Yes, and remember, he knows everything."

Hannah looked at Payton harshly, "You didn't need to tell him, you know!"

Looking back at Shelby, just as harshly, Payton hissed, "No secrets!"

Ms. Hanson stood in the doorway, tears streaming down her cheeks as she listened to what the three women were saying. It was beautiful, what was happening, and yet it broke her heart to see it. "Now," She interrupted them, and smiled when all three of them looked at her, "It's your turn to make a choice," she pointed out to the beach, "You can decide to go out there and talk to him and resolve this, or you can decide you don't want to." She looked at Payton and Shelby, "None of us will judge your decision." She smiled, "But we also won't accept it if you decide against taking this chance and then complain about it for the rest of your days."

Shelby looked at Payton, who was trying not to smile.

Hannah listened to them, torn between being mad and being so happy that she found them as friends. "I want to.....but,"

Willa put up her hands, "No excuses," her words were curt, "This is your life, you either take it or you leave it." She softened them now, "Just remember that love is the biggest gift you'll ever give and get, and it's worth it."

Nodding in agreement, both Payton and Shelby stepped forward, each offering a hand to Hannah.

Her decision made, Hannah allowed them to pull her up, and into a hug. Even Ms. Hanson joined in.

Hannah left them, and Mrs. Hanson took her place on the patio, tears in her eyes. They leaned against the railing and watched as Hannah made those steps out toward Asher. How scary was it to risk your heart again? That question made a picture of Gannon pop into her head and she swept him out, mentally. Now was about Hannah, not her.

They all were holding their breaths, hoping that Hannah and Asher would say what was in their hearts. After a few tense minutes, they were kissing.

Payton said something sassy, but Shelby just smiled, happy that Hannah found something wonderful out of all of this. The three of them went downstairs to greet the happy couple. Mrs. Hanson disappeared for a few minutes, saying she needed to send an email of all things, but she showed up with a bottle of sparkling wine and poured them all glasses.

Chapter 20

Maybe it was the whole happy ending scene with Hannah and Asher at the retreat, but the next week flew by in a wave of happy days.

Finally, it was Saturday, when she would be getting together with Gannon and she was excited.

Her first class flew by, but the second one, seemed to drag on. No one was focused and it was frustrating because Shelby was so excited to see Gannon again. After the students left, she locked the door, grabbed her bag with clothes to change into, and went into the bathroom.

Changing into an outfit of a skirt, a white blouse, and sandals that were still comfortable for walking, she looked at herself in the mirror.

She undid her braid, and let her hair fall, in waves, over her shoulders. She finger-combed it to make it look a little messy, and sprayed a little perfume on before coming out.

Looking at her phone, Shelby saw that it was only 1:30pm and she'd have to wait for Gannon to show up for a half hour. Originally, she'd wanted to give herself enough time to change after her last class, but now, she was anxious to see him. As if her thinking of him made him appear, she looked up to see Gannon just outside the door of the gym, smiling.

Walking over to the door, Shelby unlocked it, and stepped aside so Gannon could come inside. She re-locked the door behind him and turned around to face him. He looked so gorgeous, in shorts, a polo shirt, his hair a little messed, as much as it could be for as short as it was. The thing that got Shelby the most was the way he smelled, very male but sophisticated is how she would describe it. "Hello, you're early," She said, not knowing what else to say.

He was only a few steps away, so Gannon closed the distance between them, cradled the back of her head in his hands, so his fingers were tangled in her hair, and leaned down to kiss her. This time, he wanted to kiss her properly.

Shelby knew what he was going to do, and didn't mind one bit. Her last coherent thought was, 'thank goodness I brushed my teeth,' before his lips captured hers. And captured was the most appropriate word because once Gannon's lips had hers on his, he didn't seem keen on releasing them.

Her lips were soft and melded with his perfectly. He opened his mouth a little, to touch those soft lips with his tongue. Shelby knew what he wanted, and parted her lips to accommodate him.

Anything Gannon wanted, Shelby wanted just as badly. When he first kissed her, she let her arms hang down at her sides, not sure what to do with them. As soon as he deepened the kiss, Shelby had to hold on to his arms, just to keep standing up. That started a whole new barrage of need because his arms were solid muscle and she could feel the muscle shift as he moved his head back and forth, therefore her head moved and shifted his hands beneath it.

Gannon could see this turning very hot, very quickly, so he pulled away from Shelby. For a few moments, her eyes were still closed, so he had the privilege of watching her in an "after kiss" dream state. She was breathtaking. "Thank you," He said, his voice rough with need.

As Shelby's eyes drifted open, she looked up into Gannon's green ones. They looked like gems that sparkled. Instead of just her lips tingling, as was the case the night they went to dinner, now her whole body tingled. "You're welcome," She whispered. She still held on to his upper arms, now she needed to hold on for balance. The world was spinning a bit and she needed to let it settle before she'd be okay to let go.

As the fog of need cleared, Gannon spoke first, saying, "I know I told you that I'd like to go walking at a park, but if you wanted to go back to my place, or yours, I'd be okay with that too."

His words were filtering into her brain slowly, but the innuendo was apparent. He felt what she felt, a chemistry that neither of them could deny. "As much fun as I'm sure that would be," Shelby said once she found her voice, "I'm not sure I want to move quite that fast."

Gannon nodded. "Normally, I'd say that too, but damn Shelby, you do something to me and I can't keep it under control."

Teasing him, Shelby replied, "You like control don't you," her words were innocuous enough, but the meaning was straight up sexual.

Growling, Gannon said, "Yes," and pulled her to him. He didn't kiss her this time, just ran his hands over her shoulders and up her neck. He could spend hours just kissing her neck.

Shelby could feel him, his arousal, and see it in his eyes. Very little persuasion would be needed to get him into her bed. As powerful as that made Shelby feel, she couldn't just start hopping into bed with him. Not yet, anyway. If he kept kissing her like that though, her days would be numbered.

He couldn't stand there and look at her any longer. Gannon wanted her so much that he would have to try to convince her to make love with him, and he didn't need to embarrass either of them with that. Again, the gentleman in him woke up, thank goodness. "We'd better go before we get ourselves in trouble."

Nodding, Shelby couldn't agree more. She was still shaking a little when Gannon released her. Walking into the office, she drew the blinds closed, grabbed her purse, and closed the door. They left the gym, and Shelby locked the door behind them. It took her longer than normal because her body didn't want to calm down after Gannon's kisses.

"I assumed we would leave your car here, and then I'd just drop you back off here after…." His voice drifted off.

It was a relief to Shelby that Gannon was as affected by their kisses as she was. "Our date," She finished for him, and smiled. Laying her hand on his arm, she said, "Let's go before we both combust."

Never in his life had Gannon met someone who was so honest about their feelings. It aroused him for sure, but it also kind of intimidated him, and Gannon wasn't a man who was easily intimidated. "Okay," He replied, and opened up the passenger side of his SUV so Shelby could get in.

Having Gannon open up her door for her was sweet. It touched Shelby in a very different way, and made her feel safe. She noticed he did that a lot, opened up doors for women, even Kendall when he walked out to the car with her, got her door opened. After Gannon jumped into the driver's seat, Shelby commented, "I think it's very sweet that you open doors for ladies."

"My mom and dad would have my hide if I didn't," Gannon told her, and smiled, before adding, "But I like it. I like making a woman feel as though she's worth the effort."

The comment was so sweet that Shelby had to look away to avoid letting him see her eyes tearing up. She most definitely felt as though she was worth the effort, if his actions and comments were on point.

They drove into Houston, Gannon letting her know that they were going to Discovery Green Park. "It's pretty convenient to restaurants and everything so I thought we'd grab some lunch, if you're hungry, and then go walk the park."

'So, he was a thinker,' Shelby thought to herself. "That sounds great," She replied.

Gannon just turned the vehicle onto the 45 North Freeway when he asked Shelby, "So, what kind of music do you like?"

"More like," Shelby began, "What kind of music don't I like?"

That started a conversation about music they grew up with versus what they prefer to listen to now. Their tastes were similar and they even shared a few of the same favorite bands.

When they parked on the street, next to the park, Shelby was surprised by how fast the drive had been.

They ended up picking a restaurant that was literally right across the street from the park. It was American cuisine with a modern, healthy twist.

Although Shelby had never eaten there, she'd heard of it.

The hostess showed them their table, Gannon asking if they could eat outside on the patio.

Once seated, Gannon asked Shelby, "Are you okay with being outside? It isn't too humid today so I thought we'd take in the fresh air."

She appreciated his consideration, "I prefer to eat outside," she told him, "although Kent didn't." As soon as Kent's name crossed her lips, Shelby was embarrassed.

Reaching over, Gannon put his hand over Shelby's and said, "I'm going to assume that is your late husband's name." She nodded, but didn't speak. Squeezing her hand, Gannon suggested, "Why don't you tell me about him?"

Shocked, that they were talking about Kent, while on a date, Shelby didn't really know where to start.

Seeing Shelby's reluctance, Gannon smiled. "It's okay to talk about him, you know." He winked, "I think any man who was able to get your heart should be remembered."

His words touched her deeply. It was difficult for Shelby to keep the emotions out of her voice, but she started with, "We met in college. He was criticizing something I was doing on the balance beam and I basically told him to kiss my ass."

Laughing, Gannon could definitely see Shelby doing that.

"We dated through college, got engaged our senior year, graduated, and then got married." Shelby didn't know what was okay to share and what wasn't. "He was funny, a bulldozer mostly," At Gannon's questioning look, she explained, "Anytime that he wanted something, a house, the gym, anything, he just sort of did it and then asked my forgiveness afterwards."

Gannon heard the affection Shelby held in her heart for her late husband, but he didn't understand the man's attitude. He was taught that marriage was a team effort, you discussed, you decided, yes, maybe you fought, but everyone knew everything. "Did you get mad?" He asked at a break in the story.

Rolling her eyes, Shelby replied, "All the time," and then sighed, "But he would just smooth it over with a smile or kiss and all would be forgiven."

"You were a very obliging spouse," Gannon commented.

Thinking about the word he chose, Shelby frowned, then responded, "Yes, yes I was."

They placed their orders and talked about their families, the subject of Kent dropped for the moment. Shelby was shocked that Gannon and Peggy were two of six kids. Likewise, Gannon couldn't believe that Shelby was an only child.

After they finished their lunch, Shelby had a salad to be "good" and Gannon chose a burger, they went across the street and started walking the path that wove around the park. There was a little pond there, with people kayaking. It was serene, the green grass, the trees, the light breeze, and the company.

Conversation drifted from topic to topic, both of them trying to be as casual as they could.

Shelby was surprised by the little things that Gannon liked. He mentioned being more of a homebody. Since his job was stressful, it was nice to come home and decompress. Shelby preferred to be outside since she felt cooped up in the gym during the day, but wasn't opposed to evenings in with popcorn and a movie. They shared a common interest in television shows, both disliking the "reality" television and gravitating more toward dramas or comedies.

When Gannon asked Shelby about her favorite flower, she gave him a skeptical look, and asked, "Are you digging for ways to get brownie points?"

"Maybe….," Gannon said slowly, "but you didn't answer my question."

She'd give him points for his tenacity. "My favorite flower is the carnation," She answered.

Gannon looked at her, and asked, "Carnation, really?"

His being shocked at her choice made her laugh, she nudged him in the arm with her shoulder, "I like carnations," she said defensively, "They're happy flowers."

They continued to walk, with Gannon laughing at her comments regarding some people being snobbish about flower selections.

Two hours later, they were starting their umpteenth lap of the park path. It was good, getting to know one another in this type of setting. There was no pressure to be a certain way or do anything, it was just casual.

Out of the blue, Gannon announced, "I feel the need to treat you to some ice cream," then he stopped, and asked, "Do you like ice cream?"

Giving him a dry look, Shelby retorted, "I'm a woman with no lactose intolerance, Gannon, I love ice cream!"

Her explanation made him laugh again.

They made their way back to where his car was parked, Gannon holding her door open again, and got in.

This time, traffic was heavier. Gannon looked over and said, "I apologize, I forgot how congested it would be this time of day."

Reaching over, covering his hand with hers, Shelby replied, "It's fine, just more time I get to spend with you."

'Wow!' Gannon thought. The woman even made a traffic jam seem like fun.

Remembering that she meant to ask him something, Shelby inquired, "How did your parents come up with the name Gannon?"

The question was out of the blue, and it took a few moments for Gannon's brain to switch gear from awareness to coherent thought. "Uh," He started, then continued with, "Well, the meaning is Gaelic for fair skinned, but I got it because it was my great-grandfather's name."

"Oh," Shelby said, "It's such a beautiful name."

No one, in his whole thirty-one years of life, ever said his name was beautiful. He was told it was weird, uncommon, interesting, unusual, but never beautiful. Only Shelby could make it sound sexy like that. "Thank you," He told her.

Her hand was still covering his, as it sat on the center counsel of the vehicle, and his thoughts were switching back to being aware of her. Traffic moved at a snail's pace, and Gannon found he didn't even care as long as Shelby was sitting beside him.

Her phone pinged with an incoming message, so Shelby pulled it out of her purse and laughed when she read the message from her dad…..

I want you to take a picture of this Gannon guy, he's a cop so he will understand why I'm asking. Love you, be safe.

Glancing over at Shelby, Gannon asked, "What's so funny?"

Lifting up her phone, she clicked on the camera app and said, "Smile," he didn't, but she snapped a picture of him anyway.

"What was that for?" Gannon asked her, frowning because she took a picture of him when he wasn't smiling.

Chuckling, as she was sending the picture to her dad's phone, she told him, "That was my dad asking for a picture of you and saying that because you're a cop, you should understand why he wants one."

Sighing, Gannon commented, "Well, I wouldn't have looked so grumpy if you'd have explained that to me before you just snapped the picture."

Biting her lip, Shelby returned, "Yes, but I wouldn't have found it as funny."

"I'm glad I make you laugh," Gannon said, and found he meant it. For some reason, making Shelby laugh was something he wanted to do desperately. Maybe it was because he knew she was recovering from something bad. He didn't know the circumstances of her husband's death, but he knew he could find out if he wanted to.

It took them a good hour and a half to get back down to Pearland. Making good on his promise of ice cream, Gannon took her to a great ice cream place right off of the 288. Even their little trip for the sweet treat taught him things about Shelby. She loved chocolate, and mint, and ate her ice cream with a daintiness he found adorable. His was gone long before hers and he ordered the largest size the shop had.

"Sorry," Shelby apologized for her slowness. "I enjoy eating my treats slowly, so I can thoroughly enjoy the experience."

And his thoughts took a dive, right into the gutter, again. He'd like her to go slowly and enjoy an experience with him. Feeling guilty for his sexual thoughts, he cleared his throat and looked around the shop. It was kind of slow this time of day, because it was dinner time for most people. He figured the shop would be flooded in about an hour or so. It took him a few seconds before he noticed that Shelby was speaking. "I'm sorry," He asked, "What did you say?"

Licking her lips, she told him, "I was just wondering why every time I say something to you, I'm immediately flooded with sexual thoughts about it."

That honesty was going to get them both into a lot of trouble. The blood was quickly draining from his brain and traveling to other parts of his body. "Really?" His voice squeaked a little as he asked.

Chuckling, Shelby finished licking the spoon, and put it down. "What I'm wondering is, how much will power do you have?"

His smile faded. Was she serious? If she was referring to his will power against wanting to make love with her, well that was down the drain already. "Depends," He cleared his throat, "on what you mean."

Her body hummed with awareness and Shelby knew, eventually, she would make love with Gannon. Her body responded so easily, as if it were on some other conscious level than her mind was. It wouldn't be today, she was too scared, but it would be soon. She wouldn't be able to resist him, which was a clear fact. "I don't have a whole lot of it myself, will power I mean, so I'm hoping you'll be the strong one when I kiss you goodbye today."

Swallowing hard, Gannon nodded, but he sensed that she knew there was no backbone behind the nod. He was as weak as she was in this particular area. "I'll try, for you," He said, hoping he could keep his word.

She got up, threw out their ice cream cups, and walked back over to hold her hand out to him. "Let's go then."

Gannon took her hand, the feel of her skin against his driving him nuts, and followed her out to the SUV. He tucked her inside, and jogged around to the driver's side.

Chapter 21

It took a little while for them to get down Broadway, to where the gym was located. They passed Imperial on the way and gave each other a look.

Pulling up in the space beside Shelby's car, Gannon put the vehicle in park, and turned to face her. "Okay, when are we seeing one another again?" He asked, allowing the need to creep into his tone.

If more men looked and spoke to women the way Gannon was doing right now, Shelby was pretty sure there would be a whole lot more, happier women out there. She could see in his eyes how much he wanted her and could hear in his tone that he wanted to see her soon. It made her feel powerful. "When is good for you?" She asked him in return.

His face grew serious, "Shelby, if I had it my way, you would be coming home with me and I wouldn't let you out of my bed until we both had to be back to work on Monday."

A flush worked its way up through Shelby's cheeks. "Oh," She said, and was ashamed that was the only thing she could respond with. Trying to play it off, Shelby said, "I thought you were supposed to be the one with will power here."

"Sue me," Gannon growled before leaning over and kissing her. He wanted to feel her lips on his and ran one hand up her arm and the other cradled her head. He loved doing that, holding her head so he could focus on kissing her the way she deserved to be kissed......completely.

The kisses were making Shelby giddy. Her body felt like a melting candle, the wick at her center was on fire, but the rest of her was just falling away. She grabbed onto Gannon's arms, clutching his shirt, trying to pull him closer.

When Gannon was able to pull away from her, more like tearing his lips away, because they protested as soon as they were no longer pressed against Shelby's, he was breathing hard. "What is it?" He asked.

Knowing exactly what he was talking about, Shelby answered, "I have no idea."

Before he could drug her with another kiss, Shelby turned to open her door. Gannon was moving to open his own door to come around and help her, but Shelby stopped him. "Don't," She said tightly, "if you do, I won't be able to stop."

Her words were like pouring lighter fluid onto an already crazy fire. The only reason he didn't insist on getting out was because he didn't want her, or anyone else to see the state of arousal his body was in. Instead, he just nodded.

Shelby got into her car and rolled down the window. Since his SUV sat higher, he had to lean over so she could see him. "Thank you for today," She told Gannon, smiling.

"Thank you," He said back, "Text me when you get home please?" He asked her before she put her window back up. He saw her nod and was glad she would do as he asked.

When Shelby got home, she saw a text on her phone from her mother……

Not a happy looking guy, but very handsome

Shelby laughed as she got out of her car and walked inside the house. She texted her mom back…..

I didn't tell him why I was taking it until afterward. He agreed with dad.

Setting the phone down, Shelby went to the refrigerator to get a bottled water. She drank half of it before coming up for air. Her throat was parched and she tried to tell herself it was from lack of water, when it was really lack of Gannon that caused the condition. Her phone pinged, it was her mom….

How was the date?

Not wanting to share all of the intimate details, Shelby tried to figure out what to say. She finally typed…..

A gentleman and a great kisser

Rose read the text from her daughter and started to giggle. Her husband looked at her, the question in his eyes. She said honestly, "I don't think you want to know."

John, trusting his wife's opinion, went back to reading the paper. He worried about Shelby, but did not want to know anything about her dating. Police officer or not, he wanted his little girl safe.

Shelby sent a text to Gannon saying…

I'm home. I had to text my mom, she'd texted me while I was driving. I'm safe and sound and somewhat disappointed that I didn't do as you suggested.

Gannon read the text and was puzzled, he texted to ask…..

What suggestion was that?

Shaking her head at how quickly men tended to forget things, she responded……

The suggestion of going back to your place and not leaving your bed until we both had to go to work on Monday.

She was killing him! Gannon was sure he was going to die of sexual need. He hadn't felt like this since…….well, since never. Not even in high school did he feel this constant tension that Shelby created inside of him. Heaven help them both if they did end up in bed together, he may never get out. He had a sneaking suspicion that once he had Shelby, physically and emotionally, he would not want to give her up.

They texted on and off for the rest of Saturday and into Sunday. Gannon's texts were the last thing Shelby saw that night and the first thing she saw the next morning. He'd sent a text just a few minutes before Shelby woke up. Her first thought of the day included him. Looking over, she saw the picture of Kent, and sighed. She hoped he approved of Gannon.

Gannon asked her repeatedly to meet up with him today, but Shelby was reluctant. Not that she didn't want to, the problem was that she wanted to so much that she knew what would happen. If they got into that whole sex thing, how on earth could they figure it out? She remembered what happened when Hannah came back to the retreat the first time she and Asher slept together. That was a whole boat load of fun……NOT!

Her phone went off again, and it was Gannon, being insistent……

Seriously, I'll make sure we have a chaperone. Peggy already invited me over to their place for dinner. I can tell her yes, you can meet me there, and they have four kids under the age of 8 so there is no possible way we can get in trouble.

Apparently Gannon didn't understand the concept of sneaky sex. Well, neither did she really, so maybe he had a point. She answered his text......

Fine, what time?

The drive over to Peggy and Kip's house was spent giving herself a pep talk. Mostly about being out in public with people. She wasn't too keen on the socialization yet, but she was making progress. In large part, thanks to her time at the retreat. She reminded herself to text Payton and Hannah about all of this tomorrow.

Gannon's sister and her family lived in Friendswood, just to the east of Pearland so it didn't take her too long to get there. The subdivision they lived in was very nice, with large, well-kept yards. It was the kind of place where Shelby thought families should live.

She pulled up to the curb and recognized Gannon's SUV. He was coming out of the house, Kendall on his heels, when she got out of her car. With the five year-old right beside him, she was unsure about what to do. They couldn't very well make out in front of Kendall. She held back and waited to see what Gannon did.

As excited as the kids were on Christmas morning, Gannon stood by the front window of Peggy's house and watched for Shelby. He asked Kendall to go outside with him to "be the representative for her parents," and caught the look of skepticism from his sister. He shrugged, and led the way outside when he saw Shelby pull up. She was rounding her car when he walked up to her. The safe thing to do was kiss her on the cheek, which he did, but he whispered, "This is taking up every ounce of my self-control."

Just to taunt him a little more, Shelby ran her hand across his shoulder as they parted. She wanted to giggle at the way his eyes sparked with awareness.

He grabbed her hand, entwined his fingers with Shelby's and they walked up onto the sidewalk, where Kendall was waiting. The little girl looked at their joined hands and smiled.

"Hello, Kendall," Shelby said with a smile.

Waving her hand, Kendall returned, "Hello, Miss Shelby."

Curious, Shelby asked Gannon's niece, "So, how are you liking the coaches at Imperial?"

With a sigh, Kendall's eyes widened, "It's hard work, but I really like it."

Both Gannon and Shelby smiled at the drama Kendall injected into the statement.

"But, it will all be worth it when you're getting medals," Shelby told Kendall.

Nodding, the little girl ran up the sidewalk ahead of them, and opened the front door. Peggy and Kip came to the doorway as Gannon and Shelby stepped up onto the front stoop.

Greetings exchanged, they all went into the kitchen while Peggy put the final touches on dinner. The conversation was casual, mostly about jobs, kids, and weather.

Shelby found herself feeling very comfortable in Peggy and Kip's home. She accepted a glass of wine from Kip and told

Gannon, "One glass, and I won't leave until it's out of my system."

Shooting her another lustful leer, Gannon just smiled sweetly and didn't say anything. He and Kip grabbed beers out of the refrigerator and went out to the garage to talk about a project Kip had out there.

Once they were alone, Peggy asked, "So, how is it dating my brother?"

Not understanding the fascination, Shelby answered, "Uh, it's nice, he's very sweet."

Shelby thought Peggy was going to choke because when she said the word "sweet" Peggy was drinking her wine and gagged.

Making sure Peggy was okay, Shelby sat back down.

"I'm so sorry," Peggy said, her hand to her chest, "it's just that you're the first woman Gannon has dated that any of us have met."

Frowning, Shelby asked, "You mean your family here?"

Shaking her head no, Peggy told Shelby, "I mean ANY of our family. When I told my mom that he was bringing you to dinner, I thought she was going to have a heart attack."

That didn't make sense to Shelby. Gannon was open and sweet and considerate. "Why do you suppose he's never brought anyone home?" She asked Peggy.

After giving the roast a basting, Peggy closed the oven door and walked over to sit at the table next to Shelby. "Other than being thoroughly embarrassed by the sheer size of the crazy family that he has, I'm thinking he's just private. You see, Gannon was the closest to our father, God rest his soul, and

Daddy used to fill Gannon's head with "finding the right woman," thing. I seriously think Gannon took it all to heart and there must have been something between the two of you that made him take the leap."

Peggy's explanation, although charming, sent a chill through Shelby. She knew they had chemistry, but she wasn't willing to just jump into some relationship because of something a parent said to them. Her mother gave her excellent advice, but Shelby never took it as gospel. Two of the kids came in, arguing, and distracted Peggy. That left Shelby to her own thoughts and those weren't that good at the moment.

The men came in a few minutes later, and Gannon knew something happened. He smiled at Shelby, happy to see her and, although she smiled back, it didn't reach her eyes. He shot a look to his sister, who seemed completely oblivious to anything.

Peggy announced that dinner was ready and the group went into the dining room. Kip sat at one end of the table, Peggy at the other, two kids on each side, and Shelby across from Gannon in the middle.

Kip led them in grace, and Shelby bowed her head, silently asking for strength.

When dinner was served, there was conversation flying around as if the family was having a water balloon fight. It was entertaining to hear the kids tell their stories from school, and watch the toddler as he rejected the food his mother tried to feed him. Everything was okay, until Kendall started talking about Imperial.

"So, Coach Jeff said I am really progressing in my floor routine," She said to her father proudly. "He told me that Coach Kent would've really like working with me.

Not knowing the back story, Kip asked, "Who's Coach Kent?"

Being five years old, Kendall didn't know the ties between all the adults so she answered her father honestly, "He's the coach that died last year in a motorcycle accident. He was Coach Jeff's best friend and partner."

Shelby wanted to crumple up into a little ball, she was so uncomfortable. Hearing Kent's name, so casually, was like a knife piercing into her chest. When she looked up, she saw Gannon's gaze laser-focused on her. He knew. He knew how much this hurt and he couldn't do anything to prevent it. "If you'll excuse me," Shelby said quietly, "I'll just powder my nose." She quickly got up and left the room, going into the little half bath off of the kitchen.

Kip, enjoying his dinner, and still not aware of what was going on, didn't see the daggers his wife was shooting out of her eyes at him. She turned her gaze to Gannon, who looked mad.

Shelby stood at the sink in the bathroom, and let the tears fall. She should have known this wouldn't work. Hearing Kent's name in this setting was more than she was prepared to handle. It was no one's fault. Certainly she didn't think that Kendall knew what was going on and Kip was just interested in his daughter's day. But this, this had to stop and now! She took some deep breaths, wiped her eyes, and left the bathroom.

Gannon watched as Shelby took her seat at the table. He could see she'd been crying. He felt like a first rate fool for inviting her. Having Kendall go to the gym where Shelby's late husband worked was a little too close for comfort. She was still grieving. As soon as dinner was finished, he made their excuse to leave. Peggy saw through it, and Gannon hugged her quickly before getting Shelby out of the house as soon as he could. "I'm so sorry," He told her as they walked down the sidewalk in front of the house.

Stopping, Shelby placed her hands on his chest, to keep him at a distance. She could feel his heart beating as fast as hers was and that made it even harder to say what she knew she had to say, "This won't work," she started.

"No!" Gannon was emphatic, "I realize everyone is too intertwined, but we'll just keep the family out of it for a while."

Appreciating Gannon's efforts, Shelby was too emotionally compromised right now, "You don't get it." She snapped without meaning to, "They were talking about the man I was married to for six years as if he were some stranger. I'm not mad at them because they didn't know, but he wasn't some stranger, Gannon, he was my husband."

Pulling her close, Gannon wrapped his arms around Shelby, saying, "I know, baby, and I'm so sorry."

She leaned against him for a few minutes, letting herself absorb his comfort. When she calmed down, she stepped back. They were just a few feet from the cars and all Shelby had to do was cross that small space and she would be safe. She gave Gannon a look, memorizing his features, then said, "Goodbye," before turning around to get into her car.

Gannon followed Shelby as she walked around her car, and asked, "What does goodbye mean, Shelby?"

Shelby knew what he was asking. "It means that I'm just not ready," She answered, and shut the door.

Tapping on the glass, he waited for Shelby to lower the window. "I'm asking you not to say goodbye," He pleaded, "If you need space, I'll give it, but not goodbye."

The look on Gannon's face caused Shelby's chest to ache. He looked so hurt, and she didn't want to drag anyone else into her personal pain. She wouldn't do that. "I can't offer you anything," She told him, a tear sliding down her cheek.

Gannon reached in and, with his thumb, wiped the tear from her cheek. "You've given me more than anyone else."

She almost broke in that moment. Almost.

Sensing that she was leaving him for good, Gannon said, "Just don't say goodbye," and stood there as she pulled away from the curb.

When he turned around, he saw Peggy standing on the front stoop of the house.

She walked toward him, crying, and said, "Gannon, I'm so sorry, Kip didn't know and Kendall, well she's only a kid."

He shook his head, "I know all that, Peg, and so does Shelby. I think this was just too much too soon for her." His shoulders dropped and he gave his sister a quick wave before walking over to get into his SUV.

Chapter 22

The next morning was the beginning of Shelby's week at the gym. She was glad for the escape of working with the kids. It kept her mind off of Gannon.

They just finished their last class when Carrie came up to the office door and peeked inside, asking, "Hey, are you okay?"

Rubbing the bridge of her nose, Shelby made up an excuse, "I think I'm coming down with something."

Nodding, Carried told her, "Well, bulk up on vitamin C, these kids are germ factories."

Shelby chuckled at Carrie's description of their students. True, but still amusing.

She was exhausted, having stayed up most of the night before. Her time was spent crying over the pain of losing Kent and the guilt of moving on with Gannon. Not that there was anything saying they were going to end up together, it was just that he was the first man since Kent.

Dialing Dr. Mitchem's office, Shelby made an appointment for the next available opening, which happened to be that afternoon, due to a cancellation. Shelby grabbed onto the appointment like a life raft.

Her classes done, Shelby was locking up the gym when her phone went off. She pulled it out of her purse and saw a text from Gannon.....

I would've texted sooner but I was sleeping to cycle myself for third shift. I was up most of the night thinking about you. Please give us a chance?

She couldn't answer it, so Shelby just put her phone back into her purse and got into her car.

By the time she arrived at Dr. Mitchem's office, she was an emotional wreck.

Her therapist sat down across from her and noted, "I guess there's no use in asking if you've made any progress, you've had a setback."

Having seen her own reflection in the mirror, Shelby would have doubted Dr. Mitchem's therapy skills had she not noticed that Shelby was a wreck. "Yep," She answered, and dove into the story of her first date with Gannon, the scene at Galveston Retreat helping Hannah, and then the last weekend with Gannon. By the time she was done, her therapist looked almost as shell-shocked as Shelby felt.

Dr. Mitchem sat back and tapped her pen on the pad of paper, "I'm going to ask you a couple of questions and I want you to just say the first thing that comes into your mind, nothing more, okay?" She asked Shelby.

Nodding, Shelby waited.

"First," Dr. Mitchem asked, "what about hearing Kent's name mentioned in that circumstance upset you?"

Not thinking, as Dr. Mitchem instructed, Shelby answered, "Because it meant he wasn't important."

Writing something down, Dr. Mitchem said, "Okay, now, how did having Gannon outside to lean on, I'm referring to when you told me he held you after you left his sister's house, help you?"

Again, not thinking, Shelby replied, "Because I knew he wouldn't judge, he would just accept it."

Nodding, Dr. Mitchem wrote down something else. She didn't ask any more questions of Shelby, just sat there, watching.

"But he was important!" Shelby shouted, then calmed down to say, "And, I shouldn't have taken a story by a child about him to heart since Kendall didn't know him."

A slight smile on her face, Dr. Mitchem spoke, saying, "A good realization."

Thinking about her behavior toward Gannon, she told her therapist, "And I should've realized that Gannon wasn't going to give up on me, he was just trying to be supportive and I shouldn't feel guilty for having strong feelings for him since Kent wouldn't want me wallowing anyway."

Her eyebrows raised, Dr. Mitchem relayed, "I think you'd make a good therapist," to Shelby, and winked.

"No thanks, I already have a job," Shelby said, her tone proud.

The rest of the session was spent discussing what Shelby wanted to do about her current emotional state.

By the time Shelby left, she felt a lot better.

When she got home, she found her phone full of texts. The first one was from Hannah…..

(From Hannah) We're getting married in three months! I want Shelby and Payton to be my bridesmaids and Mrs. Hanson, because you're more like a mother, would you be willing to walk me down the aisle? I'm sorry to ask in a text, but I'm between errands.

(From Payton) As long as my bridesmaids dress isn't hideous, I'm in.

(Mrs. Hanson) I'm crying right now so it's hard to text, but of course.

(From Hannah) You are the best. Although, Shelby's probably in class and can't text back yet, we'll let it slide.

(From Payton) What color are the bridesmaids' dresses, I might as well decide now if I'll even do it.

(From Hannah) Pale pink

(From Payton) Okay, I look good in pale pink

(From Mrs. Hanson) Oh good, I'll wear a deep rose colored dress

For some reason, seeing the happy texts tore Shelby's emotions back up. She was happy for Hannah, of course, but wished she herself was happier. Deciding that her own personal crap shouldn't dampen her friend's happiness, she texted them....

I'm totally in. Congratulations Hannah, we'll be the best bridesmaids ever!

(From Payton) How about dinner at Chez Mr. Hanson's to celebrate?

(From Mrs. Hanson) Sure, as long as I don't have to cook

(From Payton) ☹

Shelby laughed. But, what did Mrs. Hanson expect when she was the best cook that any of them knew? She joined in the texting.....

How about a brunch?

(From Hannah) Sounds wonderful

(From Payton) Just tell me where

(From Mrs. Hanson) Again, as long as I don't have to cook

After group texting for another fifteen minutes, they settled on the following Sunday. It would be just the four of them since Asher had a daddy-daughter commitment with Skyler planned already.

Shelby wanted to text Gannon and tell him about the breakthrough with Dr. Mitchem, and about her being a bridesmaid, but she held back. She needed to take some time to figure this out.

Two days later, she still wasn't settled on it all. Her parents were over for dinner, they brought the food along, and her mother studied her closely. "You're sad again, did you and Gannon have a disagreement?" She asked her daughter.

On the verge of tears for two days, Shelby finally let them go. "Mom, Dad, I think I really am stuck," She admitted to them.

Her parents listened as Shelby talked about the dinner at Peggy and Kip's, her reaction to it all, and her saying goodbye to Gannon the way she did. They didn't comment until she was done.

John spoke to his daughter first, saying, "When I met your mom, one of the first things she told me was that she was heartbroken and she would NEVER fall in love again." He looked over at his wife of thirty years, and winked at her, before continuing, "And I knew, I couldn't be responsible for her happiness because that was up to her. All I could do was love her the best way I knew how." He smiled at his little girl, "I know you'll always have this little piece of your heart that will be bruised with missing Kent. The big question is, are you going to waste the rest of your heart missing out on happiness?"

Rose smiled at her husband, and then over at Shelby. "We're not saying that Gannon is the one, although from what you've said, he sounds like a good contender," she explained to their daughter, "There can be happy at the same time there is sad. That's a part of life, sweetheart."

"What should I do?" Shelby asked her parents.

John sighed, "Well, I think you should call, or at least text him and open up a conversation, see where that goes."

It was late evening when her parents left. She knew Gannon was working third shift, but didn't know what time he started. She sent him a text, knowing he'd get it eventually…..

I think about you all the time. I've talked to my grief therapist and my parents, and they all assure me that it's okay to care about you while missing Kent. If you can understand that emotional handicap, then I'd like to see you again.

Shelby sent the text and went into her bedroom to get ready for bed. She left the phone on her nightstand and walked into the bathroom. When she came out ten minutes later, ready for bed, she saw she had a text on her phone from Gannon……

I understand, and I'll help however I can. I do care, Shelby, and if you need to talk about Kent or mourn longer, I can wait. I think about you all the time too. Peggy feels awful, although I've told her numerous times that both you and I aren't mad at Kendall or Kip. When can I see you?

Smiling at his question, Shelby wished it was right now, but he was going to work, if he wasn't already there. She texted him back….

When can I see you? You're the one working third shifts this week. I have classes the rest of the week but I'm done by 4pm tomorrow and 3:30pm the next day

She crawled into bed, and studied the screen on her phone, waiting for his answer. Within two minutes she had one…..

I'll be at the gym tomorrow at 4pm. We'll find a place close by to have an early dinner. I have to work at 10pm so I need to say goodbye, I'll see you tomorrow. Sweet dreams!

Relief washed over Shelby, she sent one final text for the night….

Be safe!

Shelby slept deeply that night. When she woke up to her alarm the next morning, she was shocked that she slept the whole night through. Picking up her phone, she saw a text from Gannon……

Home safe after a long shift of wishing I was with you. I'm going to go to sleep now and plan to have sweet dreams of us, I hope you slept well, see you at 4pm today!

Smiling, because of his sweet words, Shelby jumped out of bed and got ready to go to the gym.

When she arrived, she brought smoothies for herself and Carrie, knowing that Carrie had a weakness for them.

Classes went well, a couple of new students joined and fell into the routine easily enough.

By 4pm, Shelby was talking with one of the parents, about Bridgette, when Gannon came through the door. He didn't say anything, just let her talk.

A few minutes later, she walked the mom out and, not seeing Gannon, walked over to the doorway of the gym. He was over to her left, looking at the posters on the wall. She walked over to him and asked, "What do you find so fascinating?"

Gannon was waiting for her, his body on high alert, his senses acute, and his need for her overwhelming. He didn't turn around right away at her question, but waited until he felt her right behind him. Then, he turned quickly, and took her into his arms, finding her soft lips with his.

The kiss took Shelby by surprise, not so much because she didn't see it coming but because of how quickly it escalated between them. Tongues touched, parted, touched, and wrapped up together, creating a delectable friction inside of her. His hands were all over her, touching her arms, her neck, her shoulders, and diving into her braid, pulling it free.

Like a teenage boy, Gannon was all over Shelby, but he couldn't help himself. She tasted so damn good, and she smelled like spring, and she felt so soft against his hardness.

Out of breath, Shelby stopped the kiss and leaned her head against Gannon's chest. She had to get a grip or she'd basically have sex with him here at the gym. She knew her body, and it wanted him. "Just give me a second," She said breathlessly.

Smiling, because Shelby was as riled up sexually as he was, Gannon held her. "I need more than a second," He told her dryly.

Chuckling, Shelby looked up at him, into his beautiful green eyes, and wanted to know what was going on inside his mind. But, she knew it was probably what was going on inside her mind, where could they go to make love. Why was she questioning? "How far do you live from here?" She asked him.

Gannon could see the wheels in her mind turning. She was asking him this for one reason. "I live about fifteen minutes away," He answered, then asked her, "Are you sure?"

Her eyebrows went up, and Shelby replied, "I'm pretty sure."

They walked out of the gym, Gannon waited for Shelby to close up the gym. When they went out to their vehicles, he gave her his address and asked her to follow him.

During the drive to Gannon's house, Shelby thought of a thousand different things. She was still on birth control, so that was okay since she just never stopped after Kent's death. She wished she was dressed a little more like a girl, the gym attire wasn't exactly lingerie. She would see Gannon look into his side mirror to make sure she was still following him every few minutes.

They pulled up to a small house, Shelby parking on the street while Gannon pulled into the driveway. His squad car was parked there already, and it made his job seem more real. She got out and looked at his house. It was adorable, small, but adorable.

"It's a bungalow according to the realtor," Gannon explained as he jumped out of his SUV and walked over to meet Shelby.

She smiled at him, "It's wonderful," she told him, and meant it.

They walked up the short sidewalk and Gannon unlocked the door. He was making small talk, telling her that the neighbors liked the fact that he was a cop, and that made them feel safer. She didn't hear all of it, she was too curious to see where he lived.

The first room was a decent sized living room, with a sectional and large screen television in it. There were a few pictures on the wall, as if his sister, or mother, came in to spruce up the bachelor pad. He showed her around, leading her into a compact, but up-to-date kitchen with eat in dining. There was a small bathroom down a hallway and then three bedrooms. One of them was converted into a small office, the second one was a guest room, and the last room, was the master bedroom. Shelby noted that it wasn't as big as hers, but it was big enough for his king sized bed, a dresser, and nightstands. There was a bathroom off of it, which was nice. She turned around to find Gannon standing in the doorway, staring at her. She smiled.

Seeing Shelby in his bedroom was like having a fantasy realized. He wasn't sure it was real just yet. He asked her again, "Are you sure?" He wouldn't pressure her in any way.

Nodding, Shelby walked over to him, kissed him deeply, and then answered, "Yes."

Chapter 23

The only light in the room came through the mostly closed blinds on a large window. Gannon looked at her, in the dim light of the late afternoon, and wondered how he ever got so lucky. "What were you thinking about on the way over here?" He asked Shelby.

"I was thinking of making sure I told you I was on the pill," When he gave her a quizzical look, she explained, "It was an issue for a friend of mine," she pulled her t-shirt up and over her head, "And then I was worried because my gym uniform isn't exactly sexy."

Stepping closer to her, Gannon pulled off his own shirt and tossed it aside. If she was willing to strip for him, he'd return the favor.

Shelby kicked off her tennis shoes, and noticed that Gannon mimicked her movements. She liked it. Reaching down she pushed her gym pants down, and slipped them off, followed with her socks. Again, Gannon shadowed her lead and undid his jeans sliding them down.

They were both standing there, in nothing but their underwear, and Shelby told him, "It's been over a year," she suddenly felt nervous, and asked, "What if I'm no good?"

Covering the last little bit of space between them, Gannon took her into his arms, lifting her up so she was straddling his torso. He kissed her, letting his lips and tongue make love to her mouth before their bodies did.

Feeling Gannon's reassurance, helped soothe Shelby's nerves. She was no longer focused on whether or not she was good in bed, she was now focused on pleasing him. As soon as his lips released hers, she focused on kissing the side of his neck, and running her nails over his skin.

"Woman, that drives me crazy," Gannon told her in a low voice before laying her down on the bed.

A knowing smile on her face, Shelby looked up at him, so strong and wanting, and said, "I want you to drive me crazy, Gannon."

Her wish was something Gannon would be pleased to fulfill. He pulled his underwear down, allowing her to look at his thick, hardness. His eyes ran over her body, and he allowed his hands to follow the trail his gaze made. He sat down beside her, gently running his fingertips up her arms, down her sides, across her belly, down her thighs, and back up again.

Her body tight with need, Shelby was getting restless, "I can see how much you want me, Gannon, feel how much I want you," she whispered and took his hand, sliding it under the fabric of her panties. When his fingers found her center, Shelby's body arched in response, and Gannon's want for her went through the roof. He moved so he was kissing her, while removing her bra with his free hand. Never once stopping his manipulations of her wetness.

Any tighter, and Shelby thought she might burst into a thousand pieces. He managed, somehow, to get her bra off and tossed it off into the room. Only leaving her long enough to slide off her panties, she sighed with missing his touch. When he got her panties off, he laid down beside her. He seemed to want to go slowly, while Shelby had no such plans. She moved, and straddled him, pulling his hands up to cup her swollen breasts. She wrapped his hardness with her hand and guided it inside of her, slowly covering him with her hot, wet, core. "Ohhhh," Shelby hissed.

Swallowing hard, Gannon was just trying to stave off the embarrassment of not satisfying Shelby the first time they made love. She was so tight, and so hot, and it had been a long time for him too. "Shelby, baby," He warned her.

"You just wait for me, Gannon," She began to move, covering his hands with hers as they squeezed her breasts, a finger flicking her nipples as she rode him. "Almost there, baby, just hold on."

Not used to having someone, especially someone who turned him inside out with just a look, take charge, Gannon held on to the last vestige of his self-control. "Okay, baby, that's it, ride me," He said, not even recognizing his own voice.

The talking did it for Shelby, it threw her up to the edge, and she yelled out, "Okay, Gannon, cum with me, baby!"

His body responded to her demands and he felt her pulse around him as his release took a hold of him. "Shelby!" He yelled out.

Her body clenched in the most overwhelming climax, Shelby only grasped his hands with her own as she rode the wave of ecstasy. A minute later, she collapsed on top of Gannon, completely spent of all energy.

Gannon laid there, holding Shelby to him for a long time. Their bodies were relaxing and sleep claimed them both within minutes.

Shelby woke up after hearing a noise. It took her a minute to remember that she was at Gannon's house. He was walking out of the bathroom, and her eyes had to adjust for a few seconds before she realized he was in his uniform.

Gannon wanted Shelby to stay at his house, but he suspected she wouldn't do it. He let her sleep and got up to get ready for work. "Hey," He said to her when he noticed she'd woken up, "I set out some cheese and crackers since I never did take you to dinner," he sat down on the edge of the bed. "You're welcome to stay here, I just have to leave for work in a few minutes."

Seeing him like this, in his uniform, shook Shelby a little. She absently ran her hand down his chest, and felt the protective vest he wore under his shirt. "I'll go home," She said, getting up.

Sensing something was going on, Gannon asked her, "Are you okay? Did I do something?"

Holding her clothes to the front of her body, Shelby told him, "No, not at all, I'm just trying to take this in," she pointed to his uniform, "this is a side of you I didn't really understand until now."

Her reaction wasn't the first time a woman felt a little overwhelmed with his chosen profession. Some took it well and some bolted. He prayed that Shelby just talked to him about it. "I'm safe when I'm out there, but others aren't always," He wasn't going to lie to her, "but I'll text you before I go on shift and when I get off."

Standing there, Shelby saw Gannon as someone who was willing to compromise with her. That's all she could really ask for. "I'd appreciate that," She said, and walked over to him, dropping her clothes so she was naked when she stood in front of him.

"Not fair," Gannon said, and kissed Shelby's breasts as she stood in front of him. "I have to go, but if you want to meet me in the morning, I'll be happy to continue this train of thought."

Chuckling, Shelby walked back over to where she dropped her clothes, and told him, "No, you need sleep. That way I can see you after I get done with work tomorrow. I'll come by, you can cook me dinner and then we'll see what we can arrange."

Standing up, Gannon, walked over to her, gave her a kiss, and said, "Be here by 5 or you forfeit dinner." He smiled, asked her to go out the garage, and gave her the code for it, before leaving for work.

Shelby got dressed quickly, and left his house. She was home by 9:30pm but felt like it was in the middle of the night. She grabbed an apple out of the refrigerator, realizing she didn't eat the cheese and crackers Gannon set out for her, and got ready for bed. Sleep beckoned her and she didn't want to argue with it tonight, within minutes she was slipping into the sweet oblivion of rest.

A few minutes later, her phone went off. Opening her eyes was tough, but it was a message from Gannon......

You have no idea how difficult it was to leave you when all I wanted to do was stay in that bed and hold you. I'm about to start work but know you're in my thoughts. Sweet dreams!

Shelby was too tired to respond so she put the phone down and allowed sleep to take her away.

The next morning, when she woke up, there was another text from him......

Had a quiet night, always a good thing. I can smell your perfume on my pillow so I'm holding it close and pretending you're here. I'll see you after work later.

Oh, the man had a way with words. He made a text message sound like a love letter. Not many men could say that.

Getting out of bed, Shelby realized she was a little sore in places that she hadn't been sore in for a really long time. It was a lovely reminder of their time together yesterday. Making love with Gannon was everything she hoped it would be, and more.

She was sitting in her kitchen, sipping coffee, when she decided to text Hannah and Payton.......

Hey gals, I don't really want to talk about this in front of Mrs. Hanson, but I wanted to let you know I've been seeing someone, the uncle of one of my former students. Last night we were "together" and it was more than I thought it could be. He's a police officer and the sweetest man. Sorry, I'm still in afterglow mode.

Putting down her phone, Shelby walked over to rinse out her coffee cup, and heard her phone ping repeatedly. 'Oh, that probably got them going,' she thought to herself. She went back to the table and read the texts....

(From Hannah) What???? I thought we were going to go shopping before your first date. Last night wasn't your first date was it??? Not that I'm judging, just strangely curious.

(From Payton) Go Shelby! Go Shelby! I'm proud of you. And, I'm no one to talk. Things have been progressing between Raleigh's father and I and I'm scared out of my mind to say anything. It didn't really work out the first time around, except for the sex part.

(From Hannah) How am I not knowing anything? Am I too focused on myself that I'm not helping you both out? I feel awful.

(From Payton) I think we just wanted to give you and Asher some time. Shelby and I are big girls, we're taking our own steps to get our lives back on track.

(From Mrs. Hanson) Shelby, if you don't want to discuss sex in front of me at Brunch that's fine, but maybe you shouldn't MMS me on your cell if you don't want me to know what you're doing. ☺

Reading the last text, Shelby blushed. "Oh crap!" She said aloud. And texted quickly......

Sorry Mrs. Hanson, I'm so sorry to imply that we should keep things from you. I just wasn't sure if you'd approve.

(From Mrs. Hanson) Well, I've probably had more sex than the three of you put together......let that sink in for a moment. Maybe not, but still, I think I know the general workings of a relationship.

Now, Shelby was really embarrassed. Mrs. Hanson has had a lot of sex? It wasn't repulsive, just difficult to process. She was a hoot that was for sure.

For the next two days, Shelby would go to the gym, and Gannon would meet her there after her classes were over. They would drive over to his house and make love. The second night he wasn't working so Shelby knew he expected her to stay over. She took a bag, but left it in her car, just in case she decided she didn't want to stay. The last couple of days/nights were heavenly, but it was nice to go home and sleep in her own bed.

Their lovemaking was intense and very involved. Gannon insisted on discovering every part of Shelby, and who was she to stop him? Besides, there was something very wonderful about having a man devoted to you, physically. He made sure Shelby was on the cusp of release before he allowed himself to let go of his own passion.

When he looked at her, he was looking into the very core of her being, and Shelby knew he wanted more, but she wasn't ready yet for that kind of commitment. What they had right now was perfect.

Out of breath, after their latest bout of lovemaking, Shelby lay on the bed, half sprawled over Gannon. She started to giggle because she imagined they looked very silly in their current physical state.

"What are you laughing about?" Gannon asked her playfully.

Looking up, Shelby propped her head on her palm and replied, "I'm hoping you don't have an overhead camera because we probably look a little ridiculous."

Gannon moved quickly, grabbing her and tucking her up beside him, laughing when she squealed in surprise. "You're lucky I don't take you over my knee and spank you."

Her eyes sparkling, "Hmmm," she said, "I've never tried that before."

Looking down at her, Gannon was amazed. He was amazed that this beautiful woman chose to spend her time with him and chose to make love with him. That's what it was to him, making love. There were times when he actually pictured her pregnant with his child. The thought sent chills down his spine; the good kind that meant you were right where you were meant to be. Unable to keep his thoughts to himself, he asked Shelby, "Do you want children?"

Panic coursed through Shelby. Not only wasn't she prepared to answer the question, it threw her up and to the right, emotionally. This was the subject of a lot of arguments between her and Kent and she wasn't ready to share that with someone else, not yet. Without saying anything, she rolled away from Gannon and got up to get dressed.

Very confused, Gannon asked, "What did I do?"

All Shelby could do was shake her head. She couldn't even answer that question either. Picking up her clothes, she dressed, and started walking out of the bedroom.

Gannon grabbed his pants and slid them on quickly, he got ahead of her just as she was about to open the front door. "Shelby, I deserve an explanation."

Rubbing her hands down her face, Shelby turned and walked over to the sectional sofa in the living room. She plopped down on the end of the sofa and dropped her face into her hands. "That question you asked, about kids," She began, "well, it was a subject of a lot of arguments between Kent and me. He wanted kids for the last three years," She held up three fingers, "but I just kept telling him no. I don't know why, we were fine financially and emotionally. Our marriage was on good footing, but I just.....I just couldn't." She looked up at Gannon, tears in her eyes, "And just three days after I start sleeping with you, you're asking about kids?"

Walking over to her, Gannon crouched down. "I couldn't possibly know that question would upset you. I find that when

I'm thinking I'm falling in love with someone, I'm curious about what they want out of their lives."

Looking at him, her eyes wide with fear, Shelby asked, "Did you say you are thinking that you're falling in love?"

It would be easy to coddle her, Lord knew that Gannon wanted to make it easy for her. But, in the long run, that wouldn't do Shelby any good. She was trying to get on with her life, not just flip it into neutral and see where she rolled. "I did."

"That scares me, Gannon. I'm not going to lie to you." She wanted to run away very fast and very far.

He cupped her chin, and held her in place so he could look into those beautiful brown eyes. "Baby, I know it does. It scares me too. I'm basically holding out my heart to you and giving you free reign to crush it. I've never done that before."

Knowing that he had his own fears did help Shelby.

Gannon got up and sat down beside her, taking her hand and putting it between his. "It's easy to run, I know, I've been doing it for a long time." He smiled when she looked over at him, "But this time is different. I don't want to run, I just want you."

His words soothed her as nothing else could. "Will I stop wanting to run?"

Turning so they were facing one another, Gannon said, "Lord, I hope so."

She started crying, "Gannon, I'm just afraid of opening up myself again, and then losing you too."

"And, that's a legitimate fear, Shelby. I know a lot of guys whose wives left them or girlfriends who won't stick around because of the job we do. It can suck, but I am determined to protect people." He held her face in his hands and leaned forward to kiss her.

As soon as his lips touched hers, Shelby was lost in the most glorious of feelings. He made her nerve endings feel as though they were set on fire and in danger of being singed. Grasping onto him, Shelby scooted forward and straddled him.

They made love there, on the sofa. Removing clothes and straining to be closer to one another. Shelby was on his lap, allowing him to cup her bottom and set the pace for their loving. She threw her head back, determined to get the most enjoyment out of the experience.

Gannon's orgasm was right there, he could feel it clawing at him, but he would not let go until he felt Shelby explode around him. When her head snapped forward, and her eyes widened, he knew she was close. "That's right, baby, let it," He told her.

Shelby wanted to fight it, for some reason, but there were some things you couldn't fight, and some things you shouldn't fight. She felt the feelings rush into her as her body climaxed, pouring all the physical and emotional needs through her. She knew, she was falling in love with Gannon. Not because he was making her feel wonderful, although he was, and not because he was so handsome and caring, which he was, but because, deep down, she knew it was her fate to be loved by someone who didn't want to push Kent out of her heart, but wanted to share her heart with Kent.

She ended up staying over, tucked into the safety of Gannon's arms.

The next morning, Shelby woke up, and felt a little trickle of fear as she didn't recognize her bedroom. It took a moment for her to get her bearings and she found it was weird not seeing the picture of Kent first thing.

Gannon knew when Shelby woke up. He'd been up for hours, and always had difficulty transitioning from third shift to first shift for work. He got an extra-long weekend, although he didn't tell Shelby that yet. He knew this would be strange for her, but he was here if/when she needed him. "Are you hungry?" He asked.

"Starving!" Shelby said dramatically.

They got out of bed, and went into the kitchen. Shelby was wearing one of Gannon's t-shirts, because it went down to her knees. They were having fun, making scrambled eggs, cutting up some fruit, and even spraying each other with the sink sprayer.

Somehow, in the middle of all that, they managed to start kissing and ended up making love right there, in the kitchen.

Chapter 24

When Shelby pulled into her driveway, she was surprised to see another car parked there. It took a moment, but then she realized it was Kent's parents' sedan. Trying to think if they had something planned, Shelby started to feel as if a brick was sitting in her stomach.

Angelica was sitting in her car, waiting. She'd come over to Shelby and Kent's house to pick up the stuff Shelby said she put aside for them. She tried to call, but ended up leaving voicemails.

Getting out of her car, Shelby felt the guilt flow over her shoulders. "Hi," She said to her mother-in-law. "I didn't know you were coming over."

Already out of her car, Angelica came around the front of Shelby's car and hugged her. It wasn't difficult to read the situation, Angelica wasn't so old that she didn't see the "morning after" look. "I just came to get the box of Kent's clothes from you."

Shelby led the way into the house, throwing her keys on the little accent table in the foyer. They went back to the bedroom, and into the closet. She grabbed the box and carried it over to the bed.

Angelica opened it up, and went through the contents, laughing and crying at the memories the clothing evoked. "He loved you so much," She told Shelby.

Just standing there and smiling, Shelby couldn't say anything. Her throat was so tight, it was impossible to speak.

A few minutes later, Angelica left, taking Kent's things, and a piece of Shelby's heart with her.

Shelby sat down on the floor of the foyer and dropped her head to her knees before she started crying.

Gannon tried to text and call Shelby for the rest of the day. She wasn't answering. He was worried so he called Peggy, who got Shelby's address form a cooperative Bridgette. He could've gone to work and gotten it, or called a friend in the department, but Gannon wasn't apt to use his job abilities for personal reasons.

He drove by and, seeing her car in the driveway, stopped in front of the house.

Hedging his bets, he decided to go up and knock on the door. When Shelby answered, he knew something had happened, she looked like she'd been crying for a long time.

"What?" Shelby yelled at Gannon. "You needed another go round of sex so you're making house calls now?" The words were full of hurt and anger that Shelby couldn't keep contained.

Looking at her, and trying not to let her incite his anger, Gannon said calmly, "No, I was calling and texting you but you didn't answer and I was worried."

Shelby didn't care right now, she wanted to be left alone, "So you just, what, called the police station and got my address? Did you hack my phone? Maybe put a tracker on my car?" Why do you need to keep tabs on me all the damn time? I'm an adult and don't need this shit!" She spewed the words out like poison.

Even though his heart was taking a brutal beating, Gannon managed to hold onto his patience. Maybe it was because of being a cop, but he looked into her eyes, and said, "I got your address from Bridgette because it would've been illegal for me to get it from work. I won't call you, text you, or stop by again. I'll thank you to do the same. Goodbye." He turned and walked back down the sidewalk to his car.

Shelby stood in the doorway, watching him go, and realizing she just made the biggest mistake of her life, but not having the strength to undo it.

The brunch was scheduled the next day and Shelby was the first one to arrive at the restaurant. She suffered from lack of sleep and the feeling of being a fool, but otherwise she was great! 'Yeah, right!' She told herself. The hostess seated her, and she waited for her friends to show up.

Payton and Mrs. Hanson happened to arrive at the same time to the restaurant, so they walked in together. Once they got to the table, and got a look at Shelby, they both frowned.

"Well, I guess you screwed up," Payton said sarcastically to her friend.

Shelby made eye contact, but didn't say anything.

Mrs. Hanson reached over and squeezed Shelby's hand, saying, "We can fix it."

A tear creeping out of her eye, Shelby swiped at it, and sighed, "I don't think so."

Just then Hannah came up to the table. She wore the glow of a newly engaged woman. She looked at the group, and asked, "What happened?" as she sat down.

Payton pointed a finger at Shelby, and answered, "She screwed up."

Shelby shot Payton a nasty look, and got a tongue sticking out at her as a reply. "We're not here to talk about my love life, or lack thereof, we're here to celebrate Hannah's engagement and talk weddings," She snapped at her friends.

Her eyebrows raised, Hannah commented, "Well, that sure does make me want to discuss fabrics and colors."

Not being able to help it, Shelby smiled, despite her best efforts not to.

Mrs. Hanson suggested, "Why don't we start with Shelby's issue, clear it up, and then we can move onto Hannah's plans?"

"Amen," Hannah chimed in.

Payton nodded, "If she'll talk, I'll listen."

The three of them sat there, staring at Shelby. Finally, the pressure got to her, and she cracked, "Fine," she started, "well, we slept together and it was so fantastic, and I stayed over, had a little wobbly moment last night, but I stayed and we made love yesterday morning, and then when I get home, Kent's mom was there to pick up some of his clothes."

All three of her friends understood the meaning of the situation so Shelby, thankfully, didn't have to explain that part.

"Did she say something to you?" Payton asked, curious.

Shaking her head no, Shelby replied, "She didn't have to, she's a woman and knows what's going on."

Lifting her hand, as if she were in a classroom, Hannah asked, "Um, if Kent's mom didn't say anything to make you feel bad, why do you feel bad?"

There was the crux of the problem, Shelby shrugged, and told them, "I don't know, but I did. Then Gannon came over and

I accused him of basically stalking me and being too close, and told him to go away."

"What did he say to that?" Mrs. Hanson asked.

Tears were now streaming down her face, Shelby told her, "He said he wouldn't text me, call me, or see me and he appreciated it if I did the same," she took a deep breath, "then he calmly walked out to his SUV and drove off."

Even Payton wore a look of shock on her face. She commented, "Wow!"

Willa had been listening to this story, feeling sad for Shelby, but knowing that this Gannon fellow must really love her to be so calm and take the nonsense that Shelby dished out to him. He must also be in love with her, or he'd have reacted differently. A plan started to form in her head. She looked at the three girls, who weren't really girls, but she would always see them that way. "Okay, I'd like you to give me this Gannon's phone number."

Shelby's eyes shot to Mrs. Hanson, and shook her head no vehemently.

Hannah was nodding, "Yes! All three of you," she pointed from one to the other, "ganged up on me to intercede, this is payback."

Giving Hannah a patient look, Mrs. Hanson told her, "Not payback, we're helping Shelby resolve some issues she's having."

"Heck, I had nothing else planned today," Payton announced, "If this means I get to see a hunky cop, I say let's go for it. If you don't want him Shelby, maybe he likes blondes."

Her face shot over to Payton, her eyes throwing daggers, Shelby said, "Here's the number Mrs. Hanson," and handed the older woman her phone while she kept staring at a laughing Payton.

Mrs. Hanson took Shelby's phone and walked outside of the restaurant. She dialed Gannon's phone number and waited.

Gannon looked at his phone, saw it was Shelby, and wanted to ignore it, but he couldn't. "What do you want?" He asked, sarcasm tinging his words.

"I'll thank you not to use that tone with me," A woman's voice said, but it wasn't Shelby's.

His eyes widening, he asked, "Who is this?" In a softer tone.

Mrs. Hanson smiled, "That's much better," she told him, then explained, "I'm Mrs. Hanson, from the Galveston Retreat."

Vaguely, Gannon remembered Shelby mentioning that name during their walk at the park last week. "Yes, ma'am."

'Good, he has manners,' Willa thought to herself. "I'm calling to ask you to come out to Galveston Retreat today. Shelby is a wreck and has realized how awful she was to you. What she failed to tell you was that her late husband's mother was waiting for her when she returned home yesterday morning, and Shelby had to get some of Kent's things out and give them to his mother. It was letting go of something precious, and Shelby felt as though she was disgracing his memory by coming in after a night spent with you."

Sitting in his living room, Gannon took in the words that this Mrs. Hanson woman was saying. He couldn't imagine what

Shelby was going through, but he knew someone who would. "Can I call you back, Mrs. Hanson?" He asked the woman.

Not sure what to make of it, Willa agreed, and said, "That's fine, I'll await your call," before hanging up.

Calling his mother, Gannon asked if she had a few minutes to talk.

Mrs. Riley very rarely had such a request from her oldest son, so told him, "Of course, what can I help you with?"

Gannon started with, "I've met a woman, and she lost her husband last year." His mother was silent, "I'd like to tell you a story and see what you think.

About fifteen minutes later, Gannon hung up with his mother, then called Shelby's phone back. Mrs. Hanson answered it. He told her, "I'll be there in an hour," and hung up.

Mrs. Hanson disconnected the call, and took a sip of her mimosa before noticing three pairs of eyes boring into her. She slowly put her glass down, and told them, "He'll be at the retreat in an hour."

Those words made Shelby feel relieved and also very afraid. "What do I say to him?" She asked her friends.

"Simple," Hannah told her, "You say what's in your heart."

Gannon was pulling into a small parking area in front of a very large house. It was Victorian and looked as though it stepped out of a different century. He saw Shelby's car, but also two other cars and wondered who else was here.

Walking up the wide front porch, Gannon knocked on the door.

An older woman, with a bright and welcoming smile answered, saying, "You must be Gannon."

"Yes ma'am," He answered, not able to keep his "work voice" out of his tone.

Smiling, Mrs. Hanson stepped aside and allowed Gannon to come inside the house. He looked around, as surprised as everyone was at the inside. "It's beautiful, isn't it?" She asked him.

Nodding, Gannon waited for her to direct him. He stood there, with his hands clasped behind his back.

"You're used to being in control," Willa observed, "and in this situation, there is no such thing is there?" She asked.

Gannon shook his head no, and replied, "No ma'am, but I'm trying very hard to be supportive."

Of that, Willa was certain. This was a very responsible man standing in front of her. She was sure that he was in love with their Shelby too.

Not wanting to pretend he was here for any other reason, Gannon said, "I'd like to see Shelby please."

Pointing up, Willa directed him, "Upstairs, the last room on the right, her name is on the door."

Wasting no time, Gannon took the stairs two at a time, and walked down the hallway. Just as Mrs. Hanson said, there was a door with a chalkboard sign that read, "Shelby." Gannon saw that the door was ajar so he pushed it open. The first thing he noticed was all the yellow. It made the room look like the brightest day just came inside. As his eyes scanned the room, he saw Shelby standing by a set of large windows. She was looking out, the breeze blowing inside and making her hair dance about her shoulders. Gannon thought she was the most beautiful sight in the world. "Are you calm now?" He asked.

Shelby stood by the window, and felt Gannon's presence when he came in. Her body was already so in-tuned with his. "No," She answered, without turning around. "I'm ashamed of yelling at you and feel like one of those taffy machines you see at the fair, all twisted up."

The analogy made him smile. Shelby would never be conventional, and God love her, he didn't want her to be. "And why are you twisted up?" He asked as he took a step closer.

Still not turning around, Shelby answered, "Because I realized the other night, as we were making love on the sofa in your living room that I was falling in love with you."

Her words gave him hope, he stepped closer to her. "You are?" He asked quietly.

Now, Shelby did turn around. "Oh yes, I am, and it scares me because I don't want to hurt anyone in the process."

"Do you mean Kent's parents?" He asked. His talk with his mother about her grief after his father's passing away went a long way to helping Gannon understand what Shelby was going through.

His mother told him that she still couldn't even entertain being with another man, but that didn't mean that she shouldn't, but that was her choice. Shelby made the choice to open herself up to Gannon, to trust that another man could love her. She explained that there would probably be more times when Shelby was torn up over her past and her future as the two intertwined, and that Gannon had the responsibility, if he truly loved her, to support her and understand that.

Shelby nodded, "Yes."

"I'd like to meet them," Gannon said softly, "I'd like to know about the type of person Kent was."

His words made Shelby start to cry, "You would?" She asked him.

Covering the last couple of steps between them, Gannon told her, "Yes, because he was the only other man who got to steal your heart. I'm very grateful to him."

Crying harder, Shelby asked, "You are?"

Nodding, Gannon looked down into her eyes, and fell in love again, "I'm grateful that he loved you enough that you were okay with finding love again, with me."

Shelby was sobbing, she reached out and wrapped her arms around Gannon. He cradled her in his arms, gently rocking her and letting her know, without words, that he was there for her, that he loved her, and that he would do everything he could to stay with her.

Gannon knew, somehow, that they would be okay, he whispered into her hair, "I know you're not ready yet, but when you are, I'm going to ask you to marry me, and we'll start it out however you want to. I'm here."

His words made Shelby so thankful. "Okay," She mumbled into his shirt.

They held one another, and somewhere, Kent was looking down and happy that his Shelby was able to find someone to help her heal.

Keep reading for an

excerpt of

Danette Fogarty's

new book

Payton's Story;

Book 3:

Love After Loss Series

Payton sat in the doctor's office, and waited. She was alone, as usual. Sebastian wasn't able to get away from work, and they got into yet another fight about him not caring about Raleigh, their daughter. She was exhausted from worrying about what was going on with her daughter, and fighting with Sebastian. It was these kinds of things that made her glad they never married.

Duke University, 2011

Payton was attending a fund raiser for the baseball team at the request of her roommate/friend, Alexandra. Alex's boyfriend was on the team and Alex promised Payton that they would have a great time.

They were sitting at their table, when there was a wave of commotion that trickled through the room. Everyone was straining to get a look at the Guest of Honor, and baseball darling of Duke University, Sebastian Trent.

Not really following baseball, but knowing the gist of the game, in large part to Alex and her love of her boyfriend, Gil. Once she saw Sebastian Trent, though, Payton thought maybe she should rethink her view on the game. If all baseball players were that good looking, then maybe she should watch more often.

As luck would have it, Sebastian, and his entourage passed right by the table where Payton was seated. He was looking around, and his eyes ran smack dab into hers. It was as if time stood still, the connection between them felt tangible. He paused, then continued up to the stage, where he was to be seated with faculty of the college.

They ate dinner, but every once in a while, Payton would look up and see Sebastian staring right at her. He made her feel so exposed, which was so hot!

"Ms. Holland," The doctor said, and brought Payton out of her thoughts.

Payton blinked, to clear her mind of the memory. "Yes," She answered the doctor.

He sat down behind his desk and looked through the folder with Raleigh's tests. His brow was serious, and Payton had a funny feeling work its way up into her spine.

All of the symptoms Raleigh was experiencing, the doctors thought were from a virus. They treated her repeatedly with antibiotics but the fevers kept coming back.

Now, her little girl was weak and Payton demanded that Raleigh's pediatrician refer them to a specialist.

There was a knock on the door, and a woman dressed in a lab coat came inside the office.

Dr. Richland, the specialist, explained, "This is a colleague of mine, Dr. Menton," he waited for the woman to sit down. "She's also a specialist and I asked her to take a look at Raleigh's tests.

If two doctors were in here with her, then Payton knew it was serious. "Okay, so what's going on with my daughter?" She asked, and could hear her voice shake.

Dr. Menton leaned forward, and told Shelby, "We are diagnosing your daughter with Acute Lymphoblastic Leukemia."

As soon as Payton heard the word Leukemia, she panicked, and asked, "My daughter has cancer?"

Nodding, Dr. Menton answered, "A form of it, yes. It's not uncommon for it to be misdiagnosed because of the symptoms. This type of leukemia affects the white blood cells and that's why Raleigh keeps running fevers and mimics the symptoms of colds.

"Okay," Payton replied. Then she asked, "How do we fight it?" Being educated at Duke University, where there was a great medical school, Payton knew there were breakthroughs all the time in cancer research and the word cancer didn't necessarily mean death.

Dr. Menton took Shelby's hand into her own. "Well, normally we would start a treatment regimen that has a reasonable remission rate."

"You said, normally," Payton noted, and the feeling of anxiety started creeping into her chest.

Dr. Richland spoke first, "Ms. Holland, Payton," he was trying to get out the words that he hated saying, "I'm afraid that Raleigh's condition is far worse than we realized." He looked over at his colleague for help.

Looking at this mother, who was sitting here alone, and trying to be strong, Dr. Menton wanted to cry. She knew she couldn't, and wouldn't, but still….. "I'm afraid that Raleigh's leukemia has advanced to a stage that the current course of treatments will be ineffective."

Tears started falling down Payton's cheeks, and she was shaking. "So," She tried to take deep breaths, "you're telling me that my daughter is going to die?" She asked the doctors.

Dr. Richland nodded first, and then Dr. Menton spoke. "We will do everything we can to make Raleigh comfortable and out of pain."

"Please?" Payton begged them, "Don't let her die! I couldn't bear it if she died."

Now, Dr. Menton did let a tear escape. She wouldn't let a parent believe that she was unfeeling in their plight. This was the worst thing in the world, telling a parent their child was sick and that you couldn't help them.